YEAR OF MYSTERY

12 Short Mysteries from 2021

LEAH R CUTTER

Knotted Road Press

Year of Mystery
A Collection of Short Mysteries
Copyright © 2022 Leah R Cutter
All rights reserved
Published by Knotted Road Press
www.KnottedRoadPress.com

ISBN: 978-1-64470-246-8

Cover and interior design copyright © 2022 Knotted Road Press
http://www.KnottedRoadPress.com

Reviews
It's true. Reviews help me sell more books. If you've enjoyed this story, please consider leaving a review of it on your favorite site.

Come someplace new…
Are you a traveler? Do you enjoy exploring strange new worlds, new cultures, new people?

Journey into the various lands envisioned by Leah Cutter.

Sign up for my newsletter and I'll start you on your travels with a free copy of my book, *The Island Sampler.*

I will never spam you or use your email for nefarious purposes. You can also unsubscribe at any time.

http://www.LeahCutter.com/newsletter/

CONTENTS

INTRODUCTION

At the end of 2020, I was faced with a dilemma, namely, what was I going to publish in 2021? I hadn't written as much as I'd originally planned in 2020, hadn't been able to focus because of everything going on in the world.

I've been publishing one item a month, every month, since October of 2017. Sometimes mysteries, sometimes fantasy, sometimes science fiction, or even non-fiction. They were never all the same length either.

I had recently started a new mystery magazine, *Mystery, Crime, and Mayhem*, also known as MCM.

It was my husband who suggested that I might try for a year of mystery. That really spoke to me. And, it would all be short fiction, short mysteries. Many of them had already been published in MCM, but a lot were brand new, never having been published anywhere.

Plus, it allowed me to revisit some of my favorite series, such as the Rabbit mysteries (*The Puzzling Case of the Exam Imposters*), Alvin Goodfellow (*The Case of the Locked Room*) and even introduce people to a new series, Angela and Frankie (*Sanitizing the Safe House* and *Favors for Old Friends*).

(I actually wrote most of a new Angela and Frankie story, *The Identity Salon*. Then my computer crashed and I lost all of it and have never wanted to go back and recreate it from scratch.)

I do have plans on continuing some of these stories, making the main character a series character. I just didn't have time to write those stories this year. That includes Jacob (*Tiny Dreams* - I have the next story already planned out, *Tiny Lives*).

In the end, I'm rather pleased with this collection. It shows a range of the types of mysteries that I like to read, as well as write. As I've said before in essays that I've written for MCM, I'll read just about most every genre of mystery.

What I want is Voice.

That's what you'll find her. Lots of characters with really strong voices.

I hope you enjoy reading them as much as I enjoyed writing them!

Some year, there will probably be a second year of mystery. I still don't know what I'm doing for 2022. It's likely to be piecemeal, at least until halfway through the year.

Hopefully you'll come along with me for that ride as well.

Cheers!

Leah R Cutter
Dec 2021
Ravensdale, WA

PINNED

I 'm telling ya, Andy didn't have a lick of sense most of the time. Not even the sense that God gave a goose. He was about as mean as one, too. Those shit machines would attack anything if they felt threatened, like if you were walking around Old Man Henry's pond looking to flush quail and you got too close to one of their nests. They'd run out of the grass, charging at you, wings spread wide and hissing. Could break a man's leg if they were feeling ornery enough.

Andy was like that sometimes too, spitting and hissing if you looked at him wrong, or came too close to the pool table where he was working his magic, or even said the wrong thing, like saying, "Good morning" instead of a simple "Hello."

I put up with him, with his moodiness and his crazy schemes. I'd known him since the first year of high school, when his family moved into the area. Andy had been there for me when my wife Jenny had been killed two years before, when a semi overturned on the state highway and crushed her little Ford Ranger. We'd been high school sweethearts, and I'd married her the summer after our graduation. We were coming up on our five year anniversary. It was supposed to be Jenny and Jason forever, you know? Particularly since the doc had told her she could never have kids, something wrong with her baby oven.

It weren't easy for the pair of us, making a living out here in Hamburg, the butthole of Iowa. But both our families were here. She worked at the gas station just down the road from our trailer, Thursday through Monday, selling more beer than gas on Friday nights. I was working for corporate, the big tire place across town. I'd always been good at fixing things.

We'd talked about moving, maybe to Des Moines, or even a bigger town in Nebraska, which was only forty-five minutes away, across the Missouri river, but we never had a chance, never took the chance. We were as stuck here as a deer in deep mud.

Andy arrived that afternoon, just after the state troopers had come in to inform me of Jenny's death. He sat there while I bawled like a baby in that cramped living room, the ugly red-striped brown couch that was older than I was soaking up my tears. Handed me a beer when I finished. Then stayed with me for a week. Got me drunk when I needed it, but he also made sure I didn't drink so much I'd die of alcohol poisoning.

After seven days, when I was just starting to look around and wonder what the hell I was going to do with the rest of my life, I woke up alone in the trailer for the first time. Andy had been sleeping on that fucking sofa the whole time, getting me through every morning.

But he'd finally gone. Wasn't sure at first if he'd just had enough of me or what. The trailer felt more empty than I could have imagined, tiny and cramped as it was. It was suddenly hard to breathe, like stepping outside in December when that first good freeze hits and your lungs aren't sure there's enough air anymore.

Sitting on the striped pillow I'd scrounged up for Andy was a revolver, an old .357 Cold, the blued finish scratched with age. I knew without picking it up that it had probably been stolen from somewhere. Might even have the serial numbers filed off.

It looked like a cold black hole sitting there, sucking all the light from the morning air into it.

Next to the gun was a note from Andy. "You got through a week and the worst of it." Funny, how he never said Jenny's name, not once, after she'd been killed. "Now, you got a choice. Move forward or join her."

It surprised me that I wasn't even tempted to use that gun on myself. But Andy had probably known that. It got me moving though, pushed me out of the living room and into a new job at the local hardware store where I got to redneck solutions with the farmers and ranchers, stretching my talents for the first time. All that kept me from diving face first into a bottle that first year.

I kept the gun. Took it out on the anniversary of Jenny's death for the past two years. Never felt the need to use it, but it was good to have a backup plan, you know? Instead of being stuck without choices, pinned in place.

But a friend like Andy, who gets you through something like that, well, I'd put up with his crazy in return.

Winter of 2018 was hard, more snow falling than the last two years combined. With the money from Jenny's life insurance, I'd been able to afford a new truck with lifts and big knbby wheels. (Who would have thought that her parents would have taken out a policy on each of their four kids? I'd heard them talk more than once that all life insurance was just a scam. But they had done it. And they'd turned over most of the money to me to get on with my life.)

Only way I made it to the hardware store through December and January was because I had higher clearance on my vehicle than most. Those mornings had felt like the end of the world, the wind blowing long ribbons of snow across the road and not another soul to be seen. Sold more orange plastic snow-fence at the start of February than anything else, the ranchers not wanting to be caught without it the coming year.

Now, no one in town believed in climate change. Not really, despite what our idiot mayor might say. All those dire predictions of the oceans raising and biblical times at hand had never come true. It was just another liberal excuse for milking us dry with higher taxes.

On the other hand, no one could deny that the weather had grown downright weird. Record highs each summer. More snow, more rain, than any of the old timers could recall in their lifetimes.

Which meant flooding.

I remember, back in 2011, when I was just sixteen, how the Missouri river had nearly broken out of its banks, the waters racing to engulf our town. At that time, the Army Corps of Engineers had raised the existing levee by eight feet. That extra height just flat saved the town.

But the lametard politicians listened to the stupid engineers and believed them when they said that the levee wasn't safe at the height that had saved us, and so allowed the Army Corps of Engineers to dismantle the levee, took it back to its original eighteen feet.

There had been fund raisers for years, people making up silly songs and marching along the main street of old downtown, trying to save the levee. As I said though, nobody around here really believed in climate change. The project never got off the ground.

So now we sat there behind a dinky little earthworks levee as the waters started to rise spring of 2019, praying that god or someone would save our butthole town.

But god wasn't listening.

I was, though, when the flood warning started coming in. It had been raining cats and dogs for most of the week. I'd get soaked just walking across the parking lot at the hardware store. Watched poor suckers trying to use umbrellas, only to have them pummeled so hard with buckets of rain that they'd collapse halfway across the asphalt.

Surprised me when Andy came strolling in that morning. Hadn't seen him in a few days. Figured he was out laying in sandbags around his parent's property, maybe stave off some of the waters that were coming.

He shook himself like a wet dog when he stepped in the door. He wore an orange protection suit, like what road crew wear when they're working in rough weather. I figure he'd stolen it last summer, when he'd worked construction for a while. He'd never had what you'd call a stable job, instead, put together a string of one-off gigs while always angling for that big score.

I was working the information booth just inside the door that morning. We gave away free popcorn at the hardware store, which was popular with the parents and their kids, though I'd seen more than one old coot snag three bags when he thought no one was looking. The store smelled of butter and oil and popcorn, even with the cold winds that blew through the door every time they opened. We'd been having problems with the sensors fooled by the amount of rain, thinking that someone was walking up. Had been forced to crank the sensitivity stupid low.

"Can I help you, sir?" I said, teasing Andy when he

finally finished shaking his head and using his hands to wipe off some of the water.

He gave me a shit-eating grin, the one that set my back up because I knew it meant craziness ahead. "Sure, ah, Jason," he said, pretending to read the name off my nametag after he'd walked over to where I was standing. "I need a good set of bolt cutters," he said. "Strong enough to cut off a lock."

"You got yourself locked out of someplace?" I was prepared not to believe a word coming out of his mouth. He was up to no good.

"Maybe," he said. "Oh, and a good prybar. For pulling hastily nailed sheets of plywood off windows."

That didn't sound right to me. If Andy had been putting plywood over his windows, he wouldn't have done it badly.

Then again, some of the folks in town had been preparing for the flood as if it were a tornado or a hurricane, putting up boards over their windows so they wouldn't get busted out by the water. We'd actually sold out of plywood sheets the day before.

"What exactly do you have in mind?" I asked.

"Payback," Andy said, turning serious.

"Against who?" I figured there were any number of people in town who Andy had a beef with, whether real or imagined.

"The queen bitch, Michelle Metzger," he said, suddenly snarling darkly. "She took my pin."

"What pin are you talking about?"

"It's a mason pin," Andy said, leaning over the counter so that no one else could hear him. "Gold, with the compass and the big G in the center, circled in diamonds. Maybe two inches across."

I whistled. "How in the hell did you get ahold of that?"

Andy sighed. "This guy didn't have the money he needed

to cover his bet with me. And he swore that his ATM card was busted."

I shook my head at Andy. He was generally better at picking his marks, making sure they had the cash before setting his hooks and starting his pool hustle. This didn't sound like him at all.

"So as collateral, he gave me this pin. He was going to the bank today to get me the cash. Then this happened," he said, gesturing toward the door and the pouring rain. "We were supposed to meet at Lucky's tonight, but the bar won't be there."

Michelle Metzger owned "Lucky's Pool Hall and Saloon" on the edge of town. She was about twice our age. She'd been running the bar since before we'd been legal to drink, and had always been a hard-ass about selling it to us. Always so high and mighty, as if being the owner of a bar made her better than the rest of us. Hence our name for her, the queen bitch.

However, Andy was a pool shark. A good one, even. Before we were legal, she'd let him come in some nights when there weren't a lot going on and practice, racking up set after set and not charging him.

Once Andy started betting and making money from his sharking, she'd started demanding that he pay her a commission. Depending on the night and how snarky Andy had been, as much as twenty-five percent went to the house.

So Andy and Michelle had a love-hate relationship, frequently with more emphasis on the hate than the love. But she had the best tables in town as well as the largest number of tables, with the most suckers passing through that Andy could fleece.

"We'll need to get there soon," Andy told me, lowering his voice. "The water's coming."

"Not sure what you intend to do," I said slowly. If the

flood warnings were accurate, Lucky's might be underwater soon.

"The place is empty right now," Andy said. "And I need my pin back. Before it gets flooded."

"You're aware that that pin ain't gonna be worth much," I warned Andy, in case he was thinking maybe he could take it up to the pawnshop north of town that dealt with jewelry. "The diamonds are probably just chips, and the pin itself gold-plated."

"Don't care," Andy said, his chin rising and a stubborn look in his eyes. "It's mine. And I want it back."

"So what are you proposing we do about it?" I said after a few mulish moments of silence between us. I knew I wasn't about to out-stubborn Andy. That would be like trying to turn a bull who was hell bent on walking a straight line. Or to get a goose to go shit someplace else.

"Water's coming," Andy said, his eyes catching that look again, the one I'd seen earlier, the crazy coming back. I knew I'd see it again, probably when I least wanted it.

"No one's at the bar right now," he continued. "We don't have to be fancy or smart when we're breaking in. Water'll wash away all the evidence."

I have to admit, I found myself nodding at that. He was probably right. We could break into half a dozen houses or businesses that were close to the river and no one would be the wiser.

"But we have to leave *now*," Andy insisted. "Before the river gets there."

I checked the time. It was close enough to my lunchbreak. I cleared it with my manager, saying I was going to help Andy shore up his place, then took off the stained green apron I always wore and put my hat back on. Had a rain slicker that would keep the worst of any storm off me. Then we headed off, into the deluge.

W ipers whipped across the windshield at their highest, fastest setting, and I could still barely see three feet ahead of me. Water was already rising close to the river. A steady stream at least three inches high raced across the street.

"We don't have much time," I told Andy as I parked in front of Lucky's. No one else was in the street, so we didn't bother to park in the back. The way the rain and the river was coming, I figured we had maybe thirty minutes before the waters would be over my front axle. And if that happened, we'd be stuck here, climbing onto the rooftop and not rescued until the storm passed.

I had a good set of boots, the kind I took duck hunting in the spring when the fields were mostly ponds. Though we were walking across the concrete, it felt as though the ground was holding onto them, sucking at them like I was walking through mud. The water already covered the tops of them, not quite to my ankles. I didn't like how fast it was moving.

One slip and that water might just carry a man away.

The rain blurred the edges of the building, making it loom ahead of us like a dark cave. None of the neon signs were on in the windows. Still, I thought I caught a glimpse of some sort of light inside. Hard to tell. But the windows weren't covered in plywood, and no external lock was on the door, so the only thing Andy pulled from the pile of tools stashed on the backseat of my truck was the sledgehammer.

I'd never paid that much attention to how the door of Lucky's locked. Hadn't ever seemed important to me. Should have known that Andy would know exactly how to get into the building, that he already had a plan.

Everyone always reinforces their doors and their locks, as well as the doorjamb. Lots of metal there, hard to get through.

No one pays attention to the wall beside it, which is just sheetrock behind the cheap wood façade and easy to break through with a sledgehammer.

"That ain't gonna be hidden by the flood," I yelled at Andy through the downpour. I felt as though my words were all carried away by the rain. He didn't even bother to shrug. Maybe he intended on putting more holes into the walls, as if maybe the flood had damaged them.

From the accurately placed opening in the wall, Andy could reach in and pull back the two deadbolts on top, then knock the door itself open.

When we got in, there were lights on, little harsh white emergency lights near the edges of the ceiling. It made the place seem colder instead of friendly, like those lights gave the people underneath them a hard edge.

A dozen empty tables were scattered across the floor of the room. The chairs had all been pushed together to one side, stacked up haphazardly in the corner, maybe in anticipation of a cleaning crew. Through the doorway to the left stood the pool tables, six of them neatly lined up in the dark.

Running across the back wall stood the bar. To the right of the bar was a door to the kitchen that served up greasy fries, hotdogs and hamburgers, and in the summertime, fried pickles and ice cream. The bar itself was a dark brown color. It looked so much older in that harsh light, a bulwark that had stood there since the town itself had been formed. Shelves behind the bar were full of bottles. Might be that some of them were calling my name, and would need to be rescued from the waters before we left.

I thought at first that there was just a pile of rags sitting on the countertop. It wasn't until after we'd taken those first few steps across the floor that the shape suddenly moved.

"Holy fuck!"

I don't know if I said the words and Andy just thought them really loudly at me, or vice versa.

The dark shape resolved itself into Michelle, the owner. She'd been lying there, making the top of the bar her bed. Her long black hair hung in oily strings across her shoulders and down the front, almost to her tits. She was wearing a tank top that showed off her wrinkly brown skin, the skin of someone who'd spent too many summers working outside without either a hat or lotion.

"Get out." The words sounded like boulders crashing together, heaved out of their place by the force of the river.

Then Michelle brought up the big, old side-by-side shotgun that had been laying beside her on the bar and pointed it directly in Andy's face.

It was only then that I realized that Andy had already pulled a hand gun out and had directed at her, a little snug .38 that he'd gotten from somewhere.

I don't know for how long we all stood there in that deserted bar, the pair of them faced off. The water had followed us inside and was starting to swirl around my feet. I wasn't looking for no Titanic moment, you know? When we'd have to push our way through the current with bobbing furniture in our way. It was too fucking cold. We'd freeze before we got outside.

It finally occurred to me that the pair of them would stay frozen like statues until the waters swept them both away.

"Can we both just put away the guns for a minute and talk?" I asked, trying to use my most reasonable voice.

That earned me a glare from the pair of them, though their guns never wavered.

"What the hell do you boys want?" Michelle asked.

Andy answered that, to my surprise. "I want my pin."

Michelle snorted. "Fat chance. Just leave now."

I wanted to turn. Wanted like hell to just walk out of there.

But Andy had been there for me. I needed to be there for him.

Finally occurred to me to ask, "What the hell are you doing here, Michelle?" I asked.

"Locking up before the flood came," she said after a moment.

"Nope. Don't believe a word you just said," Andy replied.

I blinked, surprised. Why wouldn't he believe Michelle? What she just said made sense. Despite the fact that she'd been laid out on her bar like some weird-ass theatre moment.

"Don't matter if you believe me or not," Michelle said after a few long moments. "You gotta get out of here."

"You're having money problems, aren'tcha?" Andy said after a few moments. "Hadn't believed it, not with the business I see you doing. Something's been bleeding you dry though, these last few months."

He sounded so casual, as if they'd been sitting around a table and sharing a beer instead of facing each other over guns with the flood waters rising.

"Ain't none of your business," Michelle said, her voice sounding like a judge announcing a sentence and the close of the court for the day. "Now, git."

"Not without my pin," Andy said. "You know this place is going underwater. You know it. What, you got insurance riding on it? Were you here to make sure that it went? That the river took it?"

By the growl that Michelle gave, I guess that Andy hit close enough to the mark.

"So what if I'm the only one of the so-called businessmen in the area who has flood insurance?" Michelle said after a moment. "Can't help the rest of those assholes. Just myself."

I still wasn't sure exactly what she meant.

Water now sloshed up over the tops of my feet.

"We gotta get going, Andy," I said. "While we still can."

"Nope. I'm staying here until she leaves. Then I'm taking my pin."

Good lord, how the hell did Andy get anything done when he had to cart around such a huge barrel of stupid?

I looked at Michelle, then at Andy. Would serve both of them right if I just hightailed it out of there.

But there was something else going on. Some deep current flowing between the pair of them that the floods just couldn't wash away.

"You gave me that pin," Michelle said after a bit.

Andy's chin hardened back into mule stubbornness. "And now I want it back."

What the hell were they talking about? Seemed that Andy had made up the entire story of the mason pin.

"Nope. Gonna keep it. A reminder of one of the most idiotic things I've ever done over the course of a long life of stupid shit," Michelle said.

I could tell the dig hit Andy hard. He flinched a little, trying to hide his tell.

"What pin?" I asked.

"Didn't he tell you?" Michelle said, her voice turning honeysweet. "He gave me his high school varsity pin. The gold one with the football on it."

Now, I knew that Andy had never been any sort of athlete in high school, and he sure as hell had never been on the football team. The only way he'd get one of those was to either buy one or steal it. What kind of a line had he fed Michelle? Had she actually believed it was real? And why the hell had he given it to her?

Then I remembered that Andy's dad had been a big football hero back in the day. As kids, hanging out at Andy's house, we'd been forced to listen to him go on and on about his fucking glory days.

I'd bet anything that the pin, while not earned by Andy, had been in his family for a while.

"You think I really cared for you?" Andy said, spitting angry. "I didn't. Don't."

"You mean those three long nights and days of making love was just about getting your rocks off?" Michelle sneered. "Hate to break it to you, but there weren't no *true wuv* here either."

"Wait. So you and the queen bitch had it on?" I said. I couldn't have been more surprised. "Dude." Seemed that their love-hate relationship had more love in it than I'd realized. No wonder I hadn't seen him around for a while.

Andy just shook his head. "It was a mistake," he said. His tone had lowered, growing as icy cold as the winds blowing outside. "I want my pin back."

Normally, Andy blew hot with a short fuse. Lots of lightning and thunder. Once the storm was over, he'd usually forget what he'd even been angry about.

His anger never worried me unless it grew cold, like now. He wasn't about to back down.

"I already gave it to my sister," Michelle said.

"You ain't got a sister," Andy said. "I know. I checked when I was staying at your house."

The glare Michelle gave him grew measurably colder. "Okay. So she isn't blood related. She's still family. And she's got cancer. And expensive treatments."

"You were gonna use the money from the flood insurance to pay her expenses," I said, putting it all together. That was why Andy had accused her of money problems. Because Michelle had been trying to help this sister of hers.

"Ain't none of your business," Michelle said.

"And that's also was why you're here, in the bar," I continued as if she hadn't said anything. "Because I bet you have life insurance money as well, all made out to her. But why kill yourself?" It wasn't because Andy had actually broken her heart, was it?

Michelle didn't bother to deny it. "Lots of accidents happen on days like these. Lots of lives lost. And my own cancer can't be cured. Hers can."

Holy shit. Had Michelle decided to have one last fling with Andy before she died? Three days of angry sex before drowning herself?

Wouldn't be how I'd choose to go, but I could see the appeal.

"No," Andy said stubbornly. "That's not it."

Michelle gave him an odd, half smile. "Sometimes that is the way the cookie crumbles, little boy. Now, you need to get out of here. Water's rising."

It was already up past my ankles. Who knew how high it would be in the street? If we had a chance in hell of making it out of here, we had to leave now.

"Come on, Andy," I said, taking a step backwards, toward the door. "Or I'm leaving without you."

"Damn it!" Andy said, sounding desperate. "Come with us," he told Michelle.

I don't think I'd ever heard such a begging tone in his voice before.

"No," she said softly.

"You don't have to die alone," Andy told her, his voice growing warmer.

In response, Michelle turned her gun and fired, striking the far wall. The sound was deafening in the small space. I nearly peed myself in surprise.

Then Michelle brought her gun back, pointed directly at

Andy. "That was just a warning shot," she yelled. Or I thought she yelled. It was hard to hear with the ringing in my head.

I'm not exactly sure what happened next. Andy started to lower his gun. Turn his head over his shoulder. Said something I couldn't hear. A single word.

Was it "Bye"? I'm not sure.

Because then Andy turned back, drew his gun up fast and shot Michelle straight through the heart.

Thinking back on it, I figure it was a mercy killing, so she wouldn't have to lay there on the bar, waiting while the waters rose. Took some kind of nerve to be willing to do that. I sure as hell would have respected the queen bitch for that.

However, Andy hadn't taken into account the fact that Michelle also had a gun trained on him. Her muscles twitched, and the top half of Andy's skull exploded.

He was dead before he hit the water.

A *whoosh* from behind me told me that my time had just run out. Water came pouring into the building.

The only one I could save now was myself.

I pushed my way through the rising water and managed to get my truck out of the flooded streets, though it was touch and go there for a while. I figured the waters would keep the bodies safe in the bar, that they wouldn't be washed away no matter how high the river got.

Then I drove straight to the county sheriff's office to report what had happened.

For the next couple weeks, only the roof of Lucky's was visible. I watched the footage from news helicopters, as well as got reports from locals who drove their boats through the streets.

About a month after the waters finally receded, I received a polite request from a deputy to go and visit the sheriff, not an invitation that I could have refused.

However, instead of being dragged to one of the interrogation rooms, the sheriff sat me down in one of the guest chairs of his office. The room seemed so stuffy, full of lawbooks on the shelves lining the walls, big pictures of the sheriff shaking hands with Important People, the American flag standing in the corner, beside the state flag. I knew the sheriff didn't smoke cigars, but the room still had the lingering smell of the smoke of power.

He let me know that they were officially closing the books on the double murder, as both bodies were exactly as I'd described them, Michelle with a bullet to her heart that matched the gun surprisingly registered in Andy's name, as well as the way Andy's head had been blown off.

Plus, turned out Michelle had been wearing a varsity football pin, stuck high on her shoulder, where it would have been covered by her hair.

It wasn't until after I left the sheriff's office and was back out in the street, the dull spring sunshine barely breaking through the clouds, that it all seemed to suddenly be real to me.

Andy, my best friend, was gone. Along with half of the town. There was talk that the flood might have destroyed us, that no matter how much disaster relief came in, we'd never be able to fix the place.

Loud honking made me look up. A wide V of geese were flying overhead, going north for the summer.

Maybe it was time for me to move on as well. Jenny's death had only driven me so far.

Now, with Andy's death, I was no longer pinned to this town.

Didn't know where I would go. But I made my mind up then and there that it was time to leave. Maybe only as far as the next big town. Or maybe all the way to a big city.

I got into my truck, and just started driving.

GOING DEEPER

The timer on Heather's computer popped up, blocking her view of the accounting files she was working on. Though she felt a momentary flare of irritation, Heather still dutifully stood up and started her short routine of stretches.

Every twenty minutes, she took a thirty second break and stretched. It was what her friend Chelsea had told her to do, after watching Heather work non-stop for six hours on more than one occasion.

Chelsea had devised the stretches, a different set for the two short breaks Heather took every hour. Heather did her own set of stretches at the end of the hour, during the five minutes she took for a break then. Those stretches depended on how Heather was feeling, what time of day it was, whether it was time for lunch or the end of the day.

Heather put her hands on the back of her chair and leaned forward, stretching her back.

Chelsea always asked whether or not it felt good to do the stretches. Heather could only shrug. Maybe the stretches felt good. But staying focused on work also felt good. They were both part of her routine, and routine felt good too.

Doing the stretches was one of the reasons why Heather never bothered to change out of the grey sweat pants and roomy black T-shirt she'd slept in. She never went anywhere. No one could see her. She generally didn't shower or change clothes until late afternoon or evening, when she went out to meet with clients, go to Aikido, go get groceries, and so on.

Heather straightened up, then put her hands on her waist and twisted from one side to the other. She was in her office in her underground bunker, where she always worked. There were no distractions down here. It was blissfully quiet, just the hum of the computer fan. The kitchen in her bunker was more noisy, with the fridge and the sound of the fans circulating air. She turned off the fans in her office every morning when went in there to work, and would turn them back on when she finished for the day.

Nothing adorned the plain pine walls. No artwork, no photographs, no windows. She kept the books she regularly needed on a small shelf behind her, where she couldn't see them or be distracted by their various colors or heights.

The monitor on her desk was all the view Heather needed. It was four feet across, supposedly a gaming monitor. She used its width for comparing several documents at the same time. It had been worth the expense, worth the awfulness of allowing someone else in her space even for the short time it had taken to get it delivered and installed.

The idiot delivery guy had remarked again and again about how cool it was that she lived in an actual underground bunker, that there was practically no evidence that anyone lived on the six acres of land that she owned south of Seattle.

Heather hadn't built the place. It was the product of a twisted mind, at least as far as she was concerned. Who else would build a survival bunker in which to hide away in, convinced that the world would end soon? His family hadn't wanted anything to do with the property and had sold it to her for a song, particularly given property values in Seattle and its surroundings.

Her neighbors had quickly come to understand that she didn't share the views of the former owner of the bunker. She wasn't a right-wing survivalist nut. She was a different kind of nut all together, and the bunker was a haven for her.

Heather briskly marched in place for the count of twenty. She wouldn't take a proper walk for another fifteen minutes. But she raised her heartrate slightly before she sat back down and returned to her work.

While Heather was good about her routine, even she messed up sometimes. Nothing was perfect, not even her.

However, the accounting books and paperwork she was examining for Quintakon, Incorporated, were perfect.

Heather worked as a forensic accountant. She spent most of her time crawling through bank statements and spreadsheets. It was exacting, meticulous work. She couldn't say if she loved it or not. She was good at it, though. Exceptionally good.

And no one's books were ever perfect.

Something was wrong with these accounts.

Heather didn't work off instinct. She was aware that she couldn't trust her neurodivergent brain to produce a normal reaction to anything. But the fact that she couldn't find a single mistake in the books led her to believe that they weren't real.

She spent the next fifteen minutes meticulously rechecking her work, despite the fact that she'd already checked it. Twice.

When the icon at the bottom of her screen showed an incoming call from Chelsea, Heather found herself breathing a sigh of relief, particularly since it was just about time for her next break anyway.

Chelsea was the only one who timed her calls with Heather's breaks. Though Heather had tried to explain that to her parents, they'd never grasped the concept that Heather was much more willing to talk with them during the allotted time for a break, as opposed to calling at random hours during the day.

Heather put on her headset and said, "The books are too clean."

Chelsea was also the only person who understood that while Heather could make small talk, she didn't like it.

"I know, right?" Chelsea said. "I've gone through all their accounts. There isn't a single mis-categorization or digit out of place."

Heather was surprised at the amount of relief she felt when she realized that she didn't have to fight with Chelsea, didn't have to explain herself and defend her numbers. At least, not this time. There had been other times when Chelsea hadn't been willing to take Heather's word, but that had been a while ago, before they'd started working together regularly.

It was why Heather preferred working for Chelsea, though her friend couldn't afford to just keep Heather on a retainer, and she had to take work from other clients as well.

"But there isn't anything we can testify in court about," Heather said. She got up out of her chair and started pacing. When it got bad, she counted her steps—four up, four back. But it wasn't that bad today.

Not yet.

"Yeah, I know. Judge would laugh us out of court for claiming that there was something wrong because the books didn't have any mistakes," Chelsea said with a sigh.

"Now what?" Heather said. There really wasn't much more she could do. She would type up her report, but she wouldn't mention anything about the books being too clean.

Chelsea owned a small valuation and discovery firm, whose clients included many of the big investment banks in the area. Her company did all the due diligence, advising the other firms about their intended acquisitions.

Heather worked for Chelsea part time, and had helped build the sterling reputation of her friend's company by warning them off bad deals.

"I have a proposal for you," Chelsea said slowly. "Let's do dinner tonight."

"All right," Heather said. Chelsea's proposals were generally pretty good, and brought Heather more work. On the other hand, she hated the suspense of waiting. Why couldn't Chelsea just tell her?

But she knew why. No matter what Chelsea suggested, Heather's first reaction was going to be, "No." That was just her way. Chelsea wouldn't listen to Heather's first no, which was good, because Heather didn't necessarily mean it.

They arranged to meet at a local diner in Issaquah that was fairly quiet, even if they both agreed that the food was rather pedestrian.

After they'd said goodbye, Heather continued pacing. There had to be something wrong with Quintakon's books.

She also knew that if she couldn't find it, no one could.

She shut down her computer, locking everything up, then turned on the fan as she left the room. Time for a shower. She scratched at her very short brunette hair. She kept it trimmed along the sides and only grew the top long. Chelsea had said that she preferred Heather with longer hair, but it got in the way, and Heather wasn't interested in buying then losing barrettes and hair clips to hold it back. She could shave the sides herself, and only had to go into the local barber shop to trim the top once every four months.

She glanced at herself in the full length mirror hanging from the back of the bathroom door while waiting for the shower water to warm up. She knew that looked good and kept herself in good shape. She would be thirty in nine months' time. Muscles stood out when she flexed her shoulders and arms. Her gray eyes looked large in her face, probably due to her apprehension about what Chelsea would say. Her breasts were medium sized, and she could get away with not wearing a bra when she wore looser clothing. Not when she went out running or to class. She had hips, a waist, and a chest. Not a classic hour glass figure, but that didn't matter. She still liked what she saw.

Which was something else that her parents never grasped. Sure, she may be atypical in terms of her brain. She would always remember her mother's reaction to the doctor's diagnosis of "autistic"—stating that Heather was on the spectrum. Her mom had been convinced that Heather would never be able to live on her own.

Heather had proven her parents wrong, time and again. She not only lived on her own, she supported herself very well. She had a few friends, Aikido classes she regularly went to, and did good work.

She wasn't perfect. She still made mistakes. But no one was perfect.

Not even Chelsea.

With a sigh, Heather turned away from the mirror and stepped under the hot water, washing the day away so she'd be ready for what came next.

For the whatever interesting proposal Chelsea had for her next.

"No," Heather said automatically.

Chelsea nodded and said, "You always say that."

Heather opened her mouth, then closed it again. She did. She was aware of that.

"So I'm just going to let you think about it, as I always do, and see how you really feel in a couple of days," Chelsea added.

Heather sighed. It was good to have a friend like Chelsea who knew her really well, and who understood her.

It was also bad, because Chelsea *did* know her, and knew how to get Heather to do things. Maybe even things she shouldn't.

They sat in Nicky's Restaurant, in a booth next to the windows looking out on the busy street. Nickolas was a tall Russian man with thinning hair and a booming laugh. He was always proud to serve American food—hamburgers, fries, and a Sunday pot roast—along with a couple of Russian staples, like cabbage rolls and pelmeni, a type of Russian dumpling filled with spicy pork and served with butter and sour cream.

It was a Thursday, and the diner wasn't too full. They never played the music too loudly, which made it acceptable to Heather. The lights weren't too bright either. Everything was done in shades of red and brown—booths, carpet, waitstaff uniforms. It made Heather feel as though she was in a movie from the 1980s.

Chelsea had insisted that they eat first before they talk. Heather was used to that, though she didn't like it. But she knew that no matter what Chelsea proposed, she might not be able to eat afterwards. They'd shared a warm pretzel with three different mustards for an appetizer, then had each had their own burger, Heather's with sweet potato fries, and Chelsea with regular ones.

After they'd finished, Chelsea had come up with the most outrageous proposal that Heather had ever heard.

That Heather should try to be like one of the more classic

private investigators and follow the CEO of Quintakon around, seeing if he was actually cheating on his wife.

"You've taken surveillance classes, right?" Chelsea said after a few moments of stony silence while Heather tried to process the magnitude of what her friend was asking.

Heather slowly nodded. Those had been some of the most awful weeks of her life. Having to be outside of her routine, going to a new place, trying to see everything and everyone at the same time.

There had been a series of high-priced items supposedly shoplifted from a boutique that they were investigating. The owner suspected that one (or more) of the people working for her were actually stealing the clothes.

Heather had had to go in and pretend to be a customer, had to *pass* as normal for an afternoon. It had been excruciating.

She'd also told her mentor, Steve, exactly who the thief was. Three days later, the clerk was caught red-handed.

The culprit had been obvious to Heather, though it was difficult to explain to anyone else.

Heather didn't focus on faces. Those were too hard. Instead, she watched bodies, as she'd learned to do in Aikido. She could see where tension was kept, so could figure out when someone was coiling for an attack.

The clerk who'd been stealing had been leaning into the clothes, touching them more often than the others. That was as good of a description as Heather could give.

In appreciation, the woman who owned the shop had sent Heather one of the gowns she'd tried on. It was made out of a lush green satin with a plunging neckline. Heather felt ten years older in it, and like a movie star.

She still had it in her closet, even though she'd never worn it.

"Yes, I've taken surveillance classes," Heather said

eventually when she realized that Chelsea was still waiting for an answer. "But proving that the CEO is cheating on his wife isn't going to cut it."

"Why not?" Chelsea asked, honestly confused.

"Those assholes are always cheating on their wives," Heather said with a dismissive wave of her hand. "They might even have an agreement with their wives about when and how they do it."

Chelsea didn't reply. She appeared to be pressing her lips together tightly, the place of greatest tension in her body. Why was that?

Faces. Just too hard to read.

Heather was aware that she hadn't won the argument yet. She thought for a moment, calling up the names of people she knew in the tech industry.

Seattle for all its claim of being a tech mega-capital, was still pretty small town in many ways. There weren't that many top players, and most of them knew each other, or had worked for each other in the past.

"Instead of doing something stupid like trying to follow someone, why don't I first ask around?" Heather said after a few moments. "See if I can dig up something?"

Chelsea hesitated, but eventually nodded. "All right. See if you can find some dirt on Blake Quinten, the CEO."

At least Chelsea hadn't asked Heather to break into the CFO's office to find the real numbers and books.

At least, not yet.

Heather decided to treat going out to meet Dani, one of the local tech workers she knew, the same as if she was going to court. She dressed in a navy blue, professional looking suit with a men's style gray silk blouse. Heather wasn't trying to hide that she was female, just downplay it, so people would maybe look at her face and not at her breasts.

Dani had wanted to meet in downtown Seattle, for lunch at a seafood restaurant that Heather knew she'd hate but agreed to go to anyway. She drove to airport, parked her car there, then took the light rail into downtown. She hated driving in downtown Seattle—the roads were too narrow, there were one-way streets, and she got lost even with her phone shouting directions at her.

It was too much. Too many variables, too many cars, too many people.

Noise.

The light rail was only marginally better. Heather could ride the train with her noise-cancellation headphones on so the loud sounds wouldn't bother her so much. She sat with her purse/backpack on her lap, her arms wrapped tightly around it.

She tried to distract herself by looking out the window. The trees were nice at first. Then it was through neighborhoods, down the center of a wide street with cars on either side. Finally, they reached the tunnels, which Heather preferred. Just plain concrete walls, nothing to over-stimulate her.

The Westlake station had rank homeless people lurking at the entrance. Heather didn't bother hurrying by. They wouldn't hurt her—couldn't hurt her. She had enough training to take down any of them.

She paused once she got past the gauntlet of homeless and checked her map. Court days were easier. She didn't get lost when she went to testify in court. A new restaurant meant a lot more planning on her part, and a lot more focus.

People thronged the streets, some business people, a lot of tourists. Heather felt like a salmon swimming upstream, trying to get away from the light rail station and up the street. The sun was out, which was nice. Large trucks trundled down the street, blowing stinky exhaust. Taxis and smaller cars darted in and out around them, always in a hurry.

She was so glad that she'd decided not to drive that day, but take the train. She stopped on the corner before she turned, making sure she was going in the right direction. At least there weren't as many people on the side street, though the sidewalk was dark, in the shade, and much cooler. Wind blew out of a wide garage opening, making Heather start, as if someone had just brushed by her and she hadn't noticed.

After taking a deep breath, she walked on. Fortunately, the restaurant was on the next block.

The entrance took up the entire corner, a rounded revolving door, that had been done to look old-fashioned, made out of wood and brass. Heather had never feared revolving doors, though she limited herself to just walking into the restaurant and not following the door around a couple of times. Maybe after lunch.

The first thing Heather noticed was that there was a *huge* fish tank that separated the restaurant area from the bar, and went the entire length of the space. Cool blue lights illuminated the white sand at the bottom. All kinds of fish swam there. Heather didn't know any of the names of the fish, but there were yellow round ones, and sleek long black ones and pretty green ones.

"Can I help you?"

Heather looked around and realized that she'd been ignoring the woman standing behind the reception desk, that was also round, reflecting the door.

"Oh. Hi!" Heather said, aiming to be friendly. "I'm for lunch with a friend." She gave them Dani's name and was taken to a table closer to the windows that ran along the wall.

Heather hesitated, then looked over her shoulder. "Could we sit closer to the fish?"

"Of course," the receptionist said, picking up the menus she'd already laid down and turning back into the room.

While maybe Dani would have appreciated the windows, Heather wanted to watch the fish.

"It doesn't smell fishy in here at all," she commented as she took her seat, so close she could almost touch the glass of the aquarium.

"No, it doesn't," the receptionist said.

Was that the wrong thing to say? Heather wasn't sure, but based on the tone of the woman's voice, she guessed it might have been.

Oh well.

Dani came in shortly afterward. "Hi, dearie," she said. "I should have known that you'd get us close to the tank as possible."

"Have you seen those fish?" Heather asked. "There goes the big eel again," she added as the long gliding eel snaked its way across the tank.

"It was why I chose this place," Dani said. "I figured you won't care much for the food, but you'd love the fish."

"Thank you," Heather said. "I haven't even looked at the menu."

"They have a pasta noodles and shrimp dish, in a lemon sauce, that's really nice," Dani said. "And you can get gluten free pasta."

Heather nodded, feeling guilty about all the wheat and gluten she'd eaten recently. Though she knew she shouldn't eat it, she didn't always remember to ask for a hamburger without a bun and so on.

"Why don't you order, then?" Heather said, grateful to hand over the decision to someone else.

"Sure," Dani said. She looked Heather up and down. "You look good."

"Thank you," Heather said. She paused and looked at Dani. Her friend always wore her brunette hair long, with tendrils here and there curled. She was in a pretty off-white dress that had a pattern of brown butterflies on it. Heather would notice Dani's smile more than other people's because she always wore bright red lipstick.

"You look good too," Heather said after a few moments. "You seem relaxed and sunny today."

"Thank you, dearie," Dani said.

"So what have you been up to?" Heather said, knowing that with Dani she'd have to have some small talk, she couldn't just delve into the conversation and why they were meeting.

Heather tried to pay attention, but she found herself distracted by the fish in the tank. Finally, she heard Dani ask, "So tell me about your most recent case."

"Have you heard of Qunitekon?" Heather said, glad that they'd already ordered and food was coming.

Dani tilted her head to one side. "Maybe?"

"Blake Quinten is the CEO," Heather said. "We're—"

"Stop," Dani said.

Dani's entire body had suddenly gone tense. What was that about?

"I'm under a NDA when it comes to Blake Quinten," Dani said quietly.

"Oh. OH!" Heather said. She nodded, then sighed. She couldn't ask Dani anything about the company or about Blake if she was under a non-disclosure agreement.

But that also meant that possibly Dani had at one point sued Blake, and knowing how tech worked in this town, for sexual harassment. She'd had to sign a NDA in order to get any compensation.

It meant that Blake, too, couldn't talk about it, which left Dani's reputation in the clear.

Heather paused for a moment, trying to figure out what to say next.

She remembered Chelsea talking about Blake having a reputation.

"So, I know you can't talk about your case," Heather said slowly. "Do you know if you were the only one in such a position?"

For once, Heather read Dani's smile clearly. It said, "Shark."

"I may," Dani said. "Let me make some calls."

Heather nodded and watched the fish as Dani started sending messages on her phone.

Good. It meant that Heather might not have to do something completely ridiculous, such as trying to break into the CFO's office and find the other set of books.

Heather was back in the security of her bunker, at her own desk, with the only light being from the huge monitor on her desk. She had just finished writing up her report for Chelsea, but wanted to chat with her friend before she sent it.

"What is it?" Chelsea asked immediately.

Heather already had on her headset and was pacing behind her chair. "I wanted to talk to you about Quintekon," she said.

"Oh." Chelsea gave a quiet laugh. "You so rarely call, I figured something was wrong."

Heather opened her mouth then closed it again. It wasn't that Chelsea was wrong. But sometimes Heather did call her friends, did initiate going out.

Didn't she?

"Anyway," Heather said, "I can't do anything about the books for Qunitekon. They're clean, and we both know it."

"Agreed," Chelsea said.

"However, I did find evidence of a potentially damaging nature," Heather continued. She couldn't help but grin. It was fun to put Chelsea on the side of waiting for something for once.

"And?" Chelsea said when Heather didn't continue.

"I don't have anything concrete," Heather admitted. "Just a suspicious pattern. Were you aware that six different women have sued Blake Quinten? All of them have signed NDAs, so I don't know the particulars of any of the cases. However, between the books being too clean and a pattern of behavior, I think you can advise your client to not purchase Quintekon."

"Got it," Chelsea said. "Hmmm. This is all in your report, right?"

"It is," Heather said gleefully. "Dates and names only. Can't really give you much beyond that. But it's a pattern of misbehavior."

It wouldn't hold up in a court of law, that was for certain.

But as Chelsea had pointed out, she didn't have to testify with this information. Just steer her client clear of Quintekon and the problems that might arise.

Hopefully the next woman (because there was certainly going to be a next woman) wouldn't sign the NDA. Or would get a lawyer who would argue in the interest of public safety that the details shouldn't go under an NDA.

Or maybe…

Once Heather finished chatting with Chelsea, she sat back down at her computer, opening up a new tickler. She kept track of certain individuals, setting up alerts for when their name made the news.

She was going to keep track of Blake Quinten. If she got an alert that someone else was suing him, she was going to make sure that the lawyer did his or her due diligence, and found out everything they could about that scum.

There wasn't much more she could do. She was a forensic private investigator, not one of those who specialized in surveillance.

But she could always dig deeper than anyone else.

TINY DREAMS

Jacob nodded his head, following along with whatever orchestral piece was playing on the classic radio station in his old F-150 pickup. He certainly hadn't grown up listening to classical music, but it was better than the cowboy pop his former favorite station now played.

With all the troubles in his life, Jacob didn't need the radio reminding him of heartache or worse.

He sipped his black coffee out of a dented, insulated travel mug, yet another thing that had changed for him recently, getting coffee to go instead of spending half the morning down at The Crossroads restaurant, shooting the breeze with whoever came in.

It had taken thirteen months, but Jacob was now employed again, full time, with health benefits and everything. They were kind of crappy with a huge deductible, but it was better than nothing. Even when he'd been employed recently he hadn't had any benefits at all, doing side jobs for cash under the table.

The truck sped along the two-lane back road in the pre-dawn light. Houses with large plots edged the road, plenty of room for chicken coops, goat kennels, and even the one place that had a dog run for the ugly puppies they raised. Jacob didn't envy them—too close to the street and other people. He had a spot deep in the country, a full four acres, and he couldn't see his neighbors. Growing up in the backwoods of Alaska, he'd never gotten used to having people in his space, breathing his air.

Woods sprang up between the houses, mainly Douglas Fir, wherever people hadn't gotten around to clearing them out yet. Brilliant green moss covered the limbs of the deciduous trees, like a thick winter coat that would brown with the summer heat. Ferns grew everywhere, along with blackberry bramble that was just starting to bud with silver-white leaves. It looked pretty enough, though Jacob knew what a pain it was to clear, particularly using just the machete.

Spring was on the way, and Jacob was glad of it. Working construction in an unheated warehouse was better than working outside in the Pacific Northwest cold and wet winter. But forty was already in the rearview mirror, and fifty was approaching faster than Jacob liked. He wasn't too old to do this shit, however, he could see that day coming.

Jacob slowed as he approached the Tiny Dreams facility. It was early Monday, and his turn to open up the shop.

He pulled his beater truck into the paved driveway, making sure his tail wasn't sticking out into traffic for some idiot to hit him before he turned it off. Then he sat for a moment, breathing in the quiet, taking another sip of his coffee, black and smooth, settling down in nicely on top of the egg and cheese breakfast sandwich he'd cooked up earlier.

The wide parking lot from the driveway ended at a big, one story warehouse. It was cheaply made—not much more than plywood and ugly yellow siding. On the right side of the building, three windows faced the street, along with the bright blue door. Kenny, Jacob's boss, was always bitching about how drafty they made the front office.

A huge garage door took up the other side of the building, also painted blue. A white sign attached to the front of it proudly proclaimed that this was *Home of the Tiny House of Your Dreams!*

Jacob couldn't help but roll his eyes every time he bothered to read it.

At least they didn't have to keep a fancy showroom out here. Nope, that was located in Seattle proper, in the Sodo neighborhood, just south of downtown. All they did out here at the warehouse was build the tiny houses. The office in town did the majority of the client negotiating, wheeling, and dealing.

Open fields stretched out on all sides beyond the parking lot and the building. Black Angus wandered at the far end of the field, munching placidly on the piles of hay stacked there. Derek Thompson, the owner of the farm, would herd them to one of the more green fields soon, if the rains had really paused for the week. Hopefully that would keep the smell of shit down, at least for a while.

Jacob unhooked the office keys from the carbineer he used for a key ring before he opened the door of his truck. Nanny controls beeped angrily at him, letting him know that he'd left the keys in the ignition. Like he needed a reminder. He'd never locked his keys in any vehicle he'd ever owned. He was more careful than that.

The chill of the air outside struck him hard, particularly after the warm cab of the truck. He'd grown soft living down here. Jacob pulled the red quilted flannel jacket tighter over his broad shoulders, buttoning the first three buttons across his chest. He didn't bother with a hat over his short silvering hair. Didn't bother with a beard either—it rarely got cold enough that he needed it, unlike the Alaska winters he'd grown up with. Besides, the beard was likely to be coming in mostly white now, a counterpart with his ruddy white skin. At least his blue eyes were still pretty, or at least that was what one of the waitresses at The Station restaurant told him when he flirted with them.

He stomped his heavy work boots on the ground, shaking wood dust from them and waking up his feet after the forty minute drive in. His navy blue Carhartts had dark stains of shellac and linseed oil but not yet torn—he'd get quite a few years out of them still. They'd been a good find at the local thrift shop—extra-long workpants weren't exactly common, and though Jacob was only about six foot tall, he was all leg.

The gate across the entrance to the facility was made up of two long iron arms on posts that allowed them to swing either in or out. They were painted a bright yellow so that people wouldn't bang into them, though sometimes the stupid got the better of folks, as more than one vehicle had scraped the paint off, leaving behind red rusty spots.

A heavy iron chain, each link three inches long, was wrapped around where the arms met in the center of the driveway. Jacob ambled over to it, keys in hand to unlock the padlock holding the ends of the chain together.

The padlock wasn't there.

Jacob instantly straightened up. His mouth dried out. His pulse didn't start pounding—not yet—but he felt his core temperature spike.

He carefully looked around, automatically sectioning the area in front of him and focusing on a single location at a time, as he'd trained himself to do when he'd been a teenager and it was either catch dinner for him and his ma or go hungry.

No one was in view.

He studied the front door of the building, the windows,

as well as the garage door. None of them appeared broken or forced open, at least not as far as he could tell from where he was standing.

Kenny would never forget to lock the gate. He'd been raised in one of the worst parts of the local reservation. He knew better.

Jacob peered back down at the iron chain. It looked normal enough, looped like it was supposed to be. Then again, there are only so many ways to wrap a chain across a gate.

He stalked over to one of the far ends of the gate arm, then the other, looking at the drainage ditches on either side of the driveway. They both reeked of rotting grasses, and neither of them held anything other than dirty water, drown weeds, and a couple of faded Rainer beer cans. He'd have to dredge the water to see if the padlock had been thrown into one side or the other.

Wasn't sure if that would be necessary, though. Chances were, someone had come prepared with bolt cutters and had just snipped the padlock off the chain.

What had they taken?

Jacob didn't know.

What he did know was that those thieves were going to regret it. He'd make certain of it.

Jacob walked back to his truck, grabbing his keys, silencing the annoying beeping before quietly shutting the driver door. He opened the rear door on the driver side and fished the stiletto out of the pocket on the back of the seat, slipping it into his pants where he'd have easy access to it, if necessary.

Though it was at hand, he didn't grab the metal baseball

bat he kept in the backseat. No, if he was dealing with tweakers, he didn't want to get that close. Kids who were high like that tended to be too unpredictable. He left the bat where it was, right next to the baseball mitt and ball. It wasn't that he used the mitt or the ball—they were just there for plausible deniability.

Instead, he lifted the bench seat on the driver's side. A beige gun safe sat under the seat, about a foot square, bolted to the frame of the truck. Ten black buttons stuck out on one side.

Jacob popped his head out of the truck and looked around, but he still didn't see anyone. He listened for a moment. Train was rumbling by off in the distance. Cows gave the occasional moo, sounding content, not scared or bothered by some stranger in their field. Couple of early birds were calling for their mate. Cars on the highway swished in the distance. Lifted his flattened nose to the air, sniffing. Couldn't smell much of anything—cold morning air and leftover coffee.

Everything seemed peaceful enough.

He pressed the seven-digit combination, opening the gun safe. Inside, a blue-black .357 revolver was nestled against the foam he'd carefully carved, along with a box of ammunition.

Jacob loaded the gun, then locked the truck. No one was going to come up from behind and steal it. He kept the gun in his right hand, though he went to the range often enough that he could shoot pretty well with his left if push came to shove.

Slowly, Jacob approached the closed gate. The chain felt cold and heavy in his left hand as he lifted it up, unwinding it, then as quietly as he could, coiling it back on the pavement.

Jacob swallowed, trying to work some saliva back into his mouth. His pulse was probably a little faster than normal, and he was overly warm, even in the cool morning air. The air smelled of wet cow shit and fresh grass. He still didn't hear anything other than the usual country sounds.

With the gun in his right hand, pointed at the ground, Jacob stalked silently toward the building. He didn't think he was dealing with tweakers. They wouldn't have bothered looping the chain back around the gate. Still, it was better to be prepared.

Because if any of them had remained, they were soon going to be dead tweakers.

Doors were closed and locked. Windows hadn't been broken. Nothing amiss on this side of the building.

Jacob deliberately went along the right side of the warehouse. No windows were on this side. He couldn't see in, but no one could see out, either. He glanced down at the pavement as he sidestepped silently. Couldn't see any tracks there, no one burning rubber racing around the building.

At the corner, Jacob paused, breathing in again. Still didn't hear anything out of the ordinary. Two of the mostly completed tiny houses were parked out back. They were merely waiting for final touches, like the last of the wood trim in the red Vintage model, and secondary cupboards in the black Cruiser.

Jacob took three steps along the back side of the building, gun ready, before he stopped.

He suddenly knew that the large garage door back here hadn't been touched. Chances were, nothing inside the building had been tampered with.

No. Because now he remembered that there had been *three* tiny houses out back on Friday before he'd left work for the weekend. There had been a mix-up in an order, and they'd needed to repaint the bathroom a sage-green instead of white. They'd brought the house outside so the new paint wouldn't stink up the warehouse or the two new houses they were constructing inside.

Jacob knew that the fussy young couple who'd bought and paid for the tiny house wouldn't have come to collect it over the weekend, not while the paint was still drying, that was for damned certain. They had an appointment on Tuesday.

But someone had stolen their Tiny Dreams.

J acob's gut twisted as he and Kenny sat in the front office, going over their choices.

None of them were good.

Sunlight streamed in the three windows on Jacob's right, the light partially blocked by the collection of Mariners baseball bobble-head dolls that Kenny kept well-dusted up on the ledge. The rest of the office was just as neat. On the far wall, a broad map cabinet held the architectural drawings of all the tiny house designs, not that anyone ever ordered the standard design. They were all customized, which was both the bane of Jacob's life as well as a blessing, as it kept him employed.

"Our insurance won't cover the loss of an entire tiny house, that's for damned sure," Kenny stated bluntly.

Jacob kept his sigh to himself. He wasn't sure why the insurance wouldn't be enough—seemed this was exactly the sort of thing for it to cover. But maybe the Seattle office was too cheap to pay for the replacement cost of a house. Wasn't even that much.

But given the grudging nature of his health benefits, Jacob wasn't that surprised.

"What did Seattle say when you told them about it?" Jacob asked while Kenny still perused the tome of insurance paperwork.

Kenny sighed instead of replying right away.

That was not good.

"You haven't told them yet, have you?" Jacob said, putting two and two together and not liking the four he got.

Kenny shook his head and kept his eyes on the papers in front of him.

Damn it! When the hell was Kenny going to grow up? He was old enough, just celebrated thirty-two recently with a wife and two kids.

Before coming to work for Tiny Dreams, Kenny had been selling used cars. He had an honest face and an earnest look in his black eyes that Jacob couldn't fake even on his best day. Kenny's skin was dark with a red tinge to it that showed his heritage, along with his straight black hair. He knew a little about construction, and he was willing to listen to Jacob and learn. Kenny was much better with the clients, though, casually upselling them when they came in for their first "visit" with their house. He was usually good with numbers too, making sure that the Seattle office paid them before any work started, cutting corners and getting discounts that the Seattle office never learned about.

"You need to tell Seattle about the theft," Jacob said. There was no way they could hide this. The fussy couple had made so many modifications to their tiny house. It would take them ten days, with overtime, to recreate it.

Kenny said nothing, the office growing quiet and still.

Jacob took a sip of the office coffee—which wasn't as good as the stuff he brewed at home, but he wasn't bringing in fancy beans, not here. He stayed quietly, willing to sit there all day long while Kenny finally grew a pair and dealt with the issue like an adult.

"I want to try to find it, first," Kenny said finally.

For the second time that day, Jacob felt his spine stiffen

and his mouth go dry. A slight chill touched the back of his neck, as if a cool finger had just caressed it. Goosebumps ran from his shoulders up under his shorn hair and around his ears.

"Why?" Jacob asked flatly. What the hell was Kenny hiding?

"Look, you and I both know that the tiny house craze has tapered off considerably," Kenny said. "The Seattle office is hurting. That was why I had to lay off the other two guys and just bring you in."

Jacob nodded. Kenny had been trying to do all the work himself, doing a pretty crappy job, and had fallen way behind when he'd hired Jacob.

At the time, Kenny had also given Jacob the impression that the other two had found a better opportunity, not that they'd been laid them off.

It also explained why Jacob was barely making minimum wage doing custom work.

"I'm afraid that if I tell the office about the house, they're going to insist that I lay you off," Kenny said.

Jacob sighed. He suspected that Kenny's earnest look was covering up some other sin that Jacob wasn't privy to.

That was all right. They all had their dark secrets. Kenny had never looked too deeply into Jacob's past, just at the work he did in the warehouse.

"How do you want to go about hunting the stolen house?" Jacob asked. It wouldn't be like tracking a moose through the woods. The thieves would still leave something of a trail, though, even across the hard asphalt. Jacob had some ideas for how to find the elusive track, but it would be good to know what Kenny brought to the table.

"You know Mike? Who owns the convenience store down at the corner?" Kenny said. "He has camera watching the gas pumps. Maybe our thief drove past there, and we can at least get an ID on the truck."

"That's a good idea," Jacob said, surprised that Kenny had thought of it.

Then again, given some of the stories that Kenny had told of his youth, maybe it shouldn't have been surprising to Jacob that Kenny knew the location of the nearest cameras that might have incriminating evidence.

"I'll go talk with the folks at the gardening center, the other direction," Jacob volunteered. "See if the asshole went that way instead." It had been something he'd been planning on already.

"Good," Kenny said, nodding. He pushed his chair back and stood, suddenly ready for action.

"We only have until Tuesday afternoon," Jacob said as he slowly stood.

Kenny grimaced. "Yeah, I know. I'll try to put the couple who owns the house off until Thursday or Friday, tell them that the paint wasn't an exact match and we have to special order it."

"What happens if we can't find it?" Jacob asked, stubbornly staying exactly where he was, his bulk acting like a gravity well, keeping Kenny in his place behind the desk.

"I'll have to tell the Seattle office it was stolen," Kenny said.

"And the cops," Jacob added.

Kenny's throat appeared to have gotten dry, given the way he gulped. "And the cops," he said after a few moments.

Jacob didn't know what Kenny's problem was with the cops. Not that he'd ever cared for them much himself.

He didn't bother asking what they'd do once they found the thieves. He had a pretty good idea that the cops wouldn't be involved in meting out justice, either.

Jacob and Kenny got lucky at first. The cameras on the front of Mike's convenient store did show a dark pick up, probably black, hauling away the tiny house early Saturday morning, around seven AM. It had double-rear wheels, so it was either used on a farm nearby to haul horses or cattle, or to haul one of those fancy RV trailers.

Then they ran into a dead end. No other stores were on the road nearby, and the ones who were, wouldn't share their footage. There were too many miles of empty road, too many places where a tiny house might be tucked away with no one the wiser.

Kenny and Jacob met back up at the warehouse after lunch, putting in half a day's worth of work.

While Jacob drilled holes in the studs of the tiny house they'd just started to construct, Kenny added additional security to the two tiny houses sitting in the back lot. They already had locks on the hitches to prevent someone from just driving up and taking one. That, however, had just been snipped off. Kenny added a second lock, with a chain and a concrete bolster, to keep the houses from wandering away.

Kenny had just finished his work when Jacob drilled the last stub. Silently, Kenny came into the house, helping to feed the neon-yellow Romex through the holes and starting to install the electrical outlets according to the spec. They worked in silence for an hour with very few words exchanged, just a few grunts and occasional questions.

When the electric was in, Jacob threw a questioning glance at Kenny, who just nodded. They were calling it quits for the day. Kenny had managed to convince the fussy couple to come in on Thursday to pick up their tiny house. The missing tiny house.

That gave them Tuesday and Wednesday to find the

errant house. Hopefully whoever had taken it hadn't done too much damage to it, so Jacob and Kenny could repair it before the couple came.

"Coming in late tomorrow," Jacob announced as Kenny closed up the warehouse.

That got him a silent look.

He shrugged.

There were a few people he wanted to talk with in the morning, to see if he could get a lead on the house.

And if nothing else, to inquire about a possible position if his own Tiny Dreams came to an end.

J acob sat at the long bar at The Crossroads restaurant the next morning, sipping his coffee slowly, listening to the old country ballads the radio station favored. He'd already finished off a healthy breakfast—biscuits from a mix but pork gravy done from scratch, with over easy eggs, under cooked hash browns, and a side of homemade sausage links. He didn't normally eat this heavy in the mornings but he did that morning. Plus, he stretched it out, making it last, because it was likely his only meal that day.

The restaurant had taken over an old abandoned train station—a low, yellowish brick building with wide windows on all sides, letting in whatever sunshine might deign to show itself during the winter months.

When the restaurant had gone in, they'd built a wall down the long ways of the building, dividing what had been a single room into two. On one side, booths ran under the windows, then a skinny aisle, then a breakfast bar, with red padded stools bolted into the spotless black-and-white tiled floor. The counter of the bar was covered in a light blue linoleum with chrome trim, a hipster interpretation of an old diner. The kitchen was on the other side of the wall, with a large window cut into the center of it where orders were passed through, along with the heavenly smells of bacon and fried pork sausage.

Maurine walked by holding the coffee pot like it was a tournament prize, asking silently if he'd like a refill. Jacob considered her to be a good looking woman, though he knew that she didn't fit the modern standards of beauty given her weight and age, despite her sparkling dark eyes and teasing grin. She'd just celebrated twenty-one years of sobriety, and the wrinkles in her face still showed the hard living she'd done when she'd been young and stupid.

At least she'd survived them, while so many of her friends hadn't.

Jacob could commiserate, though he'd never been addicted to alcohol or drugs. Adrenaline, perhaps, but that was a whole different kind of young and stupid.

"You seen Mitch around?" Jacob asked while Maurine poured another splash of coffee in his mug.

"Now why on earth would you be asking after him?" Maurine said. She drew the coffee pot back and held it up like a sword, ready to throw it in his face in order to defend herself.

Mitch was well known in the area for being a drug supplier. He didn't cook the stuff himself, or take it either. But he was known for traveling to the far flung labs hidden in the woods and carrying product into the city. He was small time, and tried hard not to give anyone offense, so no one would turn him in. Not that the cops had ever caught him with anything, the few times they had arrested him.

"Just have a few questions for him, that's all," Jacob assured Maurine. "Some property of mine went missing. Figured Mitch might have a clue about where it ended up."

Maurine's dark eyes took on a calculating look. "You mean like a tiny house?"

Jacob laughed and shook his head. Figured. He should have just asked Maurine first instead of coming up with some elaborate plan about forcing a drug dealer to talk.

Not that he would have necessarily minding beating the crap out of Mitch, just for the heck of it. Might still find a reason.

"Now, you didn't hear this from me," Maurine warned, setting the pot down and getting serious.

Jacob nodded. He knew that while The Crossroads restaurant was the hub of the small community of the town of Elk Mound, and gossip flowed as freely as the coffee, Maurine held the secrets of more than one of the locals. She was a mother figure for many of guys—if your mom had more ink than the local bad boy wannabes and could out-swear a career Marine.

"You know Dennis Frazer?" Maurine said quietly.

"Cattle rancher just south of Cumberland?" Jacob said, trying to place the name.

"That's the one," Maurine said. "His boy, Eddie, was in here Sunday morning, bragging about finally getting his own place. When I asked where, he said it was on his dad's property for now, but that he'd be moving it later. Made a joke about how small it was. Got me wondering about you."

A sense of relief flooded over Jacob. "Thanks, Maurine," he said. "You've just saved me a whole heap of trouble."

Not that finding Mitch and beating him up would have been that much trouble. Might still do it, just on principle.

"Eddie's fallen in with a bad crowd," Maurine added. "If you can separate him from them, that might be the most helpful."

Jacob could read between the lines easy enough.

Maurine wouldn't mind if Eddie's friends saw the inside

of a hospital and had a year or more of rehab, while Eddie should be able to shake off his beating in a week or three.

"I understand, ma'am," Jacob said solemnly.

He was used to taking orders like this, singling out specific individuals for punishment, back when he wasn't known as Jacob MacMillan but just as Mac the Muscle, who took care of situations for some Important People in Seattle.

"You're a good man, Jacob," Maurine said, nodding. "Now, put your wallet away. Cleaning up the neighborhood shouldn't go unrewarded."

"Thank you," Jacob said, not bothering to argue as he downed the last of his coffee. While Jacob could be stubborn, he'd rarely met anyone as determined as Maurine.

He picked up his quilted flannel jacket and headed out, into the soft rain, walking across the lot to his beat up truck, formulating then discarding plans of attack. He'd have to approach this sideways.

Just how sideways, well, that might depend on Eddie. And whatever luck Jacob didn't have.

The Frazer ranch wasn't on the main road that led between Cumberland and Veazie, but instead, tucked in one of the private roads, off the side, just past the Nolte State Park. The only reason Jacob knew about the place was because one of Frazer's neighbors had an estate sale at the start of the year. Frequently, whatever grandchild had inherited a farm had no idea what they were selling off. Jacob had gotten some of his best woodworking tools for a song as the kids just thought they were old and didn't see the use of them.

Unfortunately, that meant it was going to be harder to approach the house. The road was marked private. Jacob knew that the neighbors out here were likely to shoot anyone just wandering across their land, assuming tweakers or thieves.

Jacob turned off the main Cumberland-Veazie road anyway, up onto the narrow private road, then pulled his truck off the pavement, onto the grass at the side. He paused for a moment, checking his appearance in the rearview mirror. He hadn't had to use any disguises since he'd left being Mac the Muscle behind, at least five years. He figured the glue was still good, though the beard he now sported itched like crazy. It was also weird that every time he turned his head and felt hair brushing his neck. The cap helping to hold the wig on was black with the logo of a local band. Even though his nose was now longer and sharply pointed, he'd gotten used to it already. At least the brown contacts didn't make the world darker.

First thing Jacob did when he got out of his truck was to raise its hood. No one out here would look twice at an old beater on the side of the road that seemed to be broken down. High gray clouds covered what sky he could see through the trees. Unless some front came through, it probably wouldn't start raining again until later that night. Clouds kept the temperature higher as well, something Jacob was grateful for.

Jacob still had his Concealed Carry license—something else he'd maintained even after leaving the muscle business. He tucked the .357 into a shoulder holster, then zipped his jacket over it. The jacket was black and made out of a heavy, slick material that would keep off the worst of the rain as well as not get caught too easily on blackberry thorns.

Heavy leather work gloves went on next, again to protect him from the worst of the bramble. And possibly to prevent any stray fingerprints. Into one jacket pocket went heavy duty garden sheers that had already been wiped clean, to clip branches out of the way. Then he picked up the baseball bat that had also been wiped down earlier. He considered using the machete, but he didn't want to leave noticeable of a trail behind him where he was going.

The turn off for the Frazer Ranch was easy to find, particularly with the weathered sign standing next to the gravel driveway. Of course, red and white *No Trespassing* signs were posted everywhere. Jacob ignored them, cautiously walking just a few feet up the driveway before spying a game trail just to the left.

The start of the trail was narrow, but it led to a much wider path. They must have elk passing through here regularly, not just deer. He didn't see any recent scat, but he kept his eyes out. Something scurried out of the way as he walked—rabbit or chipmunk. Still too early for a lot of birds, though he did hear the twitters of bushtits once. The ground was covered with yellowing leaves from a big-leaf maple, as well as bright green moss, helping Jacob move silently. Despite the coffee Jacob had consumed earlier, his mouth was dry.

The driveway split after a few yards, one part continuing straight, the other curving away to the right. Jacob spied a nice enough rambler through the trees, probably built in the eighties, up at the top of a slope. Green grass, smooth like a carpet, spread out before it. Probably took three guys to maintain it all summer long. Jacob couldn't see the point.

The road that continued straight got a lot rougher, the gravel petering out to just rock and mud. There must be a second road from the house to the back forty of the ranch. No farmer would let a utility road fall to disrepair like this.

Up ahead, Jacob spied a disused building, longer than it was wide, with regularly spaced sagging windows. It had once been painted white, and had probably been a chicken coop. He could smell the hay moldering in it. Far off in the distance, across the green field, stood a new barn, two stories tall, painted gray with bright white trim and a sloping red roof.

It was easy to see that this part of the ranch wasn't often in use or visited.

Then why was there a two-door yellow Fiat parked in front of the former coop?

Voices carried across the quiet air.

A female voice, protesting weakly.

Jacob swallowed hard. Just what was going on?

He slipped onto the road and hurried forward.

Parked just past the coop was his missing tiny house.

A boy—probably in his late teens—was leading a girl toward the tiny house. She stumbled, drunk or stoned, possibly both. He was dressed in a jacket, jeans, and boots—appropriate wear for outside—while she was wearing just a skirt and a top, with white socks and sneakers. She had the long, lean legs of an athlete, coltish with no hips, so possibly underage.

The boy bent his dark head toward her red-haired one, saying something soothing. Jacob could only catch the tone, not the words themselves.

The girl settled for a few steps, then hesitated, drawing back again.

She wasn't a willing participant, despite whatever it was she'd been given.

As far as Jacob could tell, the boy wasn't Eddie Frazer.

Was Eddie already inside the tiny house? With another girl?

How many of them were there? Jacob had to assume at least two boys, maybe three, who'd all ditched school, piled into the Fiat and driven here.

Didn't matter. Jacob had to stop them, before that tiny house turned into a house of horrors.

Jacob considered his options for a moment, before taking a deep breath and exploding into action.

The boy heard him pounding up the driveway, running full tilt toward them. He turned, drawing the girl with him.

Good.

Jacob shifted his grip on the bat, bringing it up like he was bunting a ball. He barely paused as he punched the bat into the boy's mouth.

The thunk of flesh hitting the metal made a much deeper sound than when it struck a ball. Blood spewed out of the boy's mouth as he fell sideways, landing hard in the wet mud.

The girl gave a sharp cry, but she didn't scream. She stared at him with wide eyes, shaking.

Jacob dropped the bat next to the fallen boy. He didn't want to risk bringing blood or other trace evidence into the truck.

"Stay here," Jacob growled at the girl before rushing to the tiny house.

The door was at the far end of the building. Jacob knew that just inside, to the left, was a couch/seating area. To the right was the repainted bathroom. The kitchen was in the center of the house, with ladders leading up on either side to the two lofts.

Chances were, whoever was inside was going to be downstairs. They probably couldn't negotiate ladders, not in their current state.

Jacob yanked open the door, reaching to the left.

There was Eddie Frazer, on top of a mostly naked girl.

Though he was shirtless, his pants were still up. Only sexual assault, then, and not rape.

Not yet.

Jacob slammed his fist into the side of the boy's surprised face. The force of the blow tumbled him off the girl.

She stirred, opening her eyes, blinking sleepily at Jacob.

Jacob grabbed one of Eddie's arms and pulled him off the bench and outside.

Finally, Eddie seemed to catch a clue and started to struggle.

Jacob took a fistful of Eddie's hair and yanked hard, pulling his head back, while twisting Eddie's arm up behind his back.

"Now listen here, you little shit," Jacob said as he frog marched the boy past the edge of the chicken coop and a bit beyond the Fiat. "The only reason you're still alive right now is because there are some people in the community who think that you might still be worth a shit. After I tell them what I just saw, I wouldn't count on their good word ever again. You hear me?" Jacob said, yanking on the boy's hair again.

"Ye—ye—yes," the boy stuttered.

Jacob didn't expect a proper, "Yes, sir." Boy probably hadn't been raised to have manners like that.

"Now, I'm going to be watching you," Jacob warned as he whipped the boy around. Eddie's eyes were wide and frightened, but there was a calculating look at the back of them.

Idiot hadn't learned yet that Jacob was serious.

Jacob placed his punch to the boy's face carefully, at just the right angle, guaranteed to break his nose.

Blood gushed out in a satisfactory way. Eddie bent over and howled loudly. Jacob grabbed the boy's hair again, forcing his head up.

"Listen to me," Jacob said, the words low and heavy, flowing from his mouth straight into Eddie's ear. The rank scent of the boy's sweat mingled with the oily smell of the drugs he'd taken. Jacob's stomach rolled, but he'd do as Maurine had asked, and not slit the boy's throat with the knife in his pocket.

At least, not today.

Instead, Jacob stomped down on the boy's bare foot as hard as he could with his heavy work boots. The sound of the tiny bones breaking was difficult to hear, even in the quiet yard, particularly given how the boy shrieked in pain after that.

"If I ever hear that you've disrespected a woman again, like how you just did, next time it wouldn't be your nose and your foot. I'll break both your knees, so it will hurt every time you take a step, to help you remember better. Do you hear me?"

The boy hiccupped and cried, his world probably filled with a red haze of pain. Jacob knew that feeling, had experienced it more than once.

Really, he was getting too old for this shit.

"Do you hear me?" Jacob snarled, shaking Eddie hard, like he would a small can of paint that had sat overnight.

"Yes, yes, yes, sir," Eddie finally gulped out.

Jacob threw the boy to the ground. He tried to get up, but he couldn't stand with his broken foot.

He'd have to crawl through the mud back to the house.

Too bad.

Jacob heard noise behind him and whirled around, ready for the next assailant, but it was just the two girls, slowly making their way to the Fiat.

"Get in the back," he ordered them.

The redhead nodded, supporting her friend the brunette. They slowly made their uncoordinated way into the backseat.

As he'd expected, Jacob found the keys in the ignition. He was surprised and pleased to find that it was a manual, not an automatic. He turned the car around and sped up the gravel driveway, heading toward the main road.

"Where are you taking us?" the red head finally asked, panic giving a sharp edge to her voice.

Jacob stopped a short ways down the road, in front of the mile marker.

"You wait five minutes, then you call 911. Tell them you're on the Cumberland-Veazie road, near the intersection of south-east two ninety second. Tell them that you've been drugged and that you need help," Jacob said.

The girl gulped but nodded. "Thank you," she whispered. She pulled her phone out of her pants pocket and gripped it like a talisman to ward off evil.

Jacob didn't know how much she'd seen of his "fight" with Eddie. Hopefully enough to know that he wasn't going to be a threat. At least, not in the short run.

It would be up to her how much of the story she told the authorities, whether she sank him deeper into the shit or not.

Jacob nodded to her, then raced out of the car, up the road, running. The adrenaline was fading fast, but he had to move. Now.

Shit, he really was getting too old.

It took Jacob longer than he wanted to get to his truck. He flung the gloves as well as the jacket off into the brush. The blood on his pants wasn't obvious, not with the other work stains, and he'd somehow managed to not get any on his boots.

Jacob gunned it down the gravel driveway. He told himself that he wouldn't run Eddie over even if he was crawling up the center of it. It was probably even true.

But Eddie was no where to be seen. Maybe he'd done the world a favor and crawled off under the blackberry bramble to die. Not like Jacob would be shedding any tears over that.

It took Jacob maybe three minutes to line up his truck

hitch with the tiny house. Dumb fucks hadn't bothered to block the wheels.

Sirens were loud in the distance by the time Jacob hit the main road, heading away from the yellow Fiat. He obediently slowed down and edged toward the side of the road as Cumberland's fire and rescue truck came barreling toward him.

Then, Jacob got back onto the road and turned the music on high, hauling his Tiny Dreams behind him.

I t took Kenny and Jacob most of a day to clear out the party damage to the tiny house, setting it to rights and getting the place well aired out, long before Thursday.

Kenny asked no questions. He also made Jacob sign a time sheet that showed he was working at the facility all morning Tuesday.

Though Jacob doubted anyone would be able to place him at the scene and probably didn't need an alibi, it was still good to know that Kenny had his back.

Before Jacob left Thursday night, after the tiny house had been taken by its new owner, he stopped in the office. Kenny was sitting at the desk, going over some reports, a task that Jacob never wished to acquire. The sun was already dim, and long shadows were cast across the room, keeping Kenny in the dark, just a single light shining on the desk.

"You need any help?" Jacob asked as he leaned against the doorframe.

"Naw, I got it," Kenny said with a grin as he looked up.

"You sure?" Jacob said pointedly. "No other mess that you need cleaned up? Because there's a mess there, that needs cleaning. I can smell it."

Kenny pressed his lips together and just nodded, his

mien growing solemn. "I need a little time," he said softly. "Mess should be gone by the end of the month."

"I'm holding you to that," Jacob growled in warning.

Kenny's eyes grew large at the menace he suddenly heard in Jacob's voice. He gulped, then nodded quickly.

"Good," Jacob said. "Have a good night."

He didn't know what troubles Kenny had. Didn't want to know.

But he'd fix them for good, if need be.

———

Sunday morning, Jacob sat at the breakfast bar in The Crossroads restaurant. He'd treated himself that morning to the meat lover's special—eggs, cheese, homemade pork sausage, bacon, and ham. Had an English muffin with blackberry jelly to wipe up the remains, along with about a gallon of coffee.

After he'd finished eating and was sitting back, contemplating fetching a newspaper, and maybe later, a nap, Maurine came up with the coffee pot. She gave him a sideways glance before reaching across the linoleum and refilling his cup.

"Heard there was a disturbance earlier this week out at Frazer's ranch," Maurine said as she set the pot down. "Some wild-eyed hippy with a scraggly beard, dark eyes, and long hair beat up the Frazer boy."

Jacob nodded slowly. "What else did you hear?" he asked quietly. Was this the last time he'd be welcome here?

"Funny thing, that," Maurine said. "Seems another man matching that description helped two poor girls who'd been drugged and sexually assaulted near there."

"Hmmm," Jacob said, his heart settling down. He really

liked this place, really liked being part of a loose-knit community.

"Wouldn't be a cousin of yours, would it?" Maurine said pointedly. Her dark eyes peered at him, as if trying to pierce his secrets.

"No one I know," Jacob said blandly. "All my cousins are still up above the thirty-eighth parallel." Or in prison, but Maurine didn't need to know about that.

"I see," Maurine said. "Well, Dennis might be sending his son to a military school, at least according to Pete down at the recruiting office in Enumclaw."

"Hmmm," Jacob said again. He didn't think it would do any good. Then again, maybe some discipline would help that punk.

He'd been able to turn his life around. Maybe Eddie could too.

Maurine didn't make any mention of the other boy, so he probably hadn't died. Might still be in the hospital, though, having his skull reconstructed.

"No bill for you today," Maurine announced suddenly as she straightened up. "Probably not for any meal this month, as long as you don't try to take advantage of it."

"Would I do that?" Jacob asked, shooting for innocent but probably missing by a mile.

Maurine flashed him a large smile, big enough that he could see one of her incisors was gold.

"Thank you," Maurine said before she turned away, the goddess of the coffee having given her blessing.

Or the godmother of the community.

Whatever.

Jacob put his elbows on the breakfast bar and sipped at his coffee. The warm feeling in his chest didn't just come from the drink.

The radio started playing yet another classic country ballad from the eighties.

Maybe Jacob could get Maurine to switch over the classic station some morning, though he wasn't about to push his luck that far, at least not this morning.

RED RAGES

Ginger marveled at just how good she felt with the cocktail of cocaine, caffeine, antihistamines, and whatever the hell else was currently streaming through her veins. It certainly overcame the lethargy that COVID-19 had left her with. She'd only had a fever for a day, but the exhaustion had hit her hard.

Good thing she'd been prepared for it.

Ginger didn't regularly use drugs. Cocaine was one of those things that had just felt a little *too* good the first time she'd tried it, back in the 1980s, when she'd been in college. However, in her preparations, she'd acquired a mix of drugs just for this occasion, in case she, too, came down with the plague just when she'd reached the culmination of her plans.

She drove through the eerily empty streets of Palo Alto. Everything had been shut down for a month. People were still getting used to it. Lots of cat memes and end of the world jokes, plus sourdough, of all things. Fortunately, Ginger hadn't followed along with the rest of the idiotic herd —even at fifty-one, she didn't have a nesting bone in her body. It was all rage and fire.

Working at home had just given her the opportunity to do a deep dive into her plans and actually set things in motion.

The houses she drove by had hard edges on them, as if everything had been outlined with a black sharpie. Most of the cars she saw were parked. Getting here, she'd *never* driven down the 101 so quickly, instead of having to deal with asshole tourists weaving across lanes as they read their maps, or dumbass developers checking their phones.

It was weird seeing so many birds in the city. It wasn't like from a horror movie with them dive bombing the few people who did venture out, aiming for flesh and soft spots. Instead, it felt more like an advance guard, checking to see if it was safe.

As if any place in the world was safe.

And the birds couldn't reach the boardrooms and conference tables where the real crimes were committed.

Ginger shook her head, reminding herself to focus. It was pretty fucking hard between the drugs amping her up and the exhaustion threatening to tunnel her.

Too damned bad. She had a job to do. A plan to realize. Her plan was as resilient as she could make it. One never tried to make something foolproof. Fools were too damned ingenious. Instead, resilience was the name of the game. At least these days in the software industry.

Her plan was still pretty clever, though it relied heavily on the current state of affairs.

After all, they were no longer conducting autopsies on those who died who had COVID.

That had been a huge piece of luck on her part.

She'd friended Robert J Whitney, Jr years ago on all the social media platforms, just so she could see how he was still profiting from his father's theft. She knew it was unhealthy to compare herself to him all the damned time, wanting to do better than he was financially, even though he was only in his mid-twenties. The shrinks would have quite a bit to say about their one-sided competition.

Fuck 'em.

Still, she'd rejoiced when Robert had announced that he'd tested positive for COVID, though she'd expressed sympathy and well wishes along with everyone else.

It had certainly lit a fire under her ass, and she finally put all her plans into motion. This was a golden opportunity. She just had to reach out and take it.

Despite catching the fucking plague herself.

The drugs were still keeping her upright, but just barely. Fortunately, her rage would have to do the rest.

And she had a volcano's worth of hot burning lava to fuel her.

The neighborhood where Robert lived wasn't as posh as she would have imagined. She'd never been there before, had never allowed herself to drive through it, afraid that the temptation to lob Molotov Cocktails through his front windows would have been too great to resist.

The houses were all McMansions, of course. But the yards weren't even as large as she would have imagined. Instead, they were all postage-stamp sized, with the buildings just a couple yards apart. Some of the lots were deep enough to fit a swimming pool in the back. But not all.

The neighborhood association must have required that all the lawns be perfectly trimmed and even. Probably fucking dictated the color scheme of the flowers out front. Only brick-colored lava rock was apparently allowed beneath the plants to keep the weeds out. Bright red or black wouldn't have been tolerated.

Ginger could never live in a place like this. She'd want to paint her house chartreuse or magenta just to fuck with people.

The skies were a pale blue, as if mourning the world that used to be, like the rest of them. Although the lack of smog and pollution had made the air a fuckton cleaner. Ginger didn't know if everyone would stay working from home after the plague had passed or not.

Didn't much matter to her.

They always said to dig two graves when plotting your revenge. Ginger had done her best to cover her tracks. But if she didn't survive, well, then she'd just get to spit in young Robert's eye when she met him in hell.

As well as his old man.

Everyone was inside that morning, probably chatting on Zoom or whatever the hell else they did to avoid actually working. Only delivery cars and trucks were out cruising the empty streets.

She drove past Robert's house slowly, as if making sure that it was the right address. She'd stolen one of those magnet stickers that proclaimed her car as a delivery service, had slapped it on the driver-side door.

No one would look twice at her car. Or think anything about it if it was parked there for a while. She might have more than one delivery in the neighborhood. Maybe even catering a clandestine party.

She stopped two houses past Robert's. Then she tied on her mask and put on her gloves—how convenient those were now!—before she got out of the car.

Ginger had to pause for a moment as the world darkened around the edges. God, she was tired.

But she was so close to her target, to annihilating the cause of all her suffering.

She ground her teeth and pushed forward, too stubborn to stop now.

From the trunk of her car she pulled two large bags from

a local Thai restaurant that she knew Robert loved, given the pictures he'd posted on his social media feed.

She also stuck her hand in her pocket and pulled out what looked like an oversized phone. It was almost two inches thick, though the rest of it was about the size of the latest mini-tablet.

No one from a distance could see the prongs sticking out from the top.

Ginger had modified the taser herself, making damned sure that the new design would be unrecognizable at a casual glance, as well as pack one hell of a punch.

Of course, the sidewalk up to Robert's door had no weeds sticking out between the cracks. He paid a service to ensure that his lawn was fucking perfect as well. The azaleas were just starting to flower. He had no damned clue what they were, of course, just called them pretty.

She rang the doorbell, glad for the excuse to be wearing gloves. As well as a mask.

Robert opened the door. He looked like shit, skin pale and eyes watery. His brown hair was sticking up as though she'd just woken him. He wore a baby blue, ratty bathrobe over a stained white T-shirt.

He just gaped at her for a moment. "Did I order food?" he asked dully, as if he couldn't remember.

"You certainly ordered something," Ginger replied sharply.

Then she tasered him, knocking him hard on his ass, before stepping inside and kicking the door closed behind her.

Step one, accomplished.

Now she just had to set up his "suicide." And her revenge would be complete.

Finally.

Fuck, Ginger was exhausted. She didn't remember ever feeling this tired before. Not even pulling all-nighters just after her first product had gone live.

She'd paused after she'd shut the door, looking around his spotless front entrance. What the hell? Was he having his illegal maid service come in to clean?

It took more strength than she'd counted on to pull his unresisting body from in front of the door to the living room on the right. He must have gained weight or something.

The nest he'd made himself on the couch told her the full story: Robert hadn't moved from that spot for days. Probably only to go pee. Maybe to get food delivered, given the mountain of take-out containers stacked up.

The rest of the house was likely to be spotless just because he hadn't been anywhere else since he'd gotten sick.

Ginger didn't open any windows, though she wanted to, as the stench of sweaty, unwashed male was overpowering. She dug deep into her rage and ignored it instead of puking.

The rest of the living room was nice enough. She'd seen parts of it on social media plenty of times. The couch in the center of the long space, in front of the TV, perfect for him to wank on. Built-in bookshelves against the far wall, colorful spines of flashy books meant to impress, not that he would have read anything but the reviews or wiki page. In the far corner, a desk the size of an architect's drafting table, with three huge monitors on it.

She'd smirked when she'd seen those the first time on Instagram—over compensating for much?

It took almost all her strength to drag Robert up into his desk chair. She'd figured it would be the chair that she could easily tie him to, though she had a secondary plan for using one of the kitchen chairs if she had to. Zip-ties were in the takeout bags.

It should have taken her between two to three minutes to tie him up. She'd timed herself, practicing on a manikin in her apartment in Daly City.

She hadn't counted on the fucking plague making her hands shake, or herself as weak as a kitten.

Goddamn it!

She wanted to throw her head back and howl. The neighbors probably wouldn't notice—not given Robert's rapist tendencies.

Still, best not to risk it. Plus, such a shout might take even more of her strength. She gritted her teeth and made herself move, despite the black spots dancing on the edges of her vision.

It was just more hell for her to push through. She'd already been through worse.

Fortunately, she seemed to have a touch of luck, or Robert was really sick, as she got him all the way tied up before he came to. He was making noises through the gag, as though he was trying to talk to her, to ask her what she was doing. Too fucking bad. She'd take it off later, after she had him arranged to her liking.

Still took her for-fucking-ever. And she didn't have that much time. Sooner or later, someone would notice the delivery driver was still inside, and not out being a good minion and risking their life so that others could eat.

Finally, Ginger felt she was ready. She pushed herself up to her feet, ignoring how she swayed a little.

Okay, maybe swayed a whole hell of a lot. And the room blackened considerably for a moment.

She was *not* about to faint though, goddamn it!

She got herself back under control and finally pulled out the suicide note that she'd thoughtfully provided for Robert.

It had been printed on a printer identical to the one sitting next to his desk. That the police wouldn't find the note on his computer probably wouldn't mean that much. If they even bothered to look for it.

Crafting the note had taken time. Ginger had run a lot of Robert's feed through an AI program to analyze it, and to make damned sure that what she produced sounded *exactly* like him. It said that he was sorry for being such a shit, apologized for raping that woman, and that he could no longer live with all the things he'd done.

Fortunately, she'd been able to create the note before she'd come down with the plague herself.

She showed the note to him, with a mostly steady hand, giving him time to read it and digest the implications.

Then slowly, carefully, she reached for his gag.

"I didn't do it," were the first words out of his mouth.

"Yeah, right. Like father, like son," Ginger spit at him.

Good, this was going according to plan. She knew the little shit would deny raping that girl.

Just like his father had denied ever doing anything wrong to her.

To be fair, though, Robert J Whitney, Sr. hadn't actually raped her.

Instead, he'd stolen her idea for a new dating profile website, the math she'd discovered, the new algorithms she'd developed. He been the very first investor that she'd shown her work to. After he'd seen it, he'd blackballed her. No one else would take her calls.

When Robert Sr. went to market within the next two months, she knew what had gone on. The IPO of his company had made him a billionaire.

And little Robert Jr. had profited ever since.

Ginger had done a little dance and celebrated when the

old man had died of a sudden heart attack a little over a year before.

She'd quickly learned that it hadn't been enough to scratch that itch inside her. She still raged.

When Robert Jr. had been accused of rape, she knew she had to take him down.

Like father, like son.

"I wasn't at that party," Robert said. "I can prove it. I'd been invited, but I didn't go. I wouldn't rape a woman. I'm not my father."

Ginger just sniffed. "Too bad," she said harshly. She'd known this scum would deny everything.

"Look, my dad was an asshole. I know that," he said heatedly. "You probably won't believe this, but I celebrated when he finally died."

"So?" Ginger said. "You *profited* from my loss. Whether you hated the source of your income or not. Look at this place! You're still profiting from what your father stole from me."

"What did my dad steal?" Robert asked. The glassiness of his eyes had been replaced with a much keener look.

"The algorithms for making matches," Ginger said. She stood up taller, though all she wanted to do was to go laydown. "That was my invention."

Robert appeared to swallow hard. "I knew he hadn't come up with that himself. I was in college when the company went big."

Ginger nodded. She'd known that.

"But I've sold that company," Robert said.

"I know. It was how you afforded this place," Ginger said. She couldn't help herself. He had this huge house all to himself, while she lived in a ratty apartment in Daly City.

"No," Robert vehemently denied. "All the money from

that sale went to a trust. That money goes to an AIDS charity. I knew it was dirty and I didn't want to touch it."

"Yeah, right," Ginger said. She pulled the gun out of her bag and started putting on the full plastic raincoat that she needed to protect her clothing from the blood spatter.

"Look, I can prove that I didn't rape that woman," Robert said. He was starting to sound desperate.

Ginger didn't want to hesitate. She had to keep moving. The clock was ticking.

But there was an actual living, breathing human being in front of her. Not a damned manikin. Murder was proving to be more difficult than she'd like.

"Get my phone. The code is 77542. It has the proof that I didn't rape her," Robert said.

Ginger's head was swimming. She just had to gag him again. Put the gun in his hand. Make him pull the trigger. Didn't really matter where the bullet struck. He'd bleed out and die before anyone came looking for him.

Then she'd have to untie him. Spread the blood around where the ropes had been. It wouldn't be that hard. Right?

It all seemed like too much work, at the moment. All she wanted to do was to go lay down and sleep for a week.

"My phone. It's on the couch," Robert said. "Left side."

Ginger felt as though the air had turned viscous and she was pushing herself forward underwater. Still, she slowly walked to the couch and picked up the brand new iPhone, then entered the code.

"Where is the proof?" she said, please that at least her voice sounded strong. She started to sweat heavily. Fuck. Her own fever was probably spiking. Again.

Now, it was Robert's turn to hesitate. "Open the photos app," he said slowly.

Ginger did, then swiped down to the day in question.

Fuck. There were pictures of Robert and some guy

laughing in a bar, holding up stupid foo-foo drinks, complete with little umbrellas.

And a picture of them kissing.

They did look kind of cute together.

"I'm gay," Robert said.

Ginger was surprised at how pale he'd grown. There had never been even a hint of Robert being a homosexual on any of his social media.

"Just coming out now?" she asked. Damn it! She didn't want her voice to sound so soft. But she couldn't help it.

Robert snorted in laughter. "Yeah, what a time, right? I've never said that to anyone. Particularly not my father."

"I see," Ginger said.

Yeah, she could see that. Robert J. Whitney, Sr. was an asshole in many aspects, including homophobia.

Just because Robert was gay didn't mean he hadn't raped that woman. It did appear that he'd been somewhere else at the time, though.

Crap. What was she going to do now?

Ginger tried to take a deep breath but found she couldn't. Her chest was too constricted.

"You don't look so good," Robert said.

"Don't feel so good," Ginger said. She suddenly sat down heavily on the floor, as if gravity had overcome her rage. She still couldn't breathe.

"Look, just untie me and I won't say anything about you wanting to kill me," Robert said.

Ginger nodded weakly from where she was seated. "We won't out each other," she said.

"Exactly," Robert said. "I'm—I'm really not ready to come out just yet."

Somehow, Ginger didn't think that outing someone's sexual orientation was as dire as showing up on their doorstep with intent to kill. But she'd make that trade, in terms of secrets.

"I won't say anything to anyone," Ginger promised. "And you'll keep quiet about this visit."

"Thank you," Robert said. He sounded so relieved.

The room continued to spin. Ginger couldn't figure out how to make her legs work enough to push herself to standing.

"Say, you want to untie me before you pass out?" Robert asked, sounding nonchalant.

"Fine," Ginger said with a put-upon sigh.

"Are you sick?" Robert asked as Ginger slowly crawled across the floor to where he was seated.

"COVID. Same as you," Ginger said.

"And you fought off the exhaustion enough to get yourself over her and tie me up?" Robert said, his voice filled with admiration.

"Something like that," Ginger said. She was certain the drugs had worn off long ago, burned out of her system. She knocked over one of the takeout bags and pulled out the knife she'd stuck in there. The one she'd planned on using on the zip ties after she'd killed him.

She sighed. She was just going to have to find something else to focus on instead of her revenge.

Like maybe getting well. Talking to a goddamned shrink.

She easily cut through the zip-ties, though she stayed seated on the floor. "Just give me a moment," she said, reaching for that endless lake of rage buried deep inside her.

It seemed to have evaporated. Or maybe that was why she was sweating so hard.

"Hey, hey, don't pass out on me," Robert said. He was suddenly kneeling in front of her.

Crap. She'd let him go. Would he honor his word? Or

would he call the cops on her? She just wasn't thinking straight anymore.

"I think we need to get you to the hospital," Robert said.

Ginger shook her head. "I'll go sleep in my car, then drive myself home," she said. She pushed herself forward, onto her hands and knees, then made herself stand up. The room blackened around the edges, but she could handle that. "It was nice meeting you, finally," she said. "Too bad it wasn't under better circumstances."

Holding herself rigidly upright, Ginger started to shuffle toward the door.

She made it all the way to the front entranceway before she passed out.

Ginger woke to machines beeping and stiff cotton under her arms. She was breathing easier. Tubes were stuck up her nose, forcing oxygen into her lungs. At least she was no longer burning up.

It appeared that Robert had called an ambulance after all. She wasn't sure how she was going to pay for this—her insurance wasn't worth shit—but maybe her debt would be forgiven since it was COVID related.

As she wasn't handcuffed to the bed, she assumed that he'd kept his promise and hadn't turned her into the police. She would remember to stay mum about him being gay. It wasn't that much of a big deal to her, but maybe it was to him.

God, what had she been thinking? Had she really intended to kill him? Maybe. She had left all the gear at his house. But practicing on a dummy had been a lot different than working on a living, breathing person in front of her.

Ginger finally spotted a folded card sitting on the table beside her.

Robert had left her a note. Not a suicide note, but one that assured her that she was safe, they'd talk about his asshole of a father later, and maybe go and piss on his grave together. He even called her his new-found sister.

Maybe it was the exhaustion, but for the first time, Ginger's first reaction to seeing Robert J. Whitney, Sr's name didn't immediately fill her with rage.

Instead, Ginger healed.

THE PUZZLING CASE OF THE EXAM IMPOSTER

T he civil exam to test my knowledge of the law started in an hour.

I know, I know! I shouldn't pronounce the coming of my exams, where I'd be tested on the *Lui* land law, the same way I'd announce news of the crazed horsemen from the north sweeping across the plains and attacking my little city of Da Shan.

It wasn't even as bad as the stinking foreigners coming up from the south and buying up as much property as they could.

Still, it was a fate, and it was to be mine, this poor Rabbit.

Today would determine if I would pass from being merely an apprentice law clerk, under the service of Master Wei, to becoming a full-fledged law clerk, able to set up my own shop. Several such civil exams had been set up in recent years, including archery exams for the military and general knowledge exams for becoming a bureaucrat.

Of course, even if I passed, no one would hire me, not even with the booming business we'd had with the smelly southern foreigners. It would take many years (and possibly more exams) before I would become as respected as Master Wei and could expect to take on clients.

I would have two additional chances after this one, if I flubbed my first attempt. Three tries, total.

I *had* to pass. If for nothing else, to prove to Master Wei that his faith in me for all these years hadn't been misplaced.

The fact that Mother had declared that once I passed my civil law exams she would begin to actively start searching for a bride for me may have been a motivator as well.

First, though, I had to *get* to the Hall of Learning, at the law school nearby.

Despite my late night cramming in as much knowledge as I could, I'd still woken early that morning. The sun was just making herself known, the late spring air still cool. I could hear the soup vendors already out in the street, calling customers for warm *conji*—chicken and garlic soup with rice that had been soaked in it overnight, making it more like a thick stew.

I had dressed in my second best robe. Better to appear too humble than too proud, or at least that was what Mother said. It was the color of gray morning clouds before the sun touched them and melted them away. I didn't wear this robe to the office where I worked with Master Wei, so the cuffs were not stained with ink. However, it wasn't a new robe, and they had been replaced once already, with a light spring-green color that I actually thought looked better than the original. The collar had been replaced with the same material at my persistence, no matter the grumbling of Mother.

That had happened a lot more often recently, me insisting on something and Mother giving way.

Who knows? Maybe she would actually go and seek me a bride if I passed the exams.

I carried my own writing implements with me: my best

inkstone, inkstick, and brushes, along with a clever little tin cup for holding water. They were all rolled up in a leather case that showed much wear.

It had been my father's, one of the few items that I, as the fourth and unlucky son, had inherited after his untimely death.

I didn't bother to go see Mother. I knew she wished me well. She wouldn't be awake yet.

Instead, I made my way to Bái Huā Bàn's temple.

My friends tease me for my devotion to her. I am fully aware that she is just a little local goddess. However, she'd always looked after me, and after Da Shan. She had a special place in my heart, particularly after the old priest had died and it became my duty to find the will.

Kan Ou, the new priest for the temple, had done wonderous things over the past three years. He still looked like a farmhand, with broad shoulders and beefy hands, his eyes wide and somewhat glazed. However, he'd wielded that innocence like a knife, carving contributions out of the richer men in the neighborhood to improve the temple.

A fine floor of slate tiles now covered what had once been dirt. Actual cushions were piled up against the wall, for supplicants to use. The plain wooden walls had been painted white, and currently, Kan Ou was collecting money for the series of murals he wanted to have painted there.

Kan Ou had replaced the statue of the goddess, of course, after that thief Zhan had stolen it. (I'd met with Zhan a couple of times since then, favors owed and given freely. The man was articulate, clever, and more dangerous than the Emperor's executioners with their curved *dadao* blades.)

The new statue still had the lilting grace of the old one, and was about as tall as my arm was long. Bái Huā Bàn looked down on her followers with a tiny, half smile, as if she knew all the mysteries of the world but had no intention of sharing them. Great intelligence shone from her wide eyes and broad brow. Her robes flowed down beautifully and pooled at her feet. She held a simple blossom in her hands, offering it to her followers, a symbol of her purity and great fecundity. This new earthly representation was actually made of silver, and not just plated.

Kan Ou hadn't replaced the altar. It was still rustic and wooden, standing against the far wall. Nine mystical candles lit the area around my lady, adding to her beauty and mystery.

Bái Huā Bàn waited for me, patient as always, as I stumbled into the temple. I bowed to the four directions, to the Emperor and his golden court in the west, then to the south from where all the foreigners and their *cash* came, to the east where fairy tale monsters and huge ocean lay, then finally to the north, where the horsemen stood poised, ready to carry war to us again.

Then I centered myself, breathing deeply, and bowed once more, to the center of the sacred space, bowing to my little town of Da Shan as well as to my goddess, who still took up the heart of me.

And possibly would continue to do so, even after Mother found me a bride.

Only then did I allow myself to drop to the ground and prostrate myself, pouring out all my worries and woes to the temple goddess, begging, pleading, as well as imploring Bái Huā Bàn to watch over me that day, to prompt my overfull brain to remember what it needed to, as well as to make my words clever.

Finally, I raised up my head and hurried out. Not just because I saw Kan Ou enter the temple out of the corner of my eye and I *really* couldn't donate any more money just then. But also because I heard the morning bells tolling the double hour of the Dragon.

If I didn't hurry, I was going to be late to my exam, which were going to occur during the next half hour.

Of course, that was when all of Da Shan decided to vex me. First, there was a group of laborers carrying a large load of wood on a cart which had broken down. The beams were strewn all over the street. A group of onlookers were offering "helpful" suggestions as the poor men struggled to clear the way. Between the people and the street full of wood, it was too congested to get through.

Luckily, I'd gone on enough tours of Da Shan with Xin Chao, that great ox and one of my best friends, so I thought I knew an alley I could cut through and around.

That turned out to be a mistake, as the alley wound around and around. There was no passage out! I had not taken the first street that crossed the alley, thinking that I was making better time this way. But the alley had grown narrower as it passed behind several shops. I hopped over baskets being woven, the straw bale of a broom maker, even several (very smelly) vats of bamboo being turned into paper.

When I finally made my way out of the winding narrow alley, I discovered I was north of the law school. I tried heading toward it as quickly as I could, merely rushing and not running.

Which was of course when I tripped and fell, managing not only to rip my robes at the knee as I landed hard, but covering the front of them with dirt.

My only blessing at that point was that I'd only fallen down on a dusty road. I hadn't stepped in manure or tripped over a laborer's bucket of paint.

I tried to straighten my robe as best I could without taking off my belt, as well as brush off the dirt that now seemed embedded on my pretty green cuffs.

I didn't have time to go home and change.

I knew, *knew* the examiners were going to have a problem with me arriving in this condition.

I will admit that the old Rabbit might have stood there fretting and wringing his hands over his appearance, possibly making him later than he already was.

This new Rabbit, who I'd become over the last few years, managed to find some of that courage that Xin Chao and my other friends claimed I had. I limped forward, still determined to make it to my exams.

I reminded myself that Master Wei's eyes were no longer the best, and so he was constantly squinting at things. He frequently wore the remains of his previous meal in his long beard. He'd only acquired new robes at Mother's insistence, and they didn't stay clean for long.

Yet, Master Wei was respected by every *Xi* law office in Da Shan. He knew the law, love the law, and was intimate with every little clause or quirk within it.

And I was his apprentice. I, too, would prove that I could be respected for what I knew and not for how I looked.

I finally arrived at the school.

However, no one was waiting outside the exam room! Was I so late that the exams had already finished?

No.

The exams had been postponed for a day.

I arrived in better shape the next day, just after the hour of the Dragon. I'd had to wear my best robe, which was a beautiful yellow color, perfect for spring. My friend Long Yen, who was the son of the head of the Weaver's Guild, had gotten it for me, at a bargain as well.

Two other young men waited in line before the door. An older man stood there, verifying the identity papers of the people wanting to take the exam. He also had a rolled up piece of paper that contained the names of all those who had applied and paid their fees. He checked off each name before the person was allowed into the examination room.

He was very thorough in his examination of all the papers handed to them, reading the names out loud. It made me feel very official when he finally passed me through.

I wasn't the first to be allowed into the examination room, but the third.

Possibly my luck was changing, as I wasn't the unlucky fourth that day.

The room had low desks to accommodate twenty students. Beautiful, wistful watercolor paintings hung on scrolls between the windows. No dust was allowed to gather in the corners, no cobwebs hung from the ceiling.

It was the epitome of a clean, tidy environment.

It was also the exact opposite of the office I shared with Master Wei, which was stuffed full of scrolls, books, and old contracts, the desks like islands moored between towering mountains of paper. This room had windows that would allow delightful breezes through. We were on the second story of a courtyard that faced a dyer, and frequently the office was full of the acrid smell of the dyes, in addition to the constant smell of moldering paper.

Maybe some year I could actually have such a clean workspace myself.

In the meanwhile, I choose my desk in the far back corner, rolled up my sleeves and tied them back so I wouldn't stain the cuffs, then prepared my writing materials. I filled my cup with water from the jug up front, then poured a little bit of water into my inkstone. The inkstick I used was my favorite, the compressed ink releasing perfectly as I ground it across the inkstone.

Soon, I had the perfect ink ready to use for writing my

exam essays. The smell of it relaxed me: it was the smell of hard work, of all the contracts I'd already reviewed or put together at Master Wei's behest.

Our office was the dirty little secret of the *Xi* office: instead of doing the actual work themselves of land contracts or wills, they handed it to us. We collected a very good fee in exchange, though they were the ones who always got the credit. Yet, they were the ones who held poetry contests were considered quite accomplished scholars.

I was certain they had no idea how to deal with an unlucky widow who couldn't inherit her husband's land, which codes to use to work around the law so she and her children weren't left destitute.

By the time I'd finished preparing my ink, most of the rest of the desks were full. I knew a few of the other exam takers: we'd met once so that we could study together at one of the local tea houses. However, they'd been more interested in the pots of plum wine than in the law we were there to discuss, so I'd stopped meeting with them.

When the old man at the door read out loud the name of Jin Lo, I looked up, surprised.

I didn't know Jin Lo personally. We hadn't even been introduced. However, I'd seen him more than once at the teashop that Xin Chao's family ran. Ling-Ling, Xin Chao's older sister, was always angling for better tips from the richer families who visited their establishment. She wore her robes too tightly, and her hair too loose, a curl dangling artistically from behind her ear. I knew Mother had few kind words for her.

She'd set her sights on Jin Lo, who was from a wealthy, well-placed family. He'd bragged while flirting with her that he'd already been guaranteed a position in the local *Xi* office.

When I pointed out that didn't mean he knew anything about the law, I nearly had a lap full of tea in response.

I had thought that Jin Lo would have already passed the civil exams if he was on the way to such a lofty position in the *Xi* office.

Yet, there he was, having his papers examined before he walked into the exam room.

Except...the person who walked in wasn't Jin Lo. It was an older man, possibly as ancient as thirty, though I myself was nearing twenty-four. The man had a similar smirk to the one Jin Lo wore, but that was where the resemblance ended. This man had a wide, intelligent brow, though his eyes were placed too closely together, so he peered out with a look of low cunning. He wore light blue robes weren't as good as Jin Lo's: not only had the cuffs been replaced with a less-quality black material, but the plaques running up and down the front had been switched out for a different color blue that wasn't the best match.

Perhaps I was mistaken. Possibly this was another man with the same name.

However, I'd heard the full family name being read out loud by the old man at the door.

I was certain that it was supposed to be the same Jin Lo I'd seen at Tang's Tea Shop.

What was this person doing here?

The old man closed the door after the fake Jin Lo arrived, announcing the start of the test.

I didn't have time for any sort of inquiry. I also had to push the disturbance from my own troubled thoughts, and focus on the task at hand.

Namely, replying to the questions on the exam so well, so thoroughly, that there was never a question about my eligibility.

None of the questions in the exam book perplexed me. They were all straight forward about the sections and paragraphs of the land code.

I honestly could have answered most of them after my first year of working with Master Wei.

Was I missing something? I went back through them, checking to see if I'd made a mistake, but I couldn't find a flaw in my answers.

It was only when I turned to the essay sections that I began to worry.

This was where the heart of the exam really lay. The essays tested not only if you could recite chapter and verse of the existing codes, but seeing if you could also apply them.

I am not a poet. There are no songs in my heart that must be expressed with the prettiest of words, then worked and reworked until I could wring every ounce of nuance from each line, each character chosen specifically to do two or three times the work as another.

However, the law does sing if you're willing to listen. I poured my heart into every essay answer, citing not just the applicable codes but related ones as well, using nuance to argue my point as to why this interpretation was valid.

I found myself sweating as I wrote feverishly, quickly grinding out more ink as needed, sloshing water on my table and wiping it up with my sleeve, turning the yellow black.

Mother was going to *kill* me for staining my best robe with ink.

However, I was going to make her so proud by passing my exam on the first try.

Examinees started leaving the room. The Jin Lo replacement was one of the earliest.

Yet, I stayed were I was, adding a paragraph here or another phrase there, making sure that I had included every bit of knowledge that I'd acquired over the years onto the page.

It was a masterpiece.

I handed over my exam book only when the old man at the front called time. Even then, I knew I'd missed things, that I needed to go back and add in yet another phrase or code.

I slowly gathered together my writing implements. I had broken my inkstick at some point during my frenzied writing. I didn't remember doing so.

I felt dirty, hollowed out, and exhausted. When I pushed myself to standing, I wavered on my feet, black spots dancing across my eyes.

However, I couldn't rest. Not yet.

I first had to report to Master Wei, to talk about how the exam had gone.

Then I had to get to the bottom of why Jin Lo hadn't sat for his own exam.

F ortunately, the dyers didn't have cloths hanging to dry in our shared courtyard that afternoon. I'd run that obstacle course more than once, dodging between drops of bright orange or pale blue. I made it up the stairs to the office Master Wei rented relatively unscathed.

The office itself halted the stride in my step. Oh, it was the same mess as always. Master Wei was just lucky we'd never accidentally set a fire. All of that paper scattered everywhere would go up quickly.

It was just the *mess* that took me back. The smell of molding paper. The bright spring day had turned warm, and it felt like a furnace just getting warmed up inside. I could already feel myself start to sweat.

I don't know why the office seemed particularly bad that day. Maybe it was because the pile of contracts that Master Wei had dumped on my desk looked as though the gentlest of winds was going to knock it over. Perhaps because the pile of books next to Master Wei's desk had already been knocked over, obscuring even the small path between the stacks.

Or maybe it was the appearance of Master Wei himself, walking up from the back of the room, large and looming, looking like a gray, angry ghost.

Mind you, a gray ghost with a white beard that held crumbs of the pork roll he'd eaten for lunch.

The gray robes Master Wei wore weren't his worse stained ones, so there were still patches of gray around the cuffs. The front of the robe held long lines of brown dots—dribbles of tea, possibly also from that morning. Dirt scuffed the hem of the robe, as if it had been dragged through the dirt.

Had Master Wei shrank since he'd put on those robes? Or originally had them made?

He raised himself up to his full height. He stood taller than most of the people in Da Shan. Though I was tall and thin myself, I was still three fingers shorter than he was.

"What can I do for you?" Master Wei said with what I think he meant as a friendly smile. It looked more like a pained grimace, however.

"It's just me," I said as I stepped across the threshold.

Master Wei squinted in my direction before he said, "Of course. I knew it was you," he snapped. "I was just showing you the proper way to greet our clients."

"Of course," I said. I hurried to his side. "Are you all right, Master Wei?"

"I'm fine," he said, brushing aside my concern. "I'm just a little tired today."

This worried me, as Master Wei had been tired for almost a week now.

"Come, sit down at your desk," I said. He actually allowed me to take his arm and lead him over to his chair, which was thankfully not full of papers. "Can I bring you something? Some water, or tea, perhaps?"

"No tea, nothing to drink," Master Wei grumbled. "How about finding a copy of that damned contract I worked on last week? The one for the foreign devil and his assumption of Widow Wang's farm?"

I knew exactly the papers Master Wei was requesting. I scurried to the back, forgetting my own problems and concerns in order to help Master Wei.

I paused while standing at the back of our office, surrounded by shelves stacked to overflowing with papers, contracts, scrolls, and books.

Master Wei sat looking almost forlorn in his chair, blinking rapidly, as if to clear his eyes as he looked out the door.

How bad was his eyesight? He complained constantly that I was moving papers or contracts around on him, shuffling them so he could no longer find the piece he wanted.

Was that the case? Or was he actually having difficulty reading them now?

This morning hadn't been the first time that he'd mistaken me for a client when I came through the door.

"Now, Rabbit, and not before I keel over with age," Master Wei said without bothering to look in my direction.

There was nothing wrong with his hearing. He'd known I'd paused.

"Coming!" I called, rapidly scurrying to his side, papers in hand.

I didn't know what Master Wei would do if he could no longer work with contracts.

And I certainly wasn't looking forward to finding out.

Though it would be three days before they announced the results, I still indulged myself in a minor celebration after work by going to Tang's Tea Shop and visiting with Xin Chao.

To my surprised, Long Yen was there as well. He'd gotten married three years before. His wife had already birthed a fine boy, and was evidently pregnant again with another.

Xin Chao had also gotten married, and had a lovely baby girl now, as well as a beautiful, clever wife. She'd been the daughter of the broom maker.

I may have fancied her at one point. However, Xin Chao had never been happier since he'd gotten married.

I earnestly prayed more than once to Bái Hua Bàn that I might someday enjoy the happiness that my friends had found in their spouses. I was already married to the law. I understood that. But I hoped for some additional earthly happiness as well.

Long Yen hadn't gained weight from his marriage, even though he bragged often about the wonderful food his new wife provided for him. He still had a sharp nose sticking out of the middle of his face, a wide brow, and thin lips that looked as though he was always laughing at you.

However, his eyes had grown kinder. He no longer looked as though he would drive a bargain so hard that you'd end up losing your shirt. Maybe just the cuffs, now.

Xin Chao had gained weight. His round face had grown rounder. He was still a great ox, and spent much of his time chopping the firewood the family used to keep the pots of water for the tea boiling. But he also spent more time going on shopping excursions with his mother, searching for the best teas they could serve.

It surprised me that Ling-Ling still hadn't married. She

was older than Xin Chao. And she was beautiful. She stood at a table and did a "long pour"—slowly pouring a steady stream of boiling water into the pot sitting on a low table, without spilling or splashing a drop. Her black robe was tied too tightly of course, showing off her womanly curves.

My friends sat at a low table, just inside the shop. The front doors of the shop were wide open, and several customers sat on the steps in the fine evening air, enjoying their tea or wine.

"How did the exam go?" Xin Chao asked before I had even sat down.

I couldn't help but grin at him. "I think I did well," I said. I didn't say it too loudly. I didn't want to tempt the gods into proving me wrong.

Long Yen rolled his eyes. "Of course you did," he said. "The law is all you ever think about."

"I actually have other things I'm thinking about tonight," I said. I told them about Jin Lo, and how I believe he hadn't actually taken his own exam.

"Why are you surprised that he didn't take his own exam?" Long Yen said. "He paid someone else to take them for him."

"That's…that's not right," I sputtered. I had studied *hard* for my exam. Poured my heart into the essays. I would *earn* my placement.

Jin Lo had just bought his.

And he supposedly had a spot guaranteed to him in the local *Xi* office. If those were the sorts of people the office took, no wonder they utilized Master Wei for all their contracts.

"It isn't right," Xin Chao said, nodding. "What are you going to do about it? How are you going to stop him?"

I looked at my friend, puzzled. "Why do you think that I'm going to do something about it? Figure out how to denounce him? Anonymously, of course, so that my family name isn't dragged into such a sordid affair."

"Because that's what you do," Long Yen said with a grin. "You won't let such an injustice pass."

My friends were right. I was looking for a way to expose Jin Lo and his imposter.

"But how?" I asked. All right, possibly I pitifully moaned. I just didn't see my way clear at that point.

"I don't know," Long Yen said. "But I'd suggest you think of something. And right now. Jin Lo just arrived."

"What?" I said, looking around.

Long Yen was right. Jin Lo had just arrived. He gave a smarmy, self-satisfied grin to the entire room. He was obviously there to celebrate "his" passing of the exam.

"Go. Go now," Xin Chao urged. "I'll get Ling-Ling to help you."

"But—"

"*Now*," both of my friends insisted.

I heaved a great, put-upon sigh.

Then I pushed myself to standing, swaying as I did so.

That gave me an idea, or at least, an excuse for talking to Jin Lo.

I heard him mention that indeed, he was there to celebrate passing the exam.

I was surprised to see him celebrating by himself. Wouldn't such an important man at least have toadies to go drinking with?

Then I saw how he flirted with Ling-Ling, before she scurried off to get him his pot of wine.

Perhaps he was alone because he meant to entice Ling-Ling into something unseemly.

That would never do.

I straightened myself up, then swayed the other direction, as if I'd had too much sweet plum wine to drink. I hadn't—

my friends and I had barely consumed a single pot together. However, Jin Lo would never know that, and he would smell the alcohol on my breath.

I stumbled directly over to Jin Lo's table.

"You're here to celebrate, aren't you," I accused him.

"I am?" Jin Lo said, obviously confused.

Normally, I would *never* sit down at someone's table uninvited. I'd never even been properly introduced to Jin Lo.

But the wine I'd drunk had given me courage. That, and my friends sitting behind me.

I plumped myself down hard on the cushions beside Jin Lo. "I'm here to drown my sorrows," I confessed, playing my part to the hilt.

"Sorrows?" Jin Lo said, trying to be polite when I didn't say anything else.

"I don't think I passed my exams today," I said. I sighed. "But you think you did, don't you?"

Jin Lo gave me one of his smarmy smiles. "Of course I did," he said.

"The questions were so hard!" I wailed. "I was there the entire double hour they gave to take the exam," I added. I blinked myopically at him as I leaned closer. "Were you there? I don't remember seeing you."

"I was there," Jin Lo reassured me. "The registrar has me marked down."

"I don't think you were there," I said slowly. I gasped as if the realization had just come to me. "You weren't there! Someone else was!"

"Shhh, shhh, of course I was there," Jin Lo said, glancing around the rest of the teashop.

I knew that it didn't matter if I accused him or not. He was from an important family in Da Shan. Anything I said would immediately be discounted because of the difference in our statuses.

I heaved another great sigh. Ling-Ling returned at that point. She gave her best smile to Jin Lo, then scowled at me. However, she'd brought two metal cups for the pot of plum wine that she set on the table. I insisted on serving, pouring us both a full glass, then toasting Jin Lo for his achievement.

I only let the alcohol touch my tongue. I barely swallowed any. I needed to keep what few wits I had.

Jin Lo quaffed his entire cup. I immediately poured him a second.

"So how did you pass?" I asked, staring at him as if he held all the secrets of the universe. "What study techniques did you use?"

"It all came easily to me," Jin Lo said breezily. "It all came naturally. The law is just another extension of man's reason. It's logical."

I nearly snorted. The law was anything but *logical*. Parts of it were certainly meant to be. But there were so many twists, nooks, and crannies that had been added to the law that it was no longer smooth or anything like natural.

I didn't dispute his statements, just continued to pour out my admiration for him, while at the same time, pouring him more and more to drink.

He finished the first wine pot mostly on his own, as I was still on my first cup. When Ling-Ling brought the second pot without being prompted, she threw a broad wink my way.

Hmm. Seemed that she was in on the game, then.

"If only I could have someone as smart as you, Jin Lo, to take my exam for me!" I exclaimed while Ling-Ling was still there, fawning over him.

Ling-Ling scoffed at me. "Why would someone so important as Jin Lo perform such a favor to one such as yourself?"

"I...I would be forever in his debt," I said magnanimously. "Plus, I could pay."

"Really? How much?" Ling-Ling challenged.

I listed a sum. It was actually the amount in the accounts in my family's name.

Both Ling-Ling's and Jin Lo's eyes grew wide at that amount.

Had I actually squirreled away more money than I'd realized?

"So you would pay that much to pass the exam?" Jin Lo clarified.

I squirmed a little. "It is a lot of money," I said, downplaying it. "I'd pay at least half that, though."

Jin Lo nodded. "That's a reasonable amount," he said sagely. "Not for someone such as myself," he assured Ling-Ling. "I wouldn't be bought for such money. But I may know someone who could help you in your predicament."

"Really?" I said, delighted. "Of course, I'd pay you a finder's fee if he actually works out."

"Of course!" Jin Lo said, giving me a sloppy grin. "I'd be happy to recommend the fellow."

He gave me the name—Ren Wei—and address of the office of the person who, I was fairly certain, had been his own exam imposter.

After another broad wink, Ling-Ling went back to serving the other customers. However, I did notice her eye following me for the rest of the evening.

"Tell me," I said as I sat back, relishing my ruse so far. "Does this Ren Wei insist on a contract?"

"Of course!" Jin Lo said. "This is far too serious to be left to just a gentleman's agreement."

Fool, I thought, but didn't say out loud.

A contract meant future blackmail material, or at the very least, favors owed against some future marker.

It took me a while to extricate myself from Jin Lo and his company. I had my information. And a plan.

I'd also caught the eye of Ling-Ling, who now seemed interested in me, as she gave me a sweet smile and a small wave of her hand goodbye before I left.

This could get very sticky, with her brother being my best friend. But that was a problem to deal with on another night.

I didn't have much time to put my plan into action. The results of the exam would be announced in just a few days. If I was going to discredit Jin Lo, it had to be done quickly.

Also, before I lost my nerve.

Xin Chao caught me as I was leaving the teashop, directing me to stand with him, outside, in the shadows, unseen. The night had grown dark and the spring air, cool. I shivered unconsciously as I heard another rousing round of laughter from the teashop, people celebrating their own victories and achievements.

"Ling-Ling told me that he gave you the name and the address of the man who he used to sit his exam for him," Xin Chao said.

"He did," I said, still proud of myself for my ruse. "He also told me that he used a contract."

Xin Chao blinked his large liquid eyes at me, obviously not understanding.

"That means I can steal it, and prove that Jin Lo cheated," I said.

"Oh! You're so clever, Rabbit," Xin Chao said, shaking his head. "I would never have thought of that."

That didn't surprise me. Xin Chao didn't deal with contracts, or even the family's accounts. He'd commented more than once that no matter how hard he tried to read, the letters danced across the page.

"You are clever in your own way," I assured my friend. "Plus, you have a clever wife."

"I do," he said, beaming at me. Then he turned serious. "But you need to go and steal that contract tonight, before Jin Lo thinks twice about what he said to you."

I wanted to wail out loud. I hadn't slept well in over a month, as I'd stolen hours away from my slumber to study. I'd taken the exam that morning (that morning!) and that had drained out all my vital energies. Though I'd tried not to drink too much, I couldn't help but take a few mouthfuls.

However, Xin Chao was right.

"Fine," I said.

"The address Jin Lo gave you is in a less prosperous neighborhood," Xin Chao said seriously. "There won't be as many city guards. Or lights. It might be easier to break in."

Of course, Xin Chao would know exactly where the building lay. While he was supposedly working all day out in the courtyard behind the teashop, he frequently went on excursions through the city, exploring and finding new alleys and friends.

"Here," he said, throwing a dark cloak over my back. "Long Yen fetched this for you. It should hide you, particularly given that yellow robe you're wearing."

I settled the cloak over my shoulders. It was lightweight, but warm. When I twitched an end of it, it rippled nicely, as if showing off it daring nature.

"Thank you, and thank Long Yen for me, if you see him before I do," I said. What would I do without such good friends?

"Now, don't get caught!" Xin Chao warned before he headed back to the light and warmth of the teashop, as well as the warmth of his bed and his bride.

I sighed and stepped into the darkness of the night.

As Xin Chao had warned, Ren Wei's office was not in the best neighborhood. It wasn't as bad as say, the kilns near the west city gate, where prostitutes were said to gather. But it was barely a single step up from there.

The tavern I walked by reeked of cheap wine. The laughter that spilled out from it was rough. More than one man had barely made it out the door before passing out on the side of the street. I was just lucky I didn't accidentally kick one of the prone bodies.

Though it was difficult to see, I could recognize the scent of the candlemaker just a few doors down. You might think that such a well-thought of position wouldn't be in such a poor neighborhood. However, these were tallow candles, not fine beeswax.

Which led me to the next shop, which was a butcher's. Not a shop that I would ever patronize, as the meat sold there was absolutely *not* fresh.

Wafting through the air was the smell of the tanner's which was probably just a block away.

Ren Wei's office appeared to be sandwiched between a cooper's shop and a chicken butcher. I shuddered to think of the noise the fellow had to deal with, between the screaming of hens, the crowing of roosters, and the constant hammering of metal used to bind barrels.

Despite the smells and mess of my own office, I wouldn't have wanted to trade it for this one, that was for certain.

The front door was certain to be locked. I tried the handle just in case I had some sort of wild, weird luck, but I didn't.

Did Ren Wei sleep above his shop? I stepped back into the street, trying to make out the upper level.

There wasn't one, as near as I could tell. The buildings were all a single story. Did the owners sleep behind the shops, then? All on one level? That might make sense, in such a rough neighborhood.

I stepped back closer to the door, running my fingers over it. I was no master thief. I had no tools to jimmy a lock, or slide back a deadbolt.

Stymied, I moved to the side, still running my hand against the wall.

There was a window there. I hadn't noticed it in the dark. However, now that I was paying attention, I could just make out the outline of it. It wasn't a proper window, just shutters over an opening.

Shutters that were latched together on the inside with a simple hook.

I found a stick to slide between the edges of the shutters, then lift up to undo the latch.

The shutters fell open as if welcoming me.

I poked my head inside the room. It was very dark inside. I would have given anything for Zhan's clever lamp that gave a focused beam of light.

Then I remembered the candlemaker just a few doors up. I stole one of the candles in the display outside, leaving them a small bit of coin to repay them. A quick trip to the end of the block and the street lamps lit there provided me with the flame I needed.

Thus armed, I was able to get a much better look at Ren Wei's office.

It was deceptively simple. A kneeling desk for writing was close to the door. Additional cushions, probably for clients, lay before it.

The walls were covered in a lattice of woodwork. It took me a few moments to realize that the lattice work provided clever cubbyholes. Inside each were rolled up scrolls, probably the contracts Ren Wei had signed.

Before I pushed myself over the window ledge, I needed

to have a plan. Where would I put such a contract? There were at least a hundred cubbyholes from where I could see.

Would the most recent contracts be at the front? But that would mean a constant shifting of papers. Unless Ren Wei had an assistant, that would get old fairly quickly.

Were they alphabetized? Possibly. But by name? Or by deed?

Then it occurred to me that Ren Wei must be somewhat intelligent if he could take and pass a law exam. Possibly he'd already taken one himself, and that the majority of his contracts were for mostly legitimate work.

If I were to take on such questionably legal work, I'd keep the contracts for the less legal work separated from the others. Possibly close at hand, in case I needed to rely on them if Fat Ang, the local magistrate, came knocking.

This meant I didn't have to go through every piece of paper in the entire shop. No, I just had to figure out where there was a *lack* of such rolled up scrolls. Which cubbyholes had the fewest scrolls in them? Possibly only one or two?

I easily located that area in the rows of cubbyholes. It was near the entrance, as I'd surmised.

Pushing myself up and through the window was more difficult than it sounds. Particularly since I had a lit candle in my hand! However, not only did I get into the office without waking anyone, I only dripped hot wax on my fingers twice as I read through the contracts, finally finding the one I wanted.

I shook my head when I saw the sum entered. It was insulting, really, that a law exam cost so little. Less than a quarter of the sum I'd given. No wonder Jin Lo had been so interested in the larger amount I'd started off with!

I quickly gathered all of the illegal business contracts and slipped them into the wonderful pouch-like pockets of the cloak that Long Yen had provided to me.

Really, I was going to have to see about purchasing a cloak such as this.

I snuffed out my candle and lifted myself up and out the window before anyone awoke. I couldn't relatch the shutters, though I did close them after myself.

Ren Wei would know he'd been robbed when he saw the papers missing.

However, I knew my job was only half done.

Now, I needed to break into the college and slip the contract between Ren Wei and Jin Lo under the door of the dean.

That way, I could denounce Jin Lo anonymously. My name would never come up. My family wouldn't be implicated in his disgrace.

It took me another set of double hours to do the deed, but finally, I dragged my weary self home and collapsed into my bed, the dawn too close for me to do much other than close my eyes and nap.

I stumbled through the next day, barely able to keep my eyes open. Then, I overslept, and had to hurry on my way to Master Wei's side the next morning.

I'd spent a little bit of time the day before trying to clean up the office, but to no avail. We had too many copies of too many contracts, too many clients who we'd dealt with, too many scrolls listing the current laws.

Still, it warmed my heart to go to work that day. While the office may be a mess, it was where I got to work with the law, every day.

"Well?" Master Wei said when I came rushing in, before I'd had a chance to apologize for my tardiness.

I stopped just inside the door, blinking at him. Finally, I had to ask, "Well, what?"

"The exam results were posted on the walls of the college!" he thundered at me. "I had assumed that you had gone to check on those first, before remembering your place here."

"Oh!" I said. "Uhm, I was just coming to tell you that I would be late because I needed to go to the college..." I stammered.

Master Wei stared at me for a moment, before he waved me off. "Fine, fine," he said. "You'll be completely useless until you know your standing. Go."

I must admit, I took off as fast as a rabbit when faced with a fox nearby.

"And bring me one of those pork buns you like so much!" Master Wei called after me as I scurried down the stairs.

Of course, not just the law civil exams were posted that day. The examiners had conducted many exams over the past week, including the martial and general exams. The courtyard of the school was crowded with onlookers and busybodies, all checking to see who passed and who didn't.

Such public scores were likely to keep the town gossips busy for *months*. It was probably the best entertainment they'd had since the last sweep from the Emperor, when several officials had lost their heads to the curved *daodan* blades of the executioners.

It took me a while to find the lists for the law exam.

What surprised me was that the name of everyone who'd taken the exam was listed, organized by the day they'd taken the exam. There had been three days of exams, and mine was the last day possible.

Beside each name was generally a simple mark: Pass or fail.

My heart pounded harder as I checked the lists, searching for my name. Sweat gathered under my arms and at the small of my back, while my hands grew cold and clammy.

I was listed close to the bottom of the list. However, beside my name was merely the number three.

What on earth did that mean?

Jin Lo's name also had a number by it, but it was a two.

Finally I found the page that held a list of numbered paragraphs.

Jin Lo's note read:

Failed. Banned from retaking the exam.

I couldn't help my own smirk. Seemed that the officials didn't take kindly to having imposters take the exam.

Then I read my own note.

Come see dean of the school of law at your earliest convenience.

What on earth did that mean? Had I failed so spectacularly that they needed to redress me in person?

My heart fell to the soles of my shoes. A huge weight suddenly hung on my chest, making it difficult to breathe. The sweetness of the late spring air turned sour.

But I wasn't going to stand there wringing my hands in the middle of the school courtyard for all to see.

Mother always said, "Wear your broken arm *inside* your sleeve."

I would go and take my punishment from the dean like a man, and not like a scared rabbit.

I straightened my back, pushed my head up high, then turned and sharply marched to the dean's office. It was located at the back of the Hall of Learning. Scrolls filled with scholarly poems about the beauty and importance of learning lined the walls. Dust motes danced in the spring sunshine from the window opposite the door.

As the dean was just finishing up with someone else, I didn't have to wait too long, or before my courage faded.

Finally, it was my turn. I walked into the room. Despite my anxiety, I could still recognize that the office was meant to be comfortable. It had a low writing desk in the corner and extra pillows for guests. The bookshelf behind the desk was filled with orderly stacks of papers and scrolls. A painting of Wen Qu hung on the wall, the god of culture and learning.

The dean himself was an older man with a hawk's nose and sharp, dark eyes. His hair had streaks of black in it, showing his age. He wore formal, dark blue robes that held a certain crispness.

When I introduced myself, he rose from behind his desk and gave me a deep bow. "My dear Rabbit! It is an honor to meet you. You may call me Master Li."

Perplexed, I returned the deep bow. The man was my senior, after all.

"I suppose you wonder why you're here," Master Li said, smiling slyly. "I must admit, your essay for the exam took me back. I wasn't certain what to make of it."

I nodded, unsure when I was supposed to start apologizing.

"Then, when I read it a second time, I realized what skill you had. What cunning! It quite took my breath away, your subtle links between the subjects, as well as your extremely convincing arguments," he continued.

"Thank you?" I said, confused. Had I not failed the test?

Master Li leaned forward, as if confiding a secret. "While your family is not as high ranked as others, I believe that your skill in the law far outweighs all other considerations."

"Good?" I said, trying to prepare myself for whatever it was that Master Li was considering.

"Therefore, I have been authorized to offer you a full-time position at the local *Xi* office," Master Li concluded. "You'll be given a salary commiserate with your skill, as well as certain other benefits, such as a wardrobe allowance and to pay for the highest quality inks and brushes."

The sum he named stunned me. While I was only making an apprentice's salary, I knew that Master Wei didn't bring in that much money in a month.

Though I had bristled at the thought that I'd be given a wardrobe allowance, I did recognize that I would have a certain level of propriety to maintain being a government official.

I'd had to file contracts at the *Xi* offices more than once. The order they imposed there, with every paper in its place and a place for everything. There was no dust in the corners, no cobwebs along the ceiling. Those offices smelled of sweet incense not moldering papers.

Then I thought of poor Master Wei and his failing eyesight. He would claim that he could survive without me perfectly well. Would be insulted if I even hinted at him being less than capable of doing his job, the one he loved so well.

I took a deep breath, breathing in all the possibilities that such a position would afford me.

Then I released it, letting all those dreams go.

Though it was like a dagger to my heart, I told Master Li, "I am honored, so very, *very* honored by your more than generous offer. However, I cannot abandon Master Wei and my current position. Possibly in a few years, after Master Wei retires. But for now, I cannot."

Master Li gave me an appraising look. "Though your answer saddens me, it does not surprise me. I've known

Master Wei for many years. He is deserving of such devotion. He taught here for a few years, and I've never known anyone to have such passion for the law. Until I met you."

He smiled and gave me a short bow. "I am still honored to have met you, Rabbit. Please give Master Wei my best. And know that if you should ever have need, I am available for you to call on."

"The honor is all mine, sir," I assured the dean. I paused for a moment, then gathered together all my courage. "In the meanwhile, I would certainly enjoy getting together to discuss the law with someone as learned as yourself. Perhaps over a pot of tea sometime."

"I'd be delighted!" Master Li said, smiling.

Good. I hadn't overstepped my bounds. "I could learn so much from talking with you," I assured him.

"That may be," Master Li said. "Though I think that I, too, would be learning much."

We set a date for three days hence, to meet at the teashop that was just down the road from the school.

Then I walked back out into the spring sunshine, feeling like a changed man.

Oh, I was still the same Rabbit. Awkward and fumbling. Too devoted to the law. Still merely apprenticed to Master Wei, though I supposed that now I could draw up partner papers, and Master Wei would probably be happy to sign them.

Might even complain that I should have written them up earlier.

Yet, something inside of me had shifted. I was ready to be a man. Take on a wife. Have additional friendships, professional ones.

It was time to move forward, into my very bright future.

NANA AND HER SOAP

Stacy got out of her car slowly, standing and stretching after the long drive. Normally, going from Seattle, through Yakima, past Lake Hope and out to Horton to get to Nana's property took five to six hours. Even on a Friday, getting up stupid early and driving all day.

That weekend, though, Labor Day traffic had pushed it up to seven.

And all because of the tourists. Those stupid, fu—

Stacy stopped herself before the thought fully formed, slapping her hands over her mouth as if she'd accidentally said the word out loud.

Nana didn't abide with swearing. Despite Stacy being thirty-five, married and divorced and now living on her own, Nana would still wash Stacy's mouth out with soap if her granddaughter said a bad word. Even if Stacy just *thought* the word. Nana always knew. She'd just hand Stacy the soap and silently point toward the bathroom.

At least she'd finally arrived. Stacy stretched for a few more moments, relishing the peace and quiet out here. Of the four acres that made up Nana's property, only about half of it was developed. The rest was trees and blackberry bramble. The house itself wasn't visible from the lane, but cut off by tall, wide, cypresses. All Stacy heard were the crickets in the grass and the distant wash of the highway.

By the end of her week long vacation, all this peace and quiet would be driving her nuts.

For now, it was just lovely. The house had been built in the 1950s, a single-story rambler, solidly made out of brown brick and lovingly maintained. Large feral rose bushes stood guard on either side of the newly-painted white door. Orange and red hips shone through the green leaves, plus a few pink blossoms. When the roses were fully in bloom the entire yard smelled heavenly.

Nana and Grandpa had bought the property twenty years before as their retirement home, turning it into a hobby farm, with apples, grapes, cherries, figs, strawberries, blueberries, pears, and other fruit planted in the orchard out behind the house.

Stacy was here to help Nana with the harvest. Or at least that was what she told herself. Not just to enjoy the fringe benefits of the pies, tarts, jellies, jams, and compotes that they'd end up cooking together that week. And she certainly wasn't about to turn down any of the canned goods that Nana was sure to foist on her, all picked from her vegetable garden earlier that summer.

Grandpa had passed away six years before of an unexpected stroke. While Stacy missed him, she'd grown much closer to Nana as a result, talking with her once a week on the phone and making the long drive out four or five times a year. Next time would be for Christmas, as they'd both decided that traveling to Florida to visit Stacy's mom and her new husband was out of the question this year.

Hopefully next year.

In the meantime, Stacy walked around to the passenger

side of her little red mini-Cooper and got out her luggage, then dragged it down the immaculate sidewalk toward the house. Nana didn't much abide with weeds growing where they shouldn't. There were areas on the property that were allowed to grow wild. Just not in the civilized areas.

Stacy had texted Nana to let her know that she'd be late. Though she'd left just after six AM, it was now after one PM. She was starving.

However, the door was locked when Stacy tried it.

That was strange. Nana *always* left the door open for her when she knew that Stacy was coming.

Feeling awkward, Stacy first rang the bell, then knocked on the solid wood.

"Coming, coming!" came Nana's cheerful voice. She threw the door wide open. "Come in!"

They gave each other a huge hug. Nana still felt strong and solid in Stacy's arms, smelling of the warm buttered toast she'd just been eating.

"So good to see you," Stacy said, finally pulling back.

Nana had twinkling blue eyes that always looked as though she was one step away from mischief. She had more wrinkles than ever in her tanned face, the lines made deeper by her huge smile. Her white hair was pulled back in a bun, the slight ponytail up off her neck. She wore a faded gray T-shirt that showed tanned arms which were still muscled, and jeans with dirt on the knees, probably from working in the garden.

"You're looking well," Nana said, taking in Stacy's own black T-shirt with a white band logo on it, her cut-offs that showed off the leg and butt muscles she'd worked on all summer. "I like the new color," Nana said after a moment.

"Thanks," Stacy said. She'd found gray (gray!) hairs had started creeping in that summer, so she'd chopped most of it off then dyed her brown hair a honey blonde. It was a pain to keep up with, but Stacy found she loved it.

Eventually, she'd give into the gray, which Nana wore well. Mom did too. Stacy just wasn't ready yet.

"Why was the door locked? Had you forgotten I was coming?" Stacy teased as she dragged her luggage from the front to the right side of the rambler, where the three bedrooms were.

"Uhm, yes, that was why," Nana said.

Stacy stopped in the middle of the hallway. Nana's oil paintings covered the walls, like a mosaic of color. She turned back to look at Nana.

She was certain that Nana had just lied to her.

"Let's get you settled and get some lunch into you," Nana said, brushing past Stacy and into the bright and cheery guest room. It faced the front yard, with the roses underneath the window. Nana had painted it a bright yellow, with white trim, quilt, and rug on the dark hardwood floor. "I bet you're starving, aren't you? I made bread this morning. How does a BLT sound?"

Stacy could tell that Nana wanted her to drop the subject, and let herself be distracted by the running commentary and questions.

But Nana hadn't forgotten to unlock the door. She'd kept it locked, on purpose.

Whatever could be wrong?

Stacy and Nana picked blackberries that afternoon because the brambles were mostly in the shade by then. The next day, they started in on the apples. It was a heavy fruit year. Given their druthers, a fruit tree would only fruit every other year. They had to be trained to give fruit every year. Even after all these years, Nana's trees still preferred to fruit heavily one year and lightly the next.

However, their work wasn't finished after they carried buckets of fuji, honey crisp, Jonagold and Granny Smith apples back into the kitchen. Then they had to wash the fruit, chuck out the ones with that showed signs of bugs, and separate the apples based on quality.

Most of the fruit was going into baked goods, so it didn't matter what they looked like. Some, though, Nana gave away, and those all had to be beauties.

"I noticed you've been keeping all the doors locked, and the windows as well," Stacy finally said as she went through her pile. Ugh. That poor little apple had been pecked at by birds. The inside of it still might be usable for pie, though.

"Oh, it's nothing," Nana said. "Just heard from the Gonzales's, up the street. Seemed some of their tools went missing from their barn."

Stacy nodded, concerned. Missing tools could mean someone just wandering through. It could also mean something much worse, some sort of drug addict in the area looking for items to sell.

"Are you keeping the barn locked?" Stacy asked.

Nana nodded. "Yes, Mom," she teased. "And my studio as well."

Long before it had become popular, Nana had built herself a "she shed." It was where she did most of her crafts: her painting, her quilting, and whatever else had caught her eye that year. Most recently, it had been marbled paper. Stacy was actually looking forward to seeing what her Christmas presents were wrapped in, as they were sure to be beautiful.

"I worry about you, out here, so isolated, all alone," Stacy admitted. She'd suggested more than once that Nana retire from the countryside and come live in the city. She'd even offered to find a house someplace that would be big enough for the pair of them.

Though she was aware that Nana was likely to completely take over any space she was in. She was that much of a force of nature, and she had way too many hobbies.

Nana sighed. "I know you're worried. But living in the city would make me crazy. I need my space. My land. My gardens. My trees."

Stacy knew that as well. If she insisted on plucking Nana out of her environment, chances were she'd wither and die, like a tree with its roots exposed.

However, it would be difficult for Stacy to move out here. She worked as a paralegal in the city. While much of her work could be done remotely, some of it required in person contact. And driving back and forth from Horton to Seattle would make her crazy. Crazier. Whatever.

"It'll be fine, dear," Nana said after a few minutes, the only sound in the kitchen the splashing of water as they checked and dunked apples in the huge farm sink. "It will all work out in the end."

Stacy didn't have Nana's faith. But she was willing to let the matter rest, at least for now.

The next morning, while Nana was still washing up the dishes from the magnificent omelets they'd had that morning—tomatoes, green peppers, spinach, and chives, all from the garden—Stacy went out to the barn to get another bucket they could use for separating apples.

While Nana and Grandpa had always called it "the barn," it didn't resemble one, not much. However, Nana insisted that "barn" was the right word, even though it was actually just an equipment shed.

Admittedly, the wood sides of the barn were painted a dark red, and the trim around the windows was white. But that was about its only resemblance to a barn. Instead of being a rectangle, was a square building with a single story, about twenty feet on a side. It had two doors: one in the back that was a wide, barn-style door that was used primarily to access the riding mower, and the one in the front, which was a regular, eight-panel wooden door painted a bright blue.

The grass beside the walkway was heavy with dew and sparkled in the rising sun. For now, the air was delightfully cool. Later that afternoon it would get far too warm again. A slight wind carried the scent of the nearby pines, a smell that Stacy always relished. Bushtits chirped nearby, hunting for bugs in the trees.

Stacy felt content with the world. Maybe she could move out here.

Then she saw that the front door of the barn was ajar.

Or maybe not.

She knew, *knew*, they had locked the door the evening before. She'd double-checked it, particularly after hearing about the neighbors losing equipment. It couldn't have just blown open.

Was someone still inside?

Damn it! She'd left her cell phone in her room. Nana had a strict policy about not checking phones while at the breakfast table.

Stacy bent over, then scurried over to the barn, under the window. She listened, but she didn't hear anything but her own loudly beating heart. After a few more moments, she slowly raised up, peeking in the window, ready to race back to the house if she saw someone.

No one appeared to be in the barn, at least not as far as she could see. Not unless they were hiding in one of the corners, but why would someone do that?

Stacy walked back to the front door, then pushed it open with her toe. She didn't want to ruin any fingerprint evidence that forensics might be able to gather. (She'd seen enough police shows to know that much.)

As she'd seen from her peek through the window, everything appeared to be in place. The rakes and shovels were hanging from hooks and racks against the far wall. Storage shelves held a miscellaneous collection of boxes and supplies. The riding lawn mower still sat in its corner, and the faint smell of gas permeated the air.

Had someone broken in and then not taken anything?

It wasn't until Stacy got all the way into the barn and looked around that she see what had been stolen.

Some of Nana's gardening tools were missing. Not the bigger ones that were used in the orchard, but the smaller set, the hand tools, like the spade, the garden fork, and the clippers.

Who on earth would take those? While they were good quality—Nana was never cheap when it came to her tools—they were also very used. If someone had stolen them to sell at a pawn shop, they wouldn't get any money from them.

Shaking her head, Stacy walked back to the house.

"Did you forget the bucket?" Nana teased as Stacy walked in empty handed. Nana was already at the counter wearing her apron, large knife in hand, starting to core and quarter apples for apple butter.

"No," Stacy said. "Someone broke in. They stole your gardening tools!"

"What?" Nana asked. She seemed surprised. Then she shook her head and chuckled. "Well, they're welcome to them. They've done me good all these years."

"Aren't you going to call the police? Report the theft?" Stacy said, outraged. Really, this wasn't something to just let slide!

Nana thought for a moment. "No," she said firmly. "Poor Deputy Glenn has that new baby. Poor man isn't getting any sleep. We don't need to bother him about this."

"What if they come back?" Stacy said. Even if Nana didn't think it was anything big, Stacy could easily be upset enough for both of them.

Nana shot Stacy a hard look. Then she deliberately put down her knife, untied her apron, picked up the cutting board, and put it with its contents into the refrigerator.

"What are you doing?" Stacy asked, confused.

"Well, you're not about to let this be," Nana said, sounding reasonable. "And I'll admit, you've peaked my curiosity. Since I am not about to bother the police—not for something as trivial as this—we're just going to have to solve the crime ourselves!"

Stacy nearly groaned when she saw the twinkle in Nana's eye. How come she suddenly felt as though she was going to have to be the responsible adult here?

"Nana—" Stacy started with.

"It will be fun!" Nana assured her. "And besides, this way you'll get to meet all the neighbors up and down the lane. We can bring them some apples. And maybe some canned tomatoes. Ask them if they want apple or blackberry bars."

Stacy sighed. It was *not* going to be fun. It was actually going to be her definition of he—heck. Yes. Heck.

Nana still gave Stacy a *look*, as if she realized what Stacy was actually thinking.

Stacy gave Nana her best innocent face in return.

Though Stacy could tell that Nana wasn't fooled, at least she was willing to let it go.

Sort of.

Nana put her hands on her waist and looked Stacy up and down critically. "You need to wear something other than those shorts," she said.

"What's wrong with them?" Stacy said, looking down, confused. She liked these shorts. They were a mint-green color and made her butt look fantastic. She was also wearing a sleeveless white blouse, that had a collar and buttoned. It was a little dressed up for working out here on the property, but it had felt right that morning.

"Those pants are too tight," Nana said firmly. "Get a pair of cut-offs instead.

While Stacy might have wanted to argue, at least her grandmother wasn't making her cover up her legs.

"Fine," Stacy said after a few moments.

Changing clothes to suit her grandmother wasn't her biggest concern.

It was how could she talk Nana into moving someplace safer? At least until they'd caught the thief?

———

It turned out that three of the neighbors on their side of the lane had all been robbed. Nothing big was every taken. It was always some sort of gardening supplies. The Fredrick's had even had seeds and a bag of potting soil stolen.

It seemed as though someone was building a garden. But why? And where?

After turning down several offers of lunch, Stacy and Nana walked back down one side of the lane, towards Nana's property. The sun was hot, and Stacy was glad that Nana had insisted that Stacy wear a large floppy hat that had been Grandpa's. It was made out of green and brown camouflage and looked decidedly dorky on her. She still loved it. Nana's hat, on the other hand, was quite stylish, made out of a khaki green with a broad brim and a flap that went down the back.

Big-leaf maples, elms, birches, and pine trees lined either side of the country lane. Red and orange tinged the edges of some of the leaves. The last of the dandelions still bloomed bright and yellow just outside of the line of trees. Crickets sang loudly. A friendly breeze kept the asphalt road from being too warm.

The pair of them walked together side by side, each lost in their thoughts. If they heard a car approaching, they could move further off the edge of the lane easily enough. And chances were, no one would be going too fast. Two houses past Nana's the lane dead-ended.

"Nana," Stacy finally said, "is there any property nearby that's for sale? Or was recently sold?"

Nana thought for a moment. "Yes," she said. "Poor Mrs. Santos had to sell her land after her husband died. She moved back to Yakima, to be closer to her family. You should see the pictures she posts of her grandchildren! So adorable!"

Stacy knew that she didn't have to take any mentions of grandchildren personally. Her older brother already had three brats, so she didn't need to worry about filling that role.

"Where is her land?" Stacy asked.

"Just down past my property, across the lane," Nana replied. "You know, I've never met the new owners."

That twinkle was back in Nana's eye.

However, this time Stacy gave her a grin in return. "I think it's time we go and introduce ourselves."

"I couldn't agree more," Nana said.

They linked arms, and merrily walked down the lane together.

The house sat back aways from the lane, a dirt path leading to it. The yard hadn't been watered enough that summer and the grass was all brown and stiff. The house itself was similar to Nana's, in that it was a single story rambler made from solid brick, but the trim needed painting. Lilac bushes stood on either side of the door, the leaves looking yellow and tired.

As they approached, Stacy saw a young girl sitting on the right side of the house. She appeared to be playing in the dirt, using a hand rake to scratch at it.

She led Nana that way.

Sure enough, more than one of the tools that had gone missing from Nana's barn were scattered around the young white girl. She didn't look up as they approached, but stayed focused on the hole she was digging.

"Hello, sweetheart," Nana said.

The girl looked up, startled. She had blonde hair that the sun had bleached almost white, with large blue eyes and a round face.

The sort of round face that indicated down's syndrome.

"I'm not supposed to talk with strangers," the girl told them solemnly.

"That's right," Nana said. "We need to talk to your mother. Is she here?"

The girl stayed silent, staring at them, not saying a word.

"Mattie! Mattie!" someone called. A young pre-teen boy came careening around the edge of the house. "I told you to stay in the back!" he yelled.

"Sorry, Tommy," the girl said. "But I needed a new hole!"

Tommy sighed. "Come on," he said, extending his hand toward his sister. "You need to get back behind the house where I can watch you."

He finally looked up at Stacy and Nana. He was also white. His hair was a sandy blond, and he had the same blue eyes as his sister. He wore a clean T-shirt and shorts, though his shoes were scuffed up from the dirt. "I suppose you saw these," he said, indicating the tools and sounding resigned.

"We did," Nana said. "Where is your mother, young man?"

"I was only going to borrow them for a while!" Tommy exclaimed. "Mattie would get tired of 'gardening' sooner or later. I would have put them all back!"

"No, I wouldn't," Mattie said in her defense. "I love my gardens!"

Stacy nearly rolled her eyes. Tommy clearly didn't understand the first thing in terms of sibling control. Never tell a brother or sister they don't like something, or they'll go out of their way to prove you wrong.

"Is your mother home?" Nana asked again.

"She is," Tommy admitted with a sigh. "How much trouble am I in?"

That twinkle was back in Nana's eye. "Depends on how hard you want to work," she said, sounding stern.

With heavy steps, Tommy led the pair of them inside the house, through the back door, into the kitchen. "Ma!" he called. "Company!"

Boxes were still piled up in a corner, and things hadn't been set into place. The space was going to be lovely, though, Stacy could tell. White lace curtains hung above the sink. The cupboards were a lovely reddish wood color that complimented the golden wood floors. Tucked away in the corner was a small eating nook, covered in a colorful tablecloth with only three chairs.

The woman who stepped into the kitchen was in her late thirties, about Stacy's age. A red and white headband held back her hair, the bright color matching her lipstick. Her face was long, thin, and pale white. She had the same wide blue eyes as her children. The T-shirt she wore showed signs of her recent work, being streaked with a pale yellow paint.

After Nana made the introductions, she asked Tommy if

he had anything he wanted to say to his mother, who went by the name of Colette.

He sighed before confessing to his crimes, insisting once again that he was merely borrowing them.

Colette shook her head. "I'm so sorry," she said mournfully. "I didn't know! We'll pay you back."

"But we're house poor!" Tommy exclaimed, obviously confused.

"Yes, dear, we are," Colette said. "That doesn't mean we can steal tools from other people, just because we want them for ourselves."

"Mattie needed them," Tommy said stubbornly.

Stacy could sympathize, even though she had no children of her own. She and her ex had been house poor too—borrowing too much to pay for a house in the insane Seattle market. At least they'd been able to sell it for more than what they'd paid, before the market had collapsed. Again.

"I think I have an idea," Nana said smoothly. "How would you feel about loaning out such a strong and capable young man to do some chores around your neighbors houses? That way, he can earn his own money to purchase tools with."

Colette gave a huge grin. "I think that would be an excellent idea. Can I offer you some lunch while we work out the details? I'm afraid all I have are cheese and bologna sandwiches."

"That would be lovely," Nana said. "I'm just going to pop back to my place to collect a few things to add, if that would be all right?"

Stacy knew that Nana would probably empty half of her refrigerator and bring it back, not that Colette would take it. "Why don't I go back and get things? That way you two neighbors can chat."

Nana gave her a sharp look before she nodded. "Just pick

up a few apples, then," she said. "And maybe a jar of three-bean salad?" she asked, looking back at Colette.

"That's my favorite!" Tommy declared. "Mattie's too."

"You should go check on your sister," Colette said. "Thank you," she said after Tommy ran out of the house. "He's a handful, but his heart's in the right place."

Stacy slipped out of the kitchen while the two older women bonded. She was certain that Nana would not only have all of Colette's personal history by the time she came back, but that they were well on the way to becoming good friends.

Maybe everything would work out in the end.

Tommy came by to help every day while Stacy was there. He turned out to be very useful in the kitchen, coring apples and helping to chop them up.

Colette came over more than once as well, not just checking to make sure that Tommy wasn't making a nuisance of himself, but appearing to check in on Nana as well, making sure that the older woman wasn't doing too much and was still taking care of herself.

Stacy felt much better about Nana and her whole situation by the time she left at the end of the week. Yes, the peace and quiet had started to get on her nerves. But the laughter in the kitchen the night before had helped drive away the darkness outside.

Colette's husband drove big semi's cross-country, and so would be gone for a couple of weeks, then home for a couple of weeks. Stacy got to meet him just before she left, a large, gentle bear of a man who obviously adored his kids as well as his wife.

Just as Stacy was getting everything packed away in the

car (really, was she going to turn down any of the boxes of canned food that Nana was insisting she take?) Nana came up to her with one small box in her hand.

It was a box holding a bar of soap.

"What?" Stacy said, immediately defensive. "I've been good!" And she mostly had been. There had been a few times when she'd thought about swearing, but she hadn't. Really.

"I know my dear, and I appreciate it," Nana said. That twinkle was back in her eye. "This is for you to practice with at home. Keep the soap someplace where you can see it, so that maybe you think twice before using such language, even in the privacy of your own home."

"All right," Stacy said, a bit confused.

"There are going to be young people here, often," Nana said seriously. "This is going to become their second home. Both young Tommy and Mattie. When you come back for Christmas, you need to be well practiced in minding your tongue."

"Yes, ma'am," Stacy said, nodding.

She was glad that Nana was adopting Colette and her family. Though Tommy was only ten at this point, as he grew older he'd hopefully be able to take care of Nana. Colette and her husband certainly would.

She gave Nana a huge hug before she left. Though she still felt Nana's strength, there was a frailty there that would only increase with time.

Eventually, she and Nana were going to have to have conversations about Nana moving someplace else.

But for now, through the fortune of losing some tools, Nana was going to be taken care of.

Stacy drove off, heading back to Seattle, the bar of soap keeping her company on the passenger seat. She was *not* going to start swearing at the tourists on the road.

Not for a little while, at any rate.

BRIBING GHOSTS

Fu Ran knelt in front of her father's grave. At least she'd remembered to bring a rough, red-and-black checked blanket so her jeans wouldn't get too dirty kneeling on the ground. The August sun beat down on the back of her head from the clear blue sky, making her wish she'd wrapped her long black hair up in a bun, getting it off her shoulders and neck. She wore a short-sleeved white blouse that her father would have considered scandalous as it didn't cover her up to her neck, but it was far too warm to go around completely swaddled.

She also didn't wear any makeup—something else her father had always associated with the corrupting Western influence creeping into the mainland.

On the ground in front of Fu Ran sat a paper boat, about the size of her two hands held together. It had been cleverly folded out of bright red-and-gold "Hell" money—*joss* paper to be burned as an offering for the dead. Between the boat and the unassuming gray tombstone a few feet away, Fu Ran had stuck nine rows of incense into the ground, three sticks per row, twenty-seven total: the same as her age, hopefully a lucky number that day. Sweet smoke curled up from the lit ends, hazing the clear air.

Earlier, that spring, during the *qingming* festival, her entire family had gathered to clean the front area of the grave: her mother, her two older brothers, her grandfather, as well as one of her aunts and three of her cousins. No weeds remained, and the grass in front of the grave marker stayed short.

Now, Fu Ran knelt all alone. No one had dared come with her to visit a graveyard during *gui yue*—Ghost Month.

According to tradition, Judge Yama opened the gates of Hell on the first day of the seventh Lunar month, setting all the wild ghosts free to roam the earth. On the fifteenth of the month, there would be many celebrations and events to feed and entertain the ghosts, who would all (hopefully) leave by the end of the month.

Though Fu Ran's family had made offerings on the first day of Ghost Month to appease any hungry ancestors who came to visit, bad luck had struck them hard. Fu Ran's mother remained in the hospital after the car accident that had claimed the life of her middle brother. Her eldest brother had lost his job. And her youngest aunt had come down with the flu and was still bedridden, the doctors worried and ordering more tests.

Obviously, some ghost (or ghosts) were angry with Fu Ran and her family. She'd decided that making an offering in a temple wasn't good enough. The incense and the Hell money she burned there might get lost among all the other offerings and not go directly to her father.

Her family needed an intervention in the spirit world. Who better than her strong, calm, overly-principled father? Who'd died only three years before from cancer?

So on the eighth day of Ghost Month, Fu Ran took the hot, stinky bus all the way to the outskirts of her city,

Fuzhou, to visit her father's graveyard. The bus's air conditioning had been overwhelmed by the sheer number of bodies, with mothers and their sisters holding two children each in their laps, sullen teenagers crammed together, even ancient grandmothers stoically standing, their arms wrapped around each other's waist to hold them up.

Though her parents had given her an auspicious name —*Fu Ran* basically translated into English as lucky—Fu Ran considered herself the unluckiest girl in the whole world.

She had excelled during her college exams and had gone on to get an advanced degree in chemistry, however, no job awaited her. With the death of her father, her family had lost their Party connections. No sponsor had come forward to advocate for her.

As a result, she could only get a soul-crushing job in one of the numerous factories that lined the coast, making cheap shoes and clothes to be exported to America, but that wouldn't be putting her education to use. Plus, those jobs didn't pay well at all, and too many factories still had deadly accidents.

She didn't have a boyfriend—not even a secret crush— though her girlfriends teased her she must like *someone*, even if she didn't.

Bills were mounting up. Fu Ran wasn't sure how the family would pay not just for her brother's cremation and burial expenses, but for her mother's hospital stay as well. (It was just too inauspicious to conduct the funeral during Ghost Month, so the ceremony couldn't occur until the following month.)

Fu Ran didn't know if praying to her father would help. She'd found a paper boat because he'd always loved to go fishing on the Min River. He'd told her stories of poling a flat-bottomed boat as a boy, going upriver to where it widened out and a small pool formed where he could almost always find fish.

Fu Ran didn't know what else to do, where else to turn. Her father's old boss, the family's primary Party affiliation, had disappeared out of their lives when her father had died. None of her professors had taken her on as an assistant, despite her high grades. The loss of her brother tore at her chest like an open wound, no amount of fancy surgery could seal the hole.

After she finished her prayers, imploring that not just her father but any and all of her deceased relatives needed to help her family, she set the little boat on fire.

Maybe the boat would delight her father and get him to intervene with the ghosts targeting them.

Or perhaps he'd be dismayed at her whimsy and send more devils to haunt them.

Fu Ran defiantly stood up. The heat of the flames washed across her legs. The scorching sun beat down on her head, making her sway in place. The smell of incense swelled up and made her cough. Dark spots formed in the corners of her eyes.

She blinked.

All but one of the dark spots went away.

She turned to look at the now moving shape.

It was a man, not a ghost. Definitely not her imagination, either. White shirt, black pants, black hair, dark eyes, tanned skin.

He walked to the tombstone closest to him, then knelt down, looking around.

Then he stood and walked quickly to the next.

Who was he hiding from?

He spotted her standing. He paused and stared hard at her.

Fu Ran resisted the urge to wave at him, just to prove that she wasn't a ghost either.

He shook his head, then changed direction and came directly toward her without pausing again.

His dark eyes drilled into her very soul, holding her captive.

"It isn't safe here," the man said as soon as he drew near. He had a very cultured accent, possibly from Beijing.

He wore his black, glossy hair super short and cute. He had rolled the sleeves of his white shirt up above his elbows, showing off nicely muscled arms. Both his well-made black dress slacks and black leather shoes were scuffed and had streaks of dirt on them.

"Why isn't it safe here?" Fu Ran asked, not wanting to be chased off. This was *her* father's grave, after all. She had every right to be there. "Are you afraid of the ghosts?"

He gave a sharp, barking laugh. "Ghosts?" he asked, looking around. He spied the rows of incense almost burnt to their ends sticking out of the grave. Then he looked at her strangely. "You are a brave woman to make offerings to…" he paused, glancing at the tombstone, "your father, I'm presuming, during the middle of Ghost Month."

"Someone had to," Fu Ran explained. That was all she was planning on saying about the matter. As her aunt always said, wear your broken arm *inside* your sleeve.

The man nodded and bowed his head low to her. "I can only hope that when I have a daughter, she will be as dutiful. But for now, we both need to get out of here."

"Why?" Fu Ran asked, stubbornly crossing her arms when the man reached out to touch her, perhaps hurry her along.

The man glanced over his shoulder. "Spies," he hissed. "Taiwanese spies."

Fu Ran gasped. All her life, the Party had warned about

Taiwanese spies. Fuzhou sat directly across the strait from the renegade island. She'd had nightmares as a child about Taiwanese soldiers swarming out of their boats and taking over the city, killing everyone in her family.

She looked past the man, in the direction he'd come from.

She stiffened, shock holding her very still.

Four men stood at the very edge of the cemetery.

"Too late to run," Fu Ran told the man. She reached out and grabbed his sleeve, tugging on it. "Come. Kneel with me. They will believe you are being a dutiful son."

The man glanced over his shoulder, then back at Fu Ran. Relief flowed across his features. The smile he gave her was as dazzling as the sun overhead.

Really, it was just the summer heat that made her knees feel so weak, not his look.

"You're right," he said, gracefully kneeling down on the blanket. "They're just following a man. They don't know me by sight. I'm Zhong Di," he said, putting his hands on the ground and lowering his head.

"Fu Ran," she said as she knelt and did the same.

They each prayed in silence as the last of the smoke from the paper boat rose up into the clear sky.

Just as the men grew closer, Zhong Di reached into the breast pocket of his shirt and took out two more pieces of Hell money. He handed one to her, set his on fire with a lighter and then gestured for her to do the same.

The men abruptly swerved and walked past them.

Fu Ran felt her shoulders drop with relief. Finally, something was going right!

It wasn't until the cemetery was completely empty before Fu Ran spoke. "Why did you have Hell money with you?" she asked.

Zhong Di gave her a carefree grin that made him look

even younger and more handsome than he had initially appeared. "It's Ghost Month," he said. "And I've always believed in carrying the appropriate bribes. Who knows when you'll need them the most?"

Fu Ran nodded. A very practical answer. Though the Party decreed that this was the Worker's Paradise and everyone was equal, somehow it generally took bribes to get anything done.

Maybe that was why the Party allowed all the sacrifices during Ghost Month: they saw it as bribes for ghosts.

Both of them rose. The sun was finally hanging lower in the sky, the heat of the afternoon passing. Loud choruses of cicadas sprang up. Zhong Di helped Fu Ran first shake out her blanket, then fold it up.

"Where will you go now?" Fu Ran asked, not willing to let Zhong Di disappear like a ghost.

He sighed. "I could lie and say that I was going back to my apartment, but they might have it staked out by now."

"My middle brother just died. My mother's still in the hospital. My aunt is very sick," Fu Ran said all in a rush. "You could stay in our living room, and sleep on the sofa, but it would still be very unlucky."

She knew that it wasn't proper to invite Zhong Di home. She'd just met him! She didn't know his family or any of his friends.

Plus, he wasn't safe. He was running from Taiwanese spies. Maybe he was a spy himself.

However, she couldn't help herself. There was something about him, maybe how he held himself, or the look of confidence in his eyes, or perhaps even the strong muscles of his arms, that made her throw caution to the wind.

Then again, she'd started the day rashly, making the decision to go to a cemetery during Ghost Month. May as well continue down that same path.

Zhong Di gave her a smile that matched her reckless feelings. "I accept, but you can't ask too many questions. That wouldn't be safe for you or your family."

Fu Ran considered his statement for a moment. Again, he sounded very practical, an attribute both her mother and her father would approve of. "You will tell me what you can of your troubles?" Fu Ran asked. "Then, tell me the rest later?"

"I promise," Zhong Di said solemnly.

Fu Ran shivered. It sounded like a vow that he'd honor even unto death.

Who was this man? What mysteries filled his life? And how could she bribe him to make sure that he continued to "haunt" her, to stay with her like an old ghost?

The back door to the apartment building where Fu Ran's family lived had graffiti on it already, though it had just been painted an industrial brown not two weeks before. Black and white stickers with strident characters had been slapped on it. Plus some stupid advertisement for an illegal band.

Fu Ran sighed but didn't say anything. She pulled open the door, gesturing for Zhong Di to walk in. He carried the plastic bags containing their dinner. It had been so kind of him to buy enough food, not just for her, but for three additional people as well.

After he stepped into the dimly lit stairwell, she shut the door after him and locked it carefully. The stairway smelled of concrete and bleach. At least it no longer smelled of urine, as it had the previous month when a homeless man had snuck in and spent the night sleeping there.

"Ready for a climb?" Fu Ran asked. While there was an

elevator at the front of the building, it was often broken, always dirty, and it made clanging noises that Fu Ran didn't trust.

"After you," Zhong Di said gallantly.

Fu Ran couldn't help but give him a smile before she turned to the prospect of the six flights of stairs that they needed to climb. While she was young and in good enough shape to reach her floor without being too winded, she always felt sorry for the older people in the building. She'd frequently pass them sitting on one of the landings, wheezing and trying to catch their breath.

With Zhong Di following her, Fu Ran couldn't help but show off a little, climbing the bare concrete stairs quickly. She rarely touched the railing. Though it was painted a happy red, it was often sticky or slimy from who knew what.

The sixth floor looked cheery compared to the plain concrete staircase. Lights in red, green, and blue paper lanterns hung from the ceiling down the center of the hall. Fu Ran's family along with the neighbors had painted the walls a bright yellow. Large windows with green glass (reinforced with chicken-wire) stood on the right of each door, supposedly to supply the tiny apartments with more light. Ancient red carpet covered the floor, worn bare in many places. The hall smelled of garlic, chicken, and incense —the smells of home—with a faint undertone of more bleach.

No numbers or names marked any of the apartments, of course. It was too easy for evil spirits to follow a person home if they could easily find their address. All the doors had been painted different colors, though, to make it easier for guests to visit.

The old woman at the start of the floor, closest to the stairway, with the strongest Party affiliations, got the lucky red door. Everyone else had to settle for other colors.

Fu Ran happily stopped in front of the dark blue door of her family's apartment. They lived one apartment in from the far end and just across the hallway from the communal showers and toilets for that floor. She hoped that Zhong Di wouldn't think too poorly of them since they didn't have a private bathroom. However, at least they didn't have to go down the street to the public toilets, which were always filthy.

"I don't know who's home," she warned Zhong Di. She didn't know what kind of reception he'd get from either of her aunts, who frequently stayed with them, or her brother.

"Hopefully we have enough food to feed them," he replied with a smile.

"Thank you," she said again as she unlocked the door.

Just inside the tiny alcove, she saw only her eldest brother's shoes waiting there, a pair of worn brown-leather loafers. She hoped he wouldn't be too hard on Zhong Di. Fu Ran slipped off her shoes and put on her house slippers, then handed a pair of guest slippers to Zhong Di.

Thankfully, he wasn't too "cultured" to be ashamed of wearing guest slippers, taking off his shoes and slipping on the guest pair.

The kitchen ran along the outside wall, with a tiny stove that Fu Ran's mother had always worked miracles with, a sink that was barely big enough to hold a dinner bowl, and shelves that rose to top of the eight foot ceiling, stocked full of instant meals, dried goods, spices, bowls, and chopsticks. It still smelled of rice and pickled fish.

To the left, the apartment opened up into what had originally been one long room. Her family had divided it up to make an extra bedroom for her brothers.

Fu Ran breathed a sigh of relief when she saw the door to her brother's bedroom was closed, with a little placard hanging from the doorknob, showing a red lotus flower.

The sign meant that the person behind the door didn't want to be disturbed. The other side of the sign held a golden laughing Buddha, which, when showing, meant he would welcome company.

Though the concept of spending time alone was frowned on, both of Fu Ran's brothers, and Fu Ran herself, needed it sometimes in order to study.

And now, to grieve.

The living room itself held a low coffee table that the family usually sat around for meals. The white-and-gray top of the table barely had any dents in it from the numerous children who had banged on it over the years. The legs showed more wear, the gold paint flecking off to reveal the steel underneath. Fu Ran often slid her fingertips along them, as if she could gather strength from their sturdiness.

While the floor itself was concrete, Fu Ran's family had bought several colorful rugs to cover it. Her favorite was made from black, blue, and white cloth all braided together. It sat under the table and provided good insulation from the floor.

They had one black, scratchy couch, pressed up against the wall to her brother's bedroom. Lamps sitting on the wooden end tables at either arm of the couch made the room bright. Folded-up black metal chairs leaned against the kitchen wall, ready for guests.

The wall to Fu Ran's left held a few pictures—school graduations, important ceremonies, her father's death portrait.

Her brother's picture would join them soon enough, something Fu Ran didn't want to think about just yet.

On the right wall were two closed doors: one leading to the bedroom her parents had shared, one going to her own tiny room.

Zhong Di put the bags holding their dinner on the table, then gracefully sank down.

Fu Ran breathed a sigh of relief. At least he didn't seem to mind sitting on the floor.

They eagerly divided up the food, leaving two whole bags for leftovers. Soon, Fu Ran slurped her noodle soup, the broth having cooled to the perfect temperature, with just the right amount of tangy onions in it.

By the time she'd finished that and started in on her rice and stir-fried vegetables, she finally felt human, as well as ready to hear Zhong Di's story.

He'd seemed to come to the same conclusion, and started by saying, "I work as an inventor for…let's just say one of the big shoe manufacturers."

"Really?" Fu Ran asked. "Were you working on different rubber for the soles?"

Zhong Di blinked and nodded slowly. "In a way, I was. Why do you ask?"

Fu Ran didn't like the suspicious look in his eye. "I studied to be a chemist," she told him. "With an advanced degree."

"Oh?" he asked, surprised. "Who do you work for?"

Fu Ran looked back down at her rice. She suddenly was no longer hungry. "No one," she said. "I had good grades—the best in my class—but no one would hire me."

"I see," Zhong Di said.

Perhaps he did. It wasn't easy for someone as poor as Fu Ran to be hired into a good paying job. Particularly without Party backing.

"Anyway," he said after a few moments of silence. "I… let's just say I made an interesting breakthrough. When I showed it to my boss, Ya Du, he told me not to continue with that line of reasoning." Zhong Di sighed. He appeared to be choosing his words carefully. "Instead, two men approached me that night."

"Spies?" Fu Ran asked when he didn't speak again right away.

"I believe so," Zhong Di said. "They flattered me. And offered me a lot of money if I would sell them my discovery."

Fu Ran could tell by the way that Zhong Di hung his head that he'd originally been taken in. "What happened?" she asked.

"When it came time to give them the formula, early this morning…I just couldn't do it. I couldn't sell it to them. It was four men. I'd never seen them before. They weren't business men. They were goons. I saw them at the end of the street, then just turned and ran. They've been after me ever since." He sighed again.

"Could you sell them a formula that didn't work?" Fu Ran asked. "Alter it slightly?"

"Possibly, but that wouldn't stop them from coming after me," Zhong Di said. "And I can't turn in my boss. He has strong Party connections. It would be his word against mine. Nobody would believe me."

Fu Ran shook her head as a plan came to her.

Why did men always think they needed to do everything on their own? By themselves?

She blamed the West for that corrupting idea.

"I may have a plan," she said slowly after Zhong Di had fallen back to eating. "But it will take some careful timing on both our parts. As well as reaching out to our connections."

"Really?" Zhong Di asked, his eyes gleaming. "I knew that traveling to the cemetery was sure to bring me good luck."

Fu Ran couldn't help but giggle. That was the first time someone had found anything lucky in a graveyard.

Then again, possibly Zhong Di would bring good luck, and not trouble, to her and her family as well.

Fu Ran kept her expression professional, despite how she shook like a little girl inside. She wore a somber, light-gray blouse and a black skirt—her one, good interview outfit —with her hair pinned up in a tight bun. Tonight, she'd tinted her lips just slightly pink to make her seem younger, as well as used eyeliner to make her dark eyes look rounder and more innocent.

She didn't squirm in the hard-backed wooden chair that she sat on—that might have overplayed her hand.

Zhong Di's boss, Ya Du, sat and looked sternly at her from across the broad expansive of his oak desk. They were meeting after hours at the shoe factory. He wore the light-grey jacket currently favored by Party officials, though the top button and standing collar dug into his fat neck. His flabby lips and plump face made him look like a toad, while his black eyes were tiny and full of cunning.

The office stank of burnt rubber from the factory despite the cool air that blew constantly from the vents. Bright neon lights buzzed annoyingly above them, highlighting how dingy the place looked. Sad green paint covered the walls, scuffed and peeling. A huge picture of Xi Jinping hung on the wall just behind Ya Du, framed in bright red matting. Various Party awards hung beside it.

No school diploma, however.

"I'm glad that someone had the intelligence to come to me with this," Ya Du said. "And you're sure that Zhong Di has no idea you're here?"

"He does not," Fu Ran said, her voice steady. She suspected Ya Du was trying to figure out just how alone she was and whether or not he could just make her disappear. "Zhong Di said he was going to *hide* his discovery, instead of sharing it with the People."

Fu Ran made sure that she sounded every bit the patriot. She'd considered wearing a jacket with a red star pinned to the lapel, but it had been too warm that evening, plus it felt like overkill.

They needed for Ya Du to make Fu Ran the same deal he'd made Zhong Di.

"So you brought the formula to me," Ya Du said with relish.

Fu Ran wasn't about to tell him that it wasn't the original formula. She and Zhong Di had altered it slightly so it would be sure to fail.

"Of course I would bring it to you! You are his immediate superior," Fu Ran explained. "If he isn't going to take credit for it, you should." She hesitated, and for the first time, added some sadness to her voice. "My family has had so much bad luck this Ghost Month."

"Really?" Ya Du purred.

Fu Ran pushed down on her flush of anger. He sounded like a cat who'd just spotted a wounded bird.

"My brother was killed in a car accident," Fu Ran said softly. The pain constantly tore at her heart, and she no longer had to pretend to be sad. "My mother is still in the hospital because of it." The doctors had finally said that she might be released by the end of the following week, but then she'd have a lot of physical therapy for her broken leg and hip.

And how was her family going to pay for all of that?

"Ah," Ya Du said, sitting back in his chair. He nodded, as if he'd come to a decision. "I have some people who might be interested in such a formula."

Fu Ran frowned at him. She knew she couldn't just jump

at the chance he was offering. She had to make him convince her. "I don't understand."

"Sometimes, it's better to help each other along the path, rather than to bask in the sunshine by yourself," Ya Du said, mangling a famous Party slogan.

Fu Ran blinked. "How can we help each other?" she asked slowly, despite her rapidly beating heart.

Good patriot or not, Ya Du would also believe her to be a practical person.

"Instead of selfishly using this formula to better our American masters," Ya Du said, his face scrunching together on the last two words as if they tasted sour, "we should use it to better everyone. In particular, your family."

Fu Ran nodded as if she understood. "And you can help me do that?"

Ya Du smiled broadly at her. "I can! I can introduce you to some people who would pay you very good money for such a formula."

Fu Ran tilted her head to one side, as if considering the prospect. "Why wouldn't you take it to them yourself?" she asked as innocently as she could.

"I have more than enough!" Ya Du said, his hands spread out as if to indicate the richness of his office. "Besides, I am just a humble servant."

Fu Ran contained her scoffing snort. She'd bet that the Taiwanese agents had paid Ya Du already. And were probably pressuring him to deliver, since Zhong Di had slipped away.

The real reason Ya Du wanted her to approach the agents on her own was so that he could keep his hands clean.

She was about to make sure that Ya Du got his hands dirty, though.

"I couldn't possibly meet with such people on my own," Fu Ran said, shaking her head. "It wouldn't be safe! Or proper," she added, glaring at him.

"You are meeting me here in a factory, after hours," Ya Du pointed out.

"That's different!" Fu Ran said, indignant. "You're a married man, and an upstanding member of the Party."

"True, true," Ya Du said, nodding and preening. "How about this? We'll meet tomorrow night at the Green Tearoom, at eight PM. I'll make the introductions."

"And this is the best way to help everyone?" Fu Ran asked as if looking for reassurances. "Including my family?"

"It is," Ya Du assured her.

"Thank you so much," Fu Ran said, rising from her chair then bowing lowly, as if Ya Du were a great man.

"With pleasure," he said, smacking his fat lips together.

Fu Ran left, her insides shaking but her hands still steady.

Just one more night, and Zhong Di would be free of his foreign ghosts.

Though the Green Tearoom had been built just a few years before, it still felt ancient, with scarred wooden floors, soft amber walls, and discrete lights. The air smelled of refined green tea and lemony cakes. Beautiful pink and white orchids sat on the front reception desk. The young woman behind the dark-oak reception desk wore the replica of an old-fashioned robe and was so covered up, Fu Ran knew her father would have approved.

A large room opened up to the right of the reception desk. Low tables filled the floor, each with comfortable looking pillows scattered around them. Many men, and a few women, sat at the tables, drinking tea, eating small bites, and toasting one another.

While only the best people with the strongest influence

would be allowed in here, it wasn't a place that she ever wanted to return to. She wouldn't be comfortable here.

Perhaps Zhong Di belonged here, but not her. Even though she wore her "interview" outfit again—same black skirt, with a different white shirt, and a discreet black handbag—and maybe she could pretend as though she belonged, she would never actually fit in here. She'd grown up too poor.

The thought made her heart ache.

When the receptionist heard Fu Ran's name, instead of seating her in the public area, the woman led her down a short, closed-in hallway. At the first corridor, the receptionist took a right. Brighter lights shone down here, and soft green carpet muffled their steps. Closed wooden doors lined this corridor.

The receptionist opened the third door on her left, then waited for Fu Ran to enter.

Fu Ran nearly protested. She didn't want to wait by herself in an empty room for spies to come meet her!

Then she swallowed down her fear. She could do this.

She clutched the black handbag she held a little tighter. She wasn't completely unprepared, either.

"Come in! Come in!" she heard Ya Du's cheerful voice.

Fu Ran straightened her shoulders and marched into the room, knowing full well that it could be a trap.

Ya Du sat in the place of honor, at the head of the table. He still wore his jacket that mimicked a Party uniform.

Fu Ran didn't allow herself to sag in relief when she saw that three other places had been set at the table.

The spies would be here.

Before Fu Ran could ask Ya Du about his day, the two spies came in. They looked like the spies who had first visited Zhong Di, as he had described to her, the main characteristic being that they were both so ordinary that it would be easy to forget them. They wore their black hair fairly short. Their eyes were lighter brown, almost hazel color, and their skin looked more tanned. They'd obviously been well-fed their entire lives: good fingernails, white teeth, no pock marks on their faces. One wore a brown, western suit, while the other gray, but both were cheaply made.

After the introductions had been made and tea had been served, Mr. Gray (as Fu Ran had tagged the man in the gray suit) asked, "So, I hear that you're a chemist as well."

"I am," Fu Ran said proudly. Then she remembered her part. "But no one will hire me," she added in a meeker voice.

"We may have need of a good chemist," Mr. Brown said.

"Really?" Fu Ran asked.

She knew she was just playing a part. It wasn't hard for her to sound genuinely excited. She'd looked so long for a real job.

"We would have some tests for you, of course," Mr. Gray said. "But it could be a real opportunity."

"I'd have to think about it," Fu Ran said cautiously, as a good girl would. She didn't add that she would check with her family as well—they didn't need those complications.

Ya Du smiled beneficently at all of them, like a father making a good match for his little girl. "Good! Good! So now that I have made the introductions, I think I should leave."

Fu Ran kept a pleasant smile pasted to her face. He couldn't go. Not yet!

Thankfully, a quiet knock on the door came to her rescue.

"Sir, I—" The receptionist stepped into the room, looking flustered.

Four men stepped in behind her.

Policemen. Wearing olive green uniforms. Not blue.

That meant they were part of the Armed Police Force, who handled security measures, not regular crimes.

"What's the meaning of this?" Ya Du asked, standing and sounding offended.

"We heard there was a meeting here with two Taiwanese spies," the tallest policeman said. He glared at Mr. Gray and Mr. Black.

"These are just two business acquaintances of mine," Ya Du said.

"Right. Business," the policeman continued. "We need to see your papers."

Mr. Gray and Mr. Black reached into their jacket pockets and took out their wallets and their identification papers. Fu Ran meekly handed hers over. Ya Du huffed greatly before he fished out his own.

"What's this?" the policeman asked, waving a five-hundred yuan note, then pulling out a second and a third.

"Just to show my appreciation for the officers of the law," Ya Du stammered.

Fu Ran couldn't keep a grim smile from her face. It figured that such a good Party member would try bribing everyone he met.

"You're all going to have to come in with us," the policeman said.

"What?" Ya Du asked, puffing up his chest like a stupid peacock. "Do you know who I am? I have important friends, you know."

Another man stepped into the room, pushing past the officers.

Fu Ran blinked, surprised.

It was her father's old boss. Another Party official. Gau Wan.

"I do know who you are," Gau Wan said. He sniffed as if

he disapproved of all he saw. "And I have important friends as well."

He looked old, much older than the last time Fu Ran had seen him. Gray hair covered his head, wrinkles marked his face with lines of sorrow, and his skin hung off his cheeks as if he'd lost a great deal of weight. He wore a Western-style black suit, well-tailored, with a white shirt and shiny black shoes.

Fu Ran swallowed down her fear. He wasn't going to turn on her, was he?

As part of the plan, Zhong Di had promised to get a highly regarded Party official to come to the teahouse with the policemen. Hopefully, one who couldn't be bribed by Ya Du.

How did Zhong Di know Gau Wan? Though admittedly, Fuzhou wasn't that big of a city. It wasn't completely infeasible that the two might know each other. Zhong Di was much richer than Fu Ran, and ran in different circles. The same circles as Gau Wan.

Gau Wan had disappeared after her father's death. Other Party officials had taken note and done likewise, leaving her family adrift. What had happened to him? Some tragedy, she could tell. She suddenly felt guilty for all the angry thoughts she'd had about him over the past few years.

"Let's go down to the police station and get this all straightened out," Gau Wan said. Though he kept an easy smile on his face, his tone brooked no argument.

The two spies looked at each other.

They tensed.

They were going to make a run for it.

Everything seemed to suddenly shift to slow motion.

Mr. Gray started reaching inside his jacket pocket.

Fu Ran just as covertly reached into her purse and wrapped her fingers around the cool glass she found there.

Before Mr. Gray could pull out his weapon, Fu Ran brought out the vial she carried. Neon-green, viscous liquid filled it.

She held it up over the table.

Every eye suddenly turned to her.

"You will go quietly with the police," Fu Ran told Mr. Gray. "No heroic measures. Or I'll break this over your head and you'll die a long, drawn out, *painful* death."

Mr. Gray visibly gulped and removed his empty hand from his jacket, then raised both hands into the air.

Fu Ran turned her head and glared at Mr. Black. "I have a second one in here for you as well."

Ya Du sneered. "You wouldn't dare."

"What do I have to live for?" Fu Ran said, anger rising in her voice. "I have no father. My mother's sick. My brother is dead. One more tragedy for my family would surprise no one."

She knew even as she said the words that she lied.

She had something to live for. The hope of a relationship with Zhong Di.

However, that hope was ephemeral, as likely to disappear with the bright morning sunlight as mist from the sea.

Ya Du didn't say anything more. Mr. Gray and Mr. Black were frisked (and several more weapons discovered) before they were handcuffed and taken away. Ya Du didn't have to bear the embarrassment of handcuffs, yet he was still going to be seen by some of the more important movers and shakers of Fuzhou in the presence of police as they walked him out of the tearoom.

Finally, only Gau Wan and Fu Ran remained. She took a deep breath and sagged down, resting her elbows on the table and dropping the vial.

"Careful!" Gau Wan said, rushing over.

Fu Ran grinned. "It's just a soporific," she said. "It would have made him feel very sleepy, very quickly. Then like he'd been run over by a bus."

Gau Wan chuckled and shook his head. His smile melted the years away from him. "I need to apologize," he said softly. "For abandoning you and your family. My wife got sick the week your father died and I lost track of everything else. Zhong Di rousted me, finally reminding me of my other duties.

"I'm so sorry," Fu Ran said. And she was, though a small part of her still wanted to yell at him for disappearing years ago. However, he really did look as though he'd gone through Hell.

"How do you know Zhong Di?" Fu Ran asked as she stood up. She was still going to have to go to Party Headquarters to tell them about the attempted bribes. As well as give her statement to the police.

"He's my godson," Gau Wan explained. "I fell out of contact with him, as I did everyone else."

That explained how they knew each other, and why Zhong Di had felt he could ask for this kind of favor.

"It was the least I could do, given how I'd abandoned your family," Gau Wan added, holding open the door for Fu Ran.

"I see," Fu Ran said.

And she did. She couldn't hope for anything more, like maybe a job offer or even some money to help cover their hospital costs. Gau Wan had paid his debt by believing Zhong Di's story, by not being swayed by another Party member, and by showing up that night.

"Thank you," she said as he helped her into the back of a police car.

She didn't expect to see either Gau Wan or Zhong Di again.

They'd done their part.

Now they'd slink away into the night like the ghosts they were, and she'd be on her own again.

Fu Ran eagerly strolled through the city park. Water merrily splashed out of the mouths of the stone fish that rose in a tower in the center of the main fountain. The wind carried the smell of the sea. Though no clouds marred the bright blue sky, the breeze cooled everything down.

Just past the fountain, Fu Ran discovered Zhong Di, as the note he'd left her had promised. She told her stupid heart to stop beating so hard. She hadn't seen him for two weeks, not since the night of the police raid on the teahouse.

Ya Du had been publicly shamed and now awaited trial for treason and working with Taiwanese spies. Mr. Gray and Mr. Black had disappeared, and would probably never surface again.

Zhong Di looked so gorgeous resting against the tall edge of the fountain. His black hair shone in the sunlight, his dark eyes sparkled at her. He wore a lime-green short-sleeved shirt that showed even more muscles, gray pants, but only sandals on his handsome feet. Fu Ran couldn't help but feel as though all the air had suddenly thinned, making her light headed.

She was glad that she'd worn her prettiest skirt, pale green with the outlines of flowers done in thin black lines. It was short too—her father had hated that skirt, as it showed off her knees. She'd borrowed white sandals from one of her cousins, along with a peach-colored top.

When Zhong Di pushed himself off the fountain and started towards her, she realized that he had a string wrapped around one hand. A bright red balloon bobbed along in the air behind him.

"Hello," Zhong Di said. He sounded shy.

"Hello," Fu Ran replied. She was happy to be able to get the word out despite her desperately dry throat.

"I wanted to thank you, yet again, for helping me," Zhong Di said.

"It was nothing," Fu Ran said, disappointment stabbing her chest. Of course, that would be the only reason he'd want to see her. He couldn't be interested in her. Not like that.

"So I brought you this," he said, bringing forward the hand with the balloon attached.

"What is this?" Fu Ran asked as she reached for the string and tugged the balloon down. Then she gasped. A Chinese junk was painted on the face of the balloon, floating across a smooth sea.

Zhong Di shrugged, seemingly embarrassed. "An offering."

Fu Ran tilted her head at him, puzzled.

"I know it's tradition to burn Hell money for ghosts," Zhong Di said all in a rush. "I thought…I thought maybe we could start a new tradition." He placed his hand on the balloon string, just above Fu Ran's. "Send our offering up into the sky, straight to heaven."

Fu Ran beamed at him. "I think that's a marvelous idea," she said, letting go of the string.

Zhong Di unwrapped the string from around his palm. He pinched it lightly, then held it out to Fu Ran.

Blushing, she reached out and pinched the string as well.

Zhong Di looked up into the clear sky and said softly, "I want to thank all the ancestors who guided me a cemetery during Ghost Month, so that I might find my luck and my love." He turned to face Fu Ran, his look hopeful.

Nodding, Fu Ran turned her face up as well. "I, too, want to thank all my ancestors for prompting me visit a cemetery, even during Ghost Month, so that I might find my luck and my love."

She looked down at Zhong Di.

The smile he gave her might have been brighter than the sun.

They released the balloon together, and hand-in-hand, watched it sail up, up, up, into the clear blue sky.

PROHIBITION AT THE BOOK CLUB

The entire kitchen held the rich scent of roasted hazelnuts. Patrice shuffled over to the oven, then bent over to check the hazelnut-rosemary shortbread cookies that she was baking. They were browning up nicely. Just another minute and they'd be done.

Patrice straightened up more slowly than she liked, then took a moment to stretch her back. She used to bend over and pick up stuff from the bottom drawers of her kitchen all the time. As sixty-eight approached, she found herself getting stiffer and stiffer. Maybe it was time to take up her daughter's advice and go to a yoga class now and again.

Or to move out of the rain and the cold of Seattle, something else her daughter suggested more frequently since Owen, Patrice's husband, had suddenly died of a stroke the year before. But that was advice Patrice would ignore. Where would she go? All her friends were here.

Patrice got out the wire cooling racks and set them up on the edge of the counter, next to the rack of drying dishes. She had a dishwasher, but seldom used it, as there was only one person now in the rambling ranch house that she and her husband had raised their two children in.

On the other side of the sink, she placed her good Tupperware cookie carrier, the stacked one that let her carry three layers of cookies without worrying about them getting smooshed.

When the timer went off, Patrice pulled out both trays. She slid the parchment paper off the trays directly onto the racks. The cookies were made from almond flour and would be extra crumbly until they cooled. They weren't really a shortbread—they were dairy, egg, and grain-free for Rose, who had myriad allergies. But they had a rich buttery taste, and were a favorite with everyone.

Cookies finished, it was time to figure out how Patrice was going to carry the other "treat" she was bringing to book club that night.

The book club—named Books For Women of a Certain Age, as everyone invited into the group had to be over fifty-five—had been going strong for seven years now. They took turns hosting, and everyone always brought something to eat to the gathering. It gave them an opportunity to show off their cooking skills. Even Sue, a newcomer who had just turned fifty-six, made delicious skewers for each gathering using a combination of meat, vegetables, and a sauce that she had whipped up. As there were fifteen women who regularly attended, and they only met once a month, no one had to host too often.

Except for Jennifer. She insisted on hosting the Christmas gathering every year.

The issue was that Jennifer was a practicing Christian. On the one hand, she emphasized the "practicing" part of her religion, and not only did she go to church twice a week, she worked part-time at a foodbank. The reason why she wanted to host the Christmas gathering of the book club was because she asked for canned donations at that time.

However, also as part of being a practicing Christian, Jennifer didn't drink, and no alcohol was allowed in her house. As far as Patrice was concerned, one of the things she loved about book club was the opportunity to have a glass of wine and relax with her friends for an evening.

Now, Patrice wasn't a heavy drinker. She didn't like the taste of most cocktails, preferring the occasional glass of wine with dinner.

However, Jennifer's prohibition on alcohol had rankled Patrice. It seemed like such a double standard to her, how Jennifer always looked down her nose at anyone who had any alcohol at one of their meetings, even going so far as to change seats so she didn't have to sit beside someone who was drinking.

Yet Patrice had seen Jennifer take a hit off one of the bottles of wine once when she thought no one was looking.

So it had become a game between Patrice and Chantel—one of the other book club members—seeing how they could sneak alcohol into Jennifer's house and consume it on the premises.

The first year, they'd both hidden flasks in their purses, then made many trips to the bathroom with them. Given Jennifer's look of disapproval, they'd vowed to be more clever the following year. And they had been. Both of them had worn boots the next year, but had agreed to continue to try to surprise each other ever since.

Chantel had an ample bosom, and could easily hide a flask inside her bra. Patrice was built more along the lines of a toothpick, always had been. And she generally wore tighter fitting clothing—she figured if she still had a good body, why not show it off? So she couldn't suddenly wear a baggy sweater or jeans with extra pockets.

No, she had to be clever about hiding her forbidden drink.

This year, she'd chosen one of those tiny sample bottles of amaretto. Instead of taking a nip in secret, she'd wait until after the coffee was served, then pour a splash into her cup when no one was looking. And the smell of the alcohol was similar enough to her cookies that Jennifer should be the wiser.

Patrice couldn't carry the bottle in her pocket, that would be too obvious. She'd thought about tucking it into the waist of her slacks, then wearing a longer sweater to cover it, but the bottle might fall out at an inappropriate time. Plus, she'd never be able to lean against her chair if it was tucked into the small of her back.

No, she'd decided to carry it in her sock. She was planning on wearing knee-highs that night, so the bottle would rest up high, not around her ankle where it might be noticed.

And it would have been noticed. Patrice always wore colorful socks. Life was too short to wear dull ones. So people always wanted to see what her socks she wore.

She shuffled into the bedroom and pulled out one of her less colorful Christmas pairs, that had brown reindeer prancing across a blue sky, with a sprinkling of white snowflakes. She sat heavily down on the chair in the corner.

Ooof. She'd been standing too long. Owen would have fussed at her for it.

Patrice slipped off her comfy knitted socks and pulled on the Christmas ones. Then she slid the bottle of liqueur into the top of her right sock and pulled her pants leg down.

Hmm. She was going to have to be careful how she sat, to make sure that the bottle wasn't obvious. When she sat up straight with her knees bent and her feet on floor, no one could see it. If she decorously crossed her legs at her ankles, she'd have to be careful. As she could barely cross her legs at her knees, she didn't have to worry about that.

Then Patrice stood up and practiced getting the bottle out of her sock. Her back was going to give her problems, she could tell. She didn't want to have to sit down, though, in order to pull the bottle out.

It was too late to start getting herself more limber with yoga. Maybe next year.

Hopefully the adrenalin rush of doing something forbidden would make her movements more smooth and she wouldn't feel as though she was about to topple over at any moment.

Feeling delightfully naughty, Patrice went back out to the kitchen to pack her cookies and get ready for the party.

It was going to be deliciously fun evening.

Jennifer's house was relatively new, out in the suburbs in one of those subdivisions where every street ended in a cul-de-sac. Patrice always felt trapped when she drove in, as there was really only one street in or out of the entire place. If you missed it, you could spend days trying to escape.

The houses were on the small side for McMansions, only two stories and four bedrooms usually. Each took almost the entire plot of land they sat on, and so had neighbors peering in on either side.

Since it was Christmas, the neighbors seemed to be trying to outdo each other in terms of light displays. There were leaping reindeer and blowup Santa Clauses, with glittering icicles hanging from every eve, and even special projectors so that snowflakes danced on every wall.

Patrice was glad to see that she wasn't the first one there. Though she liked Jennifer, she didn't want to spend a lot of time with her hostess, not that particularly evening when she had an uncomfortable bottle of contraband in her sock.

Her calf was going to be bruised by the end of the night, she just knew it.

But she was willing to suffer for her forbidden treat.

Patrice rang the bell with her elbow, as she held her cookie carrier in one hand and her purse along with a paper bag filled with half a dozen cans of chili in the other.

Chantel opened it with a big grin and a hearty, "Merry Christmas!" She wore a white sweater with fuzzy blue-and-white snowflakes dancing across it, over a pair of black leggings. She wore bright blue eyeshadow, prominently highlighting her dark eyes and black skin. Her hair was pulled back from her face then frizzed out in a beautiful halo.

Hmmm. So Chantel probably wasn't carrying a flask in her bra that night, or in a pants pocket. Where was she hiding her booze?

"Merry Christmas!" Patrice said as she stepped in. Chantel took the cookie carrier while Patrice put her other items down on the floor and slipped out of her coat. Then she deliberately left her purse on the shelf underneath the jackets.

Chantel gave her a look. She knew that if Patrice left her purse near the door, then she wasn't carrying her liqueur there.

They gave each other a conspiratorial grin.

Patrice reclaimed her cookies and made her way through the empty living room that had chairs set up in a circle, back to the kitchen where everyone else had gathered based on the level of noise.

"Oh! Cookies!" Rose said excitedly as Patrice came in.

"And yes, you can eat them," Patrice told her with a knowing grin. They all tried to accommodate Rose's allergies, even it if was a challenge sometimes. Plus, Rose brought a lot of her own food that she graciously shared with everyone.

"Thank you, so much," Rose said.

Patrice knew Rose meant it. It meant a lot to her that people went out of their way to make things she could eat as well.

The kitchen felt cozy, not cramped, despite the number of people in it. All the treats had been set up on the island in the middle of the room, while the drinks—water, soda, and sparkling grape juice—stood on the counter that ran around one end of the room. At least eight people crowded around the space, laughing, talking, sharing news.

Patrice made space for her cookies then looked over the other offerings. Sue's skewers were made up of small hunks of beef alternating with water chestnuts in what looked like a tangy orange sauce. Someone had brought figs wrapped in bacon. Rose pointed out that the nacho "cheese" dip was actually dairy free, made from boiled potatoes that had been whipped in a blender to get the right gooey consistency. Frankie had baked one of her fabulous apple pies.

It all looked scrumptious. Patrice found herself a bit impatient as she piled her plate high.

While dinner was going to be lovely, she was still most looking forward to her liqueur treat later on.

Patrice studied Chantel inconspicuously all throughout the evening, trying to figure out where she was hiding her liqueur. It wasn't hidden in her hair. And she couldn't be hiding it anywhere on her body. But it had to be someplace. Where?

Just as people were starting to load up their plates with dessert and the coffee had been started, Chantel came up to

Patrice. "Did I show you my new boots?" she asked in a too-casual manner.

"No, you didn't," Patrice said, immediately looking down to study the tight black boots. How could Chantel hide anything in those? Her own calf throbbed, irritated by the bottle tucked away safely in there.

"They zip up the back," Chantel said smugly after a few moments.

Patrice shifted her attention to the tassels that dangled from the back of each boot. They looked like a ball with fringe, maybe two inches in diameter, hanging an inch down from the end of the zipper.

When Patrice looked back up at Chantel, confused, the other woman made a squeezing motion with her hand.

Patrice couldn't contain her gasp. Those balls were actually tiny squeeze bottles! Chantel had really upped her game, building her own carrier for her booze.

Patrice was going to have to step it up next year.

"Those are so cl—cute!" Patrice said, looking back up at Chantel with a huge grin. She's almost said clever, and that wouldn't have done at all.

When Chantel gave her an expectant look, Patrice pulled up the edge of her pants. "The only thing I have that's as cute are my socks." She deliberately tugged the pants to one side, showing the bulge on her calf.

"Nice," Chantel said with a nod.

After everyone had taken their dessert into the living room, Patrice got up, going back into the kitchen for her coffee. She felt herself transforming into that little old woman just down the street, the one with the shaky hands and breathless voice. Her heart pounded hard and her mouth was dry.

It was time for her to take a nip.

Dang! Monica was still in the kitchen. Maybe Patrice could pour herself a second cup of coffee later?

But Monica was almost finished making herself a cup of tea. "I don't see how you can drink coffee this late at night," she commented as she finished squeezing out her teabag.

Patrice just shrugged. Owen had asked that same question many times. Even as she'd gotten older, the caffeine had never bothered her.

Tonight, though, she might be a little hyped up afterward, particularly if she was successful getting her drink.

After Monica had left the kitchen, Patrice grabbed onto the counter with one hand to steady herself, then she slowly bent over, reaching downward.

Ooof. She'd had so much to eat! So many good things. Her belly was overly full.

Determined, Patrice stretched her hand out, clutching at the hem of her pants and slowly dragging it back up.

She paused when she thought she heard someone walking toward the kitchen.

No. Just her overactive imagination.

With a rough gesture, Patrice yanked down the top of her sock.

The bottle sprang out and hit the floor, immediately rolling away.

Patrice froze. Laughter sprang up from the other room.

She took two halting steps forward, still bent over, reaching for the bottle that had betrayed her.

And ended up right into a pair of legs that suddenly appeared in front of her.

Crap.

"Shhh. Let me help you up," came a whispered voice.

A strong hand grasped Patrice's upper arm, tugging her upright.

Double crap. Jennifer.

With a wink, Jennifer reached down and plucked up the bottle of amaretto lying between them.

Patrice felt her insides start quaking, tremors taking over her body. She wanted to protest that it had just been in fun. She hadn't meant any harm.

But before she could say a word, Jennifer cracked open the bottle and took a quick swig, then poured a dash into Patrice's waiting coffee cup.

Still frozen in shock, Jennifer had to press the bottle back into Patrice's palm before her fingers would close around it.

"Might want to stick that in your purse," Jennifer whispered.

Patrice grabbed hold of Jennifer's arm before she could turn away. "But why?"

Jennifer sighed and rolled her eyes. "It's my husband who disapproves so much of alcohol," she said. "So I really don't drink. But sometimes, I just want to have a little fun. You know?"

"But you seemed so adamant—" Patrice said, still trying to grasp Jennifer's change of attitude.

"I can't let him smell it on me," Jennifer acknowledged. "You know. There are fights that just aren't worth having, particularly after so many years together."

"I do remember that," Patrice said fondly. She and Owen had rarely fought, but partly that had been because they'd both held their tongues when necessary on occasion.

"It was smart of you to bring liqueur that tastes like your cookies," Jennifer added before she slipped away, joining the rest of the group.

Huh. Patrice found her hands were still badly shaking when she tried to pour her coffee. She hadn't expected Jennifer's at all.

After Patrice finally managed to calm down enough that she could actually get coffee into her cup rather than spilling it all over the counter, she found herself not wanting to rejoin the group immediately. She had too much to think about, too much to consider.

When Owen had been alive, Patrice had never felt lonely, not even after their children had grown up and moved away. She had her friends, her book club, her gardening club, her docent work at the Frye museum, and her own volunteer work. But not everyone had been as lucky as her and Owen.

Maybe she should invite Jennifer out to a lady's lunch sometime.

She should definitely bring more of her cookies.

And possibly, another one of those little sample bottles of something sweet.

E ND

NOT WHAT YOU'D EXPECT

I knew a spy, once.

Patty may, or may not, have fit your stereotypical ideal of a spy. She was in her late twenties, blonde, buxom, and brilliant. I found out later that she had a PhD in aeronautical engineering, along with an MBA. While her official title at one of the big airplane manufacturers in Seattle was Business Analyst, she actually worked as a corporate spy.

We met at yoga class. Thirty people packed the tiny studio three times a week. The air was always humid in there, soft and warm. Condensation covered the windows, hiding the busy street outside. Spider plants hung from the ceiling, sprouting like mad. Yoga mats filled the floor, with mere inches between them. The students tended toward younger, upper-middle-class women, wearing expensive yoga shirts and pants, but a few of us older hippies had snuck in, with our cheap tights and cut-up T-shirts.

The instructor always invited the best students to fill the first two of the four rows of students. Her reasoning was that if the people in the back couldn't see the instructor, they could still watch yogini modeling the proper poses.

I started that class in the far back corner, away from the door and the windows. I'd long since passed my fortieth birthday and fifty loomed alarmingly ahead of me. I wasn't in horrid shape, but I was beginning to feel my age.

Patty started taking classes about the same time I did, and was also relegated to the back. She wore the proper yoga uniform: sports bra, flowered yoga shirt, skin-tight yoga pants, all in coordinated blues and greens. Since we were about the same height (short) we paired up together to do partner work.

She had great breath control, and walked me through how to stop panting like a racehorse.

I'm not sure what she said that intrigued me enough to ask her to go out for tea after class.

It might just have been because she was so beautiful and I'm only human. (Though I was 95% certain that Patty didn't like girls. At least, not that way, not like me.)

Despite the chilly October winds blowing down the street, I held my jacket in one hand, letting the evening air cool me down after the over-heated room. I had my yoga mat rolled up and tucked under my arm, making sure it would also be stinking and soaking wet like the rest of me. Patty, of course, had the proper carrier for her yoga mat and strapped it to her back like a good yoga warrior.

As we walked, cars rushed by on the busy street, hurrying to their warm houses. The air carried the smell of rain and wet leaves. We talked of how we'd arrived in Seattle (me, through random choice, her, supposedly because her sister had moved out here and Patty had followed. Later, I wondered about that story, if she'd actually arrived here because of the aeronautical industry. Patty said a lot of things that I questioned afterward.)

The teashop itself was a blend of modern minimalism and hippy sensibilities: only the best organic ingredients went into the tea blends sitting in numbered canisters behind the counter; the shiny white case at the front of the store held primarily vegan and "healthy" treats; while the floor was plain gray concrete and artistic bunches of bare white branches decorated the walls.

It was hot and humid in the teashop, which was part of the reason why I hadn't worn my jacket: I knew I'd get warm again quickly. The shop always smelled of cinnamon and vanilla, with the tangy undertone of good black tea. Patty and I agreed to split a cranberry-orange scone as our treat for working so hard in class.

I volunteered to sit on the cold metal chair at our table, with my back to the room. Patty seemed to appreciate being able to sit on the cushioned bench, but also to be able to watch everyone. I wouldn't say that she was paranoid, exactly. Maybe just overly cautious, her eyes flicking up and observing every person as they walked in, cataloging them before she looked back at me.

I told Patty of my day job, working as a project manager for a well-known Seattle software company. I complained bitterly of the long hours and stress, which was also, in part, why I'd started taking yoga and meditating.

Then I asked her what she did.

"I'm a spy," she announced rather proudly.

I just nodded sagely, taking another sip of my orgasmic peppermint-and-vanilla rooibos tea. I mean, "spy" wasn't the most outrageous job title I'd ever heard of. A good friend of mine taught fighting at the CIA. He specialized in underwater hand-to-hand combat. He was the one who'd taught me not just how to defend myself, but how to fight *dirty* if it came to that, with explicit instructions, demonstrations, and practice on how to break a man's knee.

"I work in the aeronautics industry," Patty said after she sipped more of her own tea. "Mainly I do business analysis. I scrutinize every piece of literature the competition produces. Particularly their quarterly business reports."

"Okay," I said, nodding as if that sounded great, all the while thinking: *just shoot me now*. I couldn't imagine how dull it must be to have to go over those reports with a fine-toothed comb. I had to produce quarterly numbers for those damned reports for my own projects.

"But sometimes, I get to go to industry events," Patty said. She leaned a little closer over the table, as if telling me a secret. "Play the dumb blonde. Lead conversations this way and that."

I couldn't help but roll my eyes at the "dumb blonde" part. You only had to spend about two minutes in Patty's presence to realize how brilliant she was.

But men would only see what they wanted to. Particularly if someone like Patty was playing a part and showing off her fantastic breasts.

"I think that's fascinating," I told her honestly. And it made sense to me that her company would send someone like her to an event, a person who knew all the jargon, had read all the collateral, and could read between the lines of the conversations going on around her. The men would probably assume that she couldn't follow what they were talking about anyway.

Hell, the software company I worked for might do the exact same thing. They weren't the company known for "do no evil."

Patty gave me a big grin. "I knew you'd understand my position," she said. She leaned in a little closer.

I did as well. The intimacy, being that close to a beautiful woman, smelling her sweet musk, made me flush. Not that I'd cooled down that much from the yoga class.

And I'm certain that Patty saw my attraction and courted it. She wanted to use it to her advantage.

I was old enough to know what she was doing, but also flattered that she had decided I was worthy enough to be played.

"There's an event," Patty said, almost whispering. "Celebrating the industry innovators. It takes place a week from Friday. I need a date. Want to come?"

"Of course," I answered immediately. "Tell me how to dress, how to best support you."

Patty leaned back. While her eyes had shifted to something cooler and more calculating, she still said warmly, "Thank you so much! I knew you'd help me out."

I nodded, sitting back myself.

I didn't expect payment. Hell, I figured I'd never see her again after the event.

But I was planning on having one hell of an adventure in the meantime.

Patty and I chatted on the phone several times over the next week, as well as met after yoga class, going over our rolls and goals.

For the event, I wore what I called my award dress. It was black, sleeveless, and went to the ground, hugging my curves nicely. The front of it was sheer from just above my knees down to the hem. I wore my mother's amethyst necklace and matching earrings, worth a small fortune.

Of course, even with all that elegance, I still wore sensible shoes. Flat black sandals that probably weren't appropriate for the Seattle October weather. However, I didn't want to hide my beautifully painted, scarlet toenails. I'd used the same color on my fingernails, and found a lipstick color that matched as well. I wasn't about to hide my gray hair—besides, it was turning a gorgeous silver. I'd earned every single damned wrinkle in my face, so I didn't try to hide those, either. I still took extra care with my makeup, making my skin look soft and luminous.

Patty picked me up at my place. She texted me when she arrived, waiting in the taxi at the curb. I wore my long faux-fur coat, vintage and gorgeous. I knew that even in the dim evening light I presented quite a sight walking down the short staircase from my building to the street.

The driver stood by the back door of the black town car. He wore a black suit with a white shirt, and wasn't much taller than me. Cute black curls flared out under his black cap. He opened the door with a flash of white teeth against his dark skin. "Good evening, Ma'am," he said with a strong Hispanic accent.

"Thank you," I told him graciously as I slid into the car.

Patty sat in the back, her smile radiant. She also wore a black dress, though shorter than mine and gathered along her left side, giving her an asymmetric hem. She'd blown out her blonde hair that night, making it softly flow around her face like a shiny mane. Her makeup was impeccable with luscious red lips that I knew I wouldn't be kissing, but that wasn't about to stop me from thinking about it.

"Remember, you're playing a part," Patty said quietly as the car smoothly left the curb and joined traffic.

"I know," I said, keeping my voice down as well. Though there was a glass between the backseat and the driver, I knew we didn't want to be heard. "I'm just an older friend who's come into town for a vacation. I never worked outside the house, and I certainly don't know anything about those newfangled computers."

Patty grinned at me. "You look too young to use *newfangled* you know."

"Thank you," I said. "You look stunning," I said honestly. "I don't think any of the men will be able to keep their eyes off you. Or to stop themselves from talking to you, or answering your questions."

Her cover story was that she wrote up articles for one of the local neighborhood blogs in her spare time, and had thought dressing up for a night would be fun.

Patty nodded, acknowledging the truth of what I said, confident in her beauty. "Make sure you get the men to talk about their automatic control systems. Get them to explain it to you. We'll debrief after the event."

"I'll keep track of all the details," I promised her. "And will let you know if there's anything that they say that raises my interest, that I think is reaching for something new, not the standard applications."

"Thank you," Patty said. "I think this is going to be brilliant fun. I should have thought about bringing a computer specialist with me before."

Though her words brought a spike of pleasure to me, I told myself again to not get ahead of myself.

This was a one-night stand. Not forever or for keeps.

———

The event was being held out at the Museum of Flight. I'd always found the museum impressive, with the huge planes hanging from the glass roof.

I also had really good memories of my first visit, when I'd come with my dad. He'd been the crew-chief of a DC-3 during WWII, and when I was a kid, had built model airplanes out of balsa wood. He'd been familiar with almost all the vehicles we saw in the WWII wing, gave me the history as well as some of the engine flaws.

That night, tables and a banquet spread had been set up

in the southern wing of the museum. It was a smaller gathering than I'd expected: maybe seventy people. However, there were only about half-a-dozen other women there. They all seemed to be attached, wives of the men who'd been invited.

Though it was an open bar, I stuck to a single glass of red wine that I nursed through the "meet and greet" portion of the evening. It wasn't that I was a light weight, but I wanted to stay sharp all night, and any type of alcohol made me sleepy eventually.

Of course, the men all talked to themselves. Didn't want to risk girl cooties or something. I softened my stance, trying to act more like a hetero-woman, instead of an out-and-proud lesbian. I wore a nametag like everyone else, choosing a name different than my own: Elsie sounded like a good, straight, divorced, middle-aged woman to me. I had even known one, once.

There was one group of five men all huddled close to the start of the buffet line. Two wore regular suits, two had their jackets off already and were wearing dress shirts, and one wore a vintage beige plaid jacket. He even had the '70's moustache to go with it.

I knew these people: though they weren't software engineers, they were still geeks. I worked with geeks every day. I hung out at the edge of their circle, finally slipping in when they started talking about autopilot.

"Will there be pilotless airplanes someday?" I asked. "Like those driverless cars?"

"There's too many variables," said one of the men, who, according to his nametag, was called Eric. "Particularly the weather."

They all shared a shudder over that ominous creature called *the weather*.

"And you can't make the software foolproof, which the

regulators would insist on," added Floyd, the one in the plaid jacket.

"Yup. Fools are too ingenious. Particularly trained fools, like pilots," cracked another one of the men.

I rolled my eyes, but I understood what they meant. It was an old joke that translated into software engineering as well. Instead of making software foolproof or bulletproof, the focus now was on making it resilient.

I opened my mouth to make a comparison between the two industries. I shut it quickly, though, remembering the part that I played. "How about drones that carry passengers or something that's remotely controlled?" I asked. When I got a curious look from one of the men, I hastily added, "My dad built RC planes when I was a kid."

The men nodded and Floyd started explaining to me in very small words why that wouldn't work.

I tried not to bristle. While I wasn't in their industry, I wasn't an idiot.

But I was a woman. Beautifully dressed and wearing makeup. Even though the software industry didn't have that many women, it appeared that the field of aeronautical engineering had fewer.

Again, I stopped myself from putting Floyd in his place. I wasn't here as a brilliant software person, I was here to gather information. So I took a deep breath, batted my eyelashes, and at the appropriate times sighed a soft, "Really?" I may have even straightened my back and thrust out my boobs occasionally.

Inside, I continued to squirm.

This reminded me too much of when I'd been much younger and playing the part of a straight woman, pretending to be interested in guys when I all I really wanted to do was to just to make out with my best friend Amy.

I still kept to the script, thankful when muted bells rang

and we were seated at our tables. The tables all had white linens, heavy silverware, and pressed crystal glassware. At least Patty and I were seated beside each other. None of the men I'd been talking with earlier sat at our table of six: two men and a couple sat there instead.

Patty did her best to interview them, getting them to talk about their jobs and what they were working on. I had no idea if she learned anything new from them—it sounded to me as though they all had their own scripts they were working from.

The chicken with brussel sprouts that they served was as bland as I expected it to be: the caterer probably though garlic was an exotic spice. At least they served good coffee (it was Seattle, after all—their caterer's license might have been revoked if they didn't).

As desert was being served (delicious cinnamon, walnut, and raisin mini-cupcakes with vanilla buttercream frosting) the organizers of the event got up and started their speeches, intermixed with handing out the various innovators awards. The acceptance speeches from the winners were long and dry and I truly needed the caffeine to stay awake.

Once all the awards had been given, the organizers thanked us and finally sent us on our way. I needed a bathroom and probably two more cups of coffee if I was going to stay awake for the "debriefing."

Patty found me as I was leaving the restroom. "This way," she said, indicating the northern wing of the museum.

This wing held all the WWII planes. We stopped beside the Supermarine Spitfire, still looking dangerous and ready to fight. Dark sky lay beyond the glass windows surrounding us, and I could hear the soft spray of rain. The air in here still smelled of machine oil. I slipped my jacket on over my bare shoulders.

"Did you learn anything?" Patty asked softly as she pretended to admire the plane above us.

I told her my suspicions about how at least one of her competitors appeared to be working on improving pilot-assisted take-off and landing, again, difficulties primarily due to that monster called *the weather*. (It wouldn't have surprised me if most of the men in the industry didn't have a private altar where they made sacrifices to rain and storm gods, pleading for mercy.)

She merely nodded. "Yes, I've seen that in the literature. Thank you for verifying that for me. I'll dig into it more next week." She paused, then asked, "Anything else?"

I decided to be honest with her. "How do you stand it?" I asked. "Pretending to be something you aren't?"

"I was wondering if that would bother you," Patty said. She gave me a sad smile, like a teacher pronouncing that her star student had only achieved a B on their final test. "I've always played roles. Dutiful daughter despite my abusive dad. Poor college student even after the inheritance from dear old grandpa came through and made me rich. Asking stupid questions so teachers didn't expect what I tested at. Like that."

I shook my head. "I can't do it. Not anymore. I did it for too long when I was your age. Pretending to be something I wasn't. Never again." I shivered, hearing the hard edge to my tone.

The evening had unsettled me more than I had realized.

Patty, however, giggled. "That's okay. You did help. And I got some interesting leads. We should go home, though."

I followed her out of the darkened wing, still uncertain of myself.

Patty's next words didn't surprise me at all. "Oh, and I won't be taking any more yoga classes," she told me.

"Why not?" I asked, expecting to hear a lie.

"The physical part is great," Patty admitted. "I love all the stretching. But the meditation part, and truly studying the path, that's trying to change my soul."

I didn't say it, but I still thought it: *and you don't have one.*

That was how she was able to be a spy. To play a part. To delight in pulling something over on everyone.

I still had my story to tell at the end of the night. And a sweet kiss from Patty at the very end, though I knew it was all calculated and not real.

Like I said, Patty wasn't what you expected.

Or maybe she was.

SANITIZING THE SAFE HOUSE

Paper burns differently than wood. Particularly when you're dealing with bound items, like weekly planners, old yearbooks, sheaves of letter tied together with pink ribbon. It takes time to destroy all that evidence of a life well lived, time to build a fire hot enough to burn through all the photographs and old recipes.

Time I didn't have. My client had been compromised, and I had to get him the hell out of Dodge.

Or Topeka, actually, where my current charge had been living.

This particular safe house was a really nice place, well taken care of. It had been built back in the early fifties—a brick rambler with a stand of pine trees to block the winter winds whipping across the prairie. Backyard was wide open, just a short wooden fence to mark the property line. It would have been a great place to raise kids, with more trees just past the fence, as well as a small creek.

Idyllic, really. Norman Rockwell come to life.

Except for the meth lab that had sprung up at neighbor's.

The area was now crawling with ATF, FBI, and every

other three-letter acronym department you could think of, as well as a few you've never heard of.

Officers hadn't started looking hard at my client. But they would. And while my team was good, even they made mistakes. Some official would find something and come to question my guy. And me, I was just a contractor for one of those three-letter acronyms, so my boss preferred for us to fly under the radar at all times.

Better for the authorities to just not find my client.

So I had to move him. Give him yet another new identity. Remove all the evidence of his former existence. Sanitize the place while still leaving behind enough debris to make it look as though he'd just moved, not like a professional had come through.

Luckily, it was still spring. Burn bans only happened late in the summer, when the sun had baked the weeds to dry husks and the dirt the combines threw up made the air hazy. I wasn't the only house on the road with a bonfire in the backyard that afternoon—the sun was shining for the first time that week, even though the wind still blew cold.

I stirred the ashes with a long, pointed stick, spreading out the pages so they'd burn more quickly. I'd dumped the boxes of paper on top of the wood already piled in the backyard pit, figuring that the wood would burn eventually.

"Why, look at what my favorite firebug is doing."

That voice. A smoky alto. Caramel cream, threaded through with cherry brandy. At least half my dreams featured that voice. It also starred in a similar number of nightmares.

It was complicated.

"Hello, Angela," I said without bothering to turn around. If she wanted to shoot me, she already would have.

"Hello, Frankie," she replied, coming to stand beside me. She wore a practical outfit: heavy black work boots that probably had steel-reinforced toes, sturdy cargo pants, and a navy blue windbreaker with a three-letter acronym on it.

A contrasting reflection of what I wore—flannels and jeans, baseball cap from the local feed store, nothing to make me stand out. Just a regular guy, mid-thirties, Hispanic.

After the silence had dragged on, I finally dared to look at Angela's face. She still looked like an angel to me, though her blond hair was pulled sharply back and she wore "workday" makeup—a touch of mascara, pink lipstick, and only the wind adding color to her pale cheeks. Her nose turned up the slightest bit at the end, and I could still see the pictures of her as a kid with long braids and freckles on that cute nose.

"You look good," Angela said cautiously. "You taking care of yourself?"

I heard the word *finally* tacked onto the end of that. I *was* more fit than the last time she'd seen me—five? No, six years ago. I was eating my veggies and working out again. Free weights had broadened my chest and slimmed my waist. I'd had to buy all new pants as the old ones had started falling off my butt.

"Whatcha want?" I asked instead of replying. Wasn't about to tell her that going to the gym was a sure sight better than trying to drink away my regrets, as I had the first few years after she'd left.

"Who's living here?" Angela asked. "You're latest insurgent?"

"My, ah, *client*, has already moved on," I assured her.

"And what was he, she, hiding from?" she said.

"Hmmm. Let's call him Larry, as in Larry the Lounge Lizard," I told her.

"You always did hang out with a certain class of folks."

"What does that say about you?"

She rolled her eyes. "Get on with it."

"Seems like ol' Larry made some accounting errors for some important people. Now, Larry tried to prove that they were just honest mistakes, until someone found Larry's *other* bank account. You know. The one overseas."

"I see," Angela said. "And I suppose your boss, being the generous guy that he is, decided to help ol' Larry out?"

I beamed at her. "You got it! And since Larry hadn't signed anything like a non-disclosure agreement, all the intel he gave about his old operation was legal and everything."

"Riiiight," Angela said. "So you wouldn't happen to know where ol' Larry is right now, would you?"

"Not a clue," I told her cheerfully while I poked at the fire. More paper caught, burning brightly. "I'm just a cleaner."

"I know, I know. Your hands are never dirty," Angela said. She shook her head. "You wouldn't mind if I searched the place, now, would you?"

"Only if you have a warrant," I told her. "I am a law-abiding citizen, and I expect my police force to be just as law-abiding."

"Fine," Angela said. "Will there be anything left for us to discover?"

"Nope!" I lied. "Though…the ashes might still be warm."

"Thanks for the warning." The sarcasm could have been cut with a knife.

She paused, looking out over the yard. Then she sighed, loud enough for me to hear over the wind and my pounding heart.

Looked like we were about to get to the meat of things.

"I recognize the yard," she said softly. "From the pictures you sent."

I stopped poking the fire and looked up, trying to see what she did. The trees in the far back had been a lot smaller, but maybe the fence was the same.

"A lifetime ago," I finally said.

"Many lifetimes ago," Angela replied. "When there could have been a 'we'."

Before our choices led us down different paths.

"I'm sorry I never came to visit before now," she continued.

"As you said, many lifetimes ago." I was proud at how casual my voice remained. "Now, officer, unless there's something else?" I didn't want another fire between us: it would burn me to a crisp this time.

"Nothing, citizen," she said. "Happy cleaning."

"Thanks," I told her.

It had been a bad idea to stick ol' Larry here. I hadn't known what to do with the place, though. I couldn't sell it. Not without giving up all hope of…her.

When the police had first come knocking on his door, Larry had called me immediately, demanding to be moved. I'd assessed the situation and had agreed.

However, there was something fishy going on. Larry was all packed up by the time I arrived a day later, which he couldn't have been, not given the timeframe.

Plus, he must have been in contact with someone from his old life. There were too many pictures from his previous life, too many letters and old books. He couldn't have accumulated this much even after a decade.

He knew it was against the rules, but Larry also wasn't the sharpest knife in the bunch.

Was Larry trying to figure out a way of sliding back into his old life? Did he really think his old boss was the type to forgive something like embezzlement? Not to mention working for the government now?

Something else was going on. And I didn't have time to figure it out.

I thrust my stick into the ashes, frustrated. Picked up one

of the boards buried underneath the boxes of paper and heaved it upward.

Huh. More paper was trapped underneath the wood already piled there.

Mapa de Costa Azul caught my eye. Plus other tourist brochures.

Crap. Just what had Larry been up to?

I hadn't been lying to Angela. Technically, I didn't know where Larry was when she'd asked about him. Pat was one of the best on my team: a big-boned Irish woman with red curly hair and laughing green eyes who I never would have bet against in a bar fight. She'd stashed Larry in a hotel along one of the barren stretches of highway leading away from the city, a truck stop that had high turnover and wouldn't think twice about somebody paying cash.

I took extra time cleaning out the house, wiping down fingerprints, removing DNA traces, then planting false clues in case Angela was stubborn enough to send a team through.

It was close to midnight by the time I finished. When I finally left the house, the sky was clear and full of stars—more than I ever saw in the city. The air felt chilled and crisp, with just traces of smoke from this afternoon's fire. A single car raced by on the country road, the sound echoing across the empty fields.

If I'd moved here with Angela, as we'd planned so many years ago, I would have planted more trees out front. A grove thick enough to block what little traffic noise there would be, while not giving good enough coverage for surveillance or snipers.

I shook my head. That was a dream best left burned in the backyard with all the other memories of our past lives.

She liked being a cop too much. While I could have left my job—it wasn't a vocation—we were never sure whether it would actually let me leave. Too many officials knew my number and weren't afraid to call day or night. I wasn't a fixer, but I frequently did clean up messes.

Still. I would have made a go of a new life with a job I could have talked about, if she'd been willing, if she hadn't backed out at the last minute, after I'd already bought this place.

I zipped my jacket up higher, ignoring the chill I felt creeping across my shoulders. I turned to look, but no one was there, watching me. Nobody but my ghosts, anyway.

Then I yawned. God, I was tired. An entire day of hard cleaning left me wrecked. Despite all the work at the gym, I wasn't twenty anymore. I had enough cash saved up for a long retirement if I was careful. I just didn't know where I wanted to go, what I wanted to do.

Or as Angela would have put it, I still didn't know who I wanted to be when I grew up.

No one was on the highway as I drove out to it. I sat in the driveway for a little while with the lights off, staring, making sure that no one was there, hidden and watching me. And no car lights immediately came up behind me once I started down the road.

I knew I was being paranoid, but that caution had saved me more than once.

I called Pat while I was driving. She gave me the address of the truck stop hotel, along with a cheery "Hell, no," when I propositioned her as usual.

I didn't mean it. She knew that. It was a game between the pair of us.

She could probably see that my heart still belonged to Angela, and always would.

The truck stop hotel was perfect. The smell of diesel fuel

and burned grease hung in the air. Lots of traffic all hours of the night. Tons of semis parked in the back. Too many people coming and going for some clerk to pay attention to a short, balding, accountant like Larry.

Of course, there were also too many camera to hide from, but we weren't doing anything that wasn't above the board.

Pat had told me the room number. Third floor, in the back, close to the stairs. The hotel smelled dank, like the spring rains had molded the carpets. Dim lights, but no one else was in the narrow hallway.

I knocked on the door. Nothing complicated—we weren't some sort of spy team with fancy codes.

"Door's open!" came Larry's cheerful voice.

I shook my head. Larry was far too trusting.

"Now, Larry, you know better—" I said as I walked through the door.

Stopped.

Two single beds in the center of the room. Larry sitting on one, looking pleased.

Couple of goons on the other bed. One goon with a gun pointed at Larry, the other, now, pointed at me.

"Sorry! Wrong room," I said, immediately starting to back up.

"Stay right where you are," commanded a more familiar voice.

From the small bathroom came, let's call him Mouse. Larry's old boss. Face like a rat, only softer, squishier, so Mouse fit him better. Gray fuzz covered his chin, two-day-old stubble that was probably supposed to make him look tougher, but just rounded his face out more, like a homeless bum. Wore a blue denim work shirt and black pants, so clothing a little nicer than his goons who were dressed like the locals, in flannels and jeans.

Mouse also had a gun pointed at me.

"I don't want any trouble," I said, closing the door behind me. Maybe that was a mistake, cutting off my easy getaway. But I didn't want any innocent bystanders getting shot either.

Though given the paper thin walls of this place, any bullets would probably go straight through and end up in the parking lot.

"Sit," Mouse ordered, indicating the bed next to Larry.

"Larry, what did you do?" I asked as I complied.

"Mouse here is giving me back my old job!" Larry said with a huge grin.

"And you believed him?" I said.

"Got me an insurance policy," Larry bragged. "Better one than last time. Gonna get out for good, go south and stay there."

"They why are they here with guns pointed at you?" I said, indicating the goons on the bed opposite us. "Is it because they trust you?"

Larry blinked owlishly at me for a moment. Then he looked at the goons, looked at Mouse, then back at me. "They're not just pointed at me!" he said, sounding like a bratty boy.

"What do you intend to do with me?" I asked. I didn't want to know what they intended to do to poor Larry, didn't want to be an accessory to the crime. Ol' Larry was on his own this time.

"Ransom you back to your boss," Mouse told me cheerfully.

I blinked, surprised. Then I laughed. Couldn't help myself. "I'm an independent contractor," I told him. I knew the agency who'd hired me sure as shit wouldn't pay anything. They'd probably gleefully cancel the contract, happily so if I ended up not being able to send them a bill.

Mouse narrowed his eyes at me, then turned to glare at Larry. "This is the guy, right? The fixer?"

Larry nodded vigorously while I just shook my head. "I'm just a cleaner. I've spent all day cleaning up the house where this guy was living. I'll help him move, again, but then I'll just go back to cleaning again."

"He's a *fixer*," Larry insisted. "He makes people disappear."

"Only metaphorically," I said.

Larry gave me a blank look.

It was probably too big of a word for him. "I give people new identities," I translated. "New lives. They disappear from their old lives, only to start new ones. I don't kill people. I don't even carry a gun."

Technically, that was true. My gun was in my car, as usual. My boss gave me grief about that, and I didn't care.

Always easier to talk yourself out of a situation if you weren't carrying.

Mouse nodded. "They'll still pay to get you back," he said.

I shrugged. "So you plan on kidnapping me and holding me for ransom?"

"That's right! Larry did say you were a bright guy," Mouse agreed.

"POLICE!"

The door came banging down.

My avenging Angel came through, leading the charge.

Angela and the others hadn't been following me, not exactly. They *had* been following Mouse, and were quite interested when our paths intersected. When I got him to admit to a crime, they decided to act.

Or Angela had, regardless of the chain of command.

Though Angela's three-letter acronym department had made the bust, the inter-departmental squabbling was interminable. And giving me a headache.

I sat in the back of the operations vehicle watching. We were located close to where I'd started, one of the farmers loaning his field to the officials, most of whom were here for the original meth lab bust that had sprawled out.

It surprised me how much grief Angela's CO gave her, busting her chops in front of everyone.

Finally, after sworn statements and sworn secrecy and at least one phone call to my boss, the officials turned me loose. My head was pounding and I was bone tired, but I still waited an extra hour until Angela came walking out from under the tent as well.

"Buy you a cup of coffee?" I asked, falling easily into step with her as she walked out into the open field. The stars were starting to fade and the horizon had an orange glow to it. The air had gotten much colder, making me pull out my gloves.

Angela glanced at me and kept trudging toward her rental car. I knew it had to be a rental—she'd grown up in Wisconsin, and never would have voluntarily bought a white vehicle, a moving snow bank as she called them.

"What's your CO got against you?" I said as she beeped her car open.

Angela sighed and finally said, "You."

"Me?" I asked, surprised. I didn't know the woman, had never met her.

"She knew me back...before," Angela said.

I nodded. I understood what she meant by before—that time long ago when there had been an us.

"She couldn't believe I was going to give up my career, give up everything, for some guy," Angela said. "She was the one who talked me out of it, eventually. And she's never forgiven me for even considering it."

"That was ten years ago," I pointed out. Suddenly, the realization hit me. "And you're still on the bottom rung of your department, aren't you? She's never let you advance."

Angela took a deep breath, then let it all out in a loud sigh. "I hadn't wanted to believe that she would sabotage me, my entire career, but she has."

"So what do you want to do about it?" I said cautiously. Though it was growing lighter by the minute, it still felt as though a huge pit of darkness lay before us.

"I could fight it. Fight her." She shrugged. "I'm not sure it's worth it, anymore."

"The career? The badge? The job?" I asked cautiously. I couldn't kill the hope rising in me.

Slowly, Angela nodded her head.

I didn't want to get burned to a crisp. I was older, wiser.

I still didn't care. This was Angela. My angel.

I turned and casually leaned against her car, looking back over the east, toward the rising sun and my farm. Pink clouds now lay streaked across the sky. The smell of ashes was far away.

"So what do you want to do?" I asked as Angela also turned and leaned against the car beside me. She wasn't close enough to touch, but I could still feel the heat of her body all along my side.

"Sleep for twelve hours? Drink some coffee, have a really good meal, then sleep for another twelve?" she suggested.

"And then? After that?"

In a broken voice, Angela replied, "I don't know. I don't know what I want to be when I grow up."

I blinked, surprised. "Neither do I," I told her.

My heart pounded so hard I was surprised it wasn't making the empty car I leaned against echo like a drum. My fingers were both cold and sweating inside my gloves. The coffee I'd had earlier was burning its way through my stomach as well as threatening to come back up.

But it was now or never.

"You want to go someplace and maybe try to figure it out? Together?" I asked, the words hardly above a whisper.

"Us?"

"Us," I said. "We."

Angela shuddered as though ice water had just been dripped down her bare neck. She stood still for so long I had to glance over to see if she'd been frozen in place, or possibly even died of shock.

She still stared straight out at the horizon. She didn't look back at me, but I felt her hand brush against mine, then our pinky fingers intertwined.

I stared back out at the horizon with her, watching the sunrise.

"So, have you ever been to Costa Azul?"

FAVORS FOR OLD FRIENDS

The whole *thing* with Frankie and the others started with the customs agent at the Dallas/Fort Worth International airport.

She looked tall and lanky behind the bullet-proof glass of her booth. I couldn't say if she was a natural blonde or just paid very close attention to her roots. She had bangs that kissed the top of her perfectly shaped eyebrows. Hair like that would have annoyed the hell out of me, but then again, I was used to being in the field in all kinds of weather. I'd never had a cushy job sitting in an air-conditioned booth.

"Traveling for business or pleasure?" the agent asked Frankie after he slid his passport to her.

He turned and gave me a rakish grin. "Definitely pleasure," he said.

I was *not* about to blush, though the last few nights when he and I had actually been physically in the same location had been very pleasurable. It had taken us both a few weeks to bust out of our obligations in order to go on this two-week long vacation together.

We were both in our early thirties, and had realized that

neither of us had ever really taken off that much time from our various employers. It was about damned time.

As there were no direct flights to Coasta Azul, in Uruguay, we'd agreed to break our trip and spend a few nights in Bogotá on the way down.

While we'd made plans, we had stayed in constant contact via texts, email, and long, steamy phone calls.

"Pleasure? I see," the agent…purred?

What the hell? Her professional tone changed completely.

"Do you have time for a private, *thorough*, strip search then, Francisco José?" the agent asked, smiling up at him. "Come on, Frankie. Turnabout *is* fair play."

I bit my lips together to prevent myself from laughing out loud. Let's see how Frankie got himself out of this one.

"Ah, no, no, that won't be necessary," Frankie said, snagging my hand, then holding our intertwined fingers up for the agent to see.

The agent glanced up and looked at me, then shrugged. "I'm not picky," she said. "She could watch. Or help. Whatever she's into."

Wait, was I not her type? Or not good enough?

"No," Frankie said firmly. "Thank you for the kind offer. I'm off the menu from now on."

The agent pouted, sighed, then said, "Fine." She gestured for me to hand over my passport for examination.

The agent's eyebrows shot up to the top of her forehead when she got a look at my name.

"*The* Angela?" the agent asked Frankie sharply.

"*My* Angela," Frankie replied. He gave our still-joined hands a squeeze, and threw a gentler smile toward me.

That was one thing I knew about Frankie. While he might talk a good game, or flirt outrageously, he only had eyes for me. That had been the case ten years ago, and was the same now. There was never any reason for me to be jealous, or so I told myself regularly.

"Good luck," the agent said, sliding our passports back under the glass.

The unspoken, *you're going to need it* echoed after us.

"Old flame?" I couldn't help but ask as we stepped out of the quiet custom's area into the louder airport terminal.

"Old fling," Frankie corrected.

I paused, waiting. I could tell he wanted to say more. With Frankie, it was as much about reading his silences as his words.

He sighed, shrugged, and finally said, "She wasn't you. None of them were. You know?"

I did, but I didn't, not really. I hadn't dated much in the ten years since I'd called off our engagement. First, I was too married to the job, trying to prove myself to a boss who would never give me a fair deal. Then, I don't know. Dating seemed like too much effort.

Hell, I'd even gone to a relationship coach for a few months, trying to figure out what my problem was. The counselor never came out and directly said, "You're still in love with Frankie," but she'd definitely hinted at it.

Still, Frankie's continued avowal of devotion made my insides melt.

We walked hand in hand to the gate. Our connecting flight had gotten us there early, at my insistence. (Frankie would have taken a flight that left no time between connections, enjoying the thrill of running through the terminal. Me? I'd rather have a little breathing room, even if that meant killing some time at the airport.)

Our options were now to sit at the gate, go get some coffee from the mermaid on the one side, or get something alcoholic on the other. I was just about to ask Frankie what he preferred when an excited voice started calling, "Joey! Hey, Joey!"

When Frankie started looking around, I wondered again what exactly he'd been doing for the last ten years. His "official" position was working as a cleaner, tidying up safe houses.

Unofficially? I suspected that the term "fixer" might have been more appropriate at times.

A balding, used-car-salesman type came bounding up. His skin had that bronze color that came straight from a bottle, not from being out in the sun. His teeth were way too white, and probably glowed in the dark. He wore a blue-and-white pinstriped seersucker jacket with an ivory shirt, cheap brown dress-pants, and white loafers, no socks.

"Hey, Joey!" the man said, coming directly up to Frankie, hand out, ready to pump his arm off. "So good to see you! It's been years, am I right?"

Honestly, I wasn't sure whether to laugh or be horrified. Or maybe a bit of both.

"Ah, Walter," Frankie said, obviously searching for either the new name, the old name, or some amalgamation of the two. "I'd like you to meet Pamela."

Walter's eyes grew distinctly cooler. "Your handler?" he guessed. His posture changed as well, growing more stiff.

I could see him already labeling me as a NARC.

"She's a little of this, a little of that," Frankie said, bringing our intertwined fingers up again.

"Oh. *Oh*," Walter said. He leaned forward and whispered. "Sorry. You're on the job, aren't you. Didn't mean to blow your cover."

I wasn't about to correct him. Let Frankie handle this.

Walter leaned back and said in his loud, booming voice, "Have a good vacation, you two lucky kids." He paused, then added, "Be sure to look me up the next time you pass through. We'll go out for drinks. Talk about…things."

With a smirk thrown in my direction, a brief wave at Frankie, Walter headed back to his gate.

"Client?" I asked.

"Of a sort," Frankie said.

"I know, I know, you can't talk about it," I said. I wondered if this was going to be a sore spot between us, his mysterious past, the time I'd spent at the agency.

"You're right, I can't talk about some of it, just as you can't talk about some of the cases you worked on," Frankie said seriously. "But…I will tell you what I can."

"Promise?" I asked, staring into his amazing dark brown eyes. They were like melted chocolate. And they showed nothing but love for me.

Kind of amazing to be someone's entire world. A little intimidating as well.

For a moment, it was just us in that loud, busy terminal.

"Anything. Everything," Frankie breathed out after a timeless moment. "And more."

I had no words. I could only draw him closer for a quick smooch. Nothing too intimate or indecent. More like a peck, with the promise of more, so much more, later.

Of course, that was when the flight attendant had to interrupt us, wanting to talk with Frankie.

———

"So, is this going to be a thing?" I asked as little Miss Perky Boobs said goodbye after touching Frankie's arm way too many times.

"No, this is not going to be a thing," Frankie said. He sounded a little put out.

I gave him a look, showing how much I believed him.

"It's already a thing," I told him. "Are we ever going to be able to go to a place without you knowing someone?"

He shrugged. "I can't help it. I know a lot of people." .

"I thought you were all about fitting in, being discrete, being the regular *Joey* that no one will remember."

"When the job calls for that, yeah, I am," Frankie said. "Like now." He was dressed in a pale green shirt with a standup collar that looked delicious against his dark colored skin. His black hair was the perfect amount of mussed, not as though he'd just crawled out of bed but more like he was willing to crawl back in with a minimum amount of persuasion. He wore dark brown cowboy boots that were obviously hand stitched, and jeans that fit his ass just right.

"Boyfriend, you are *not* blending in," I told him. "You look like you could own one of these planes." Or possibly a Mexican drug-lord, though I wasn't about to tell him that out loud.

"That *is* fitting in. We're flying first class, you know," he said. "As well as staying in the presidential suite at the hotel. Need to look the part of someone with that kind of money." He paused, then added, "And maybe not as though we've been wearing the same shoes for the last ten years."

"They're comfortable!" I told him, looking down at my practical, brown leather walking shoes.

Okay, so maybe they were a bit scuffed and could use a good polish.

In addition, I had on jeans and simple light-blue top. My brown hair was pulled back into its usual ponytail, and I wore "workday makeup"—nothing fancy or extravagant. Just some color to pink up my lips, tone down the pale white of my cheeks, and only the shirt to highlight my blue eyes.

"I could be a waitress on her way to work," I said, comparing my getup to Frankie's.

Though, given Walter's reaction, I obviously still screamed *cop*.

Frankie gave me an assessing look, then shook his head. "Naw. The clothes will work. We'll worry about those shoes later. What you need is some bling."

"Excuse me?" I asked, though I followed Frankie back through the terminal to the duty free shop right outside of the customs' hall.

"See, I told you that it would be fine to wear your jewelry through security," Frankie said, patting my hand as we walked up to the counter.

I was *not* going to slap him for that patronizing tone. At least, not in public.

"So now we need to get you dressed up right," he added, throwing a wink at the woman behind the jewelry counter.

"What did you have in mind?" the saleswoman asked, dividing her attention between me and Frankie, obviously unsure of the power dynamic and who would spend the biggest bucks.

"I'd like a Channel-type piece," Frankie told the woman. "With large white beads and red gems strung between, either garnets or rubies."

Even I knew Channel was a fashion designer. When had Frankie started to pay attention to such things? Or had he always had this other side to him that he'd just never shown me before?

"I don't have anything exactly like that, but I think I know the look you're going for," the woman said.

She pulled out a necklace that did have round white beads, each about the size of a quarter, with small, metallic-gray polished stones in between.

I would never have bought something like that for myself. It was too big, too gaudy. It screamed, "Pay attention to me!"

Before I could protest, however, Frankie was already reaching for it.

"Exactly what I had in mind," Frankie said. "Here, let me put this on you," he insisted, attaching the beads around my neck. "Matching earrings?" he asked the saleswoman.

"Of course," the woman said.

If this was a cartoon, she'd have dollar signs in her eyes, thinking about the commission she was about to get.

I held the earrings up to my ear with one hand, held up a mirror in my other hand, then looked at myself critically.

I had to admit with just that little bit of bling, I suddenly looked the part too.

"We'll take them," Frankie said.

"Really?" I asked. The set cost more than a month's rent for my apartment.

However, Frankie had hinted that he had quite a nest egg saved up. We were going to have to talk finances. Soon.

"Yes," Frankie said seriously. "This won't be the only time we travel like this. These can be your traveling jewels."

"My what?" I asked him.

"Traveling jewels. Just for when we're traveling. Like this," Frankie said, smoothly handing the woman one of those black, fancy credit cards. The kind that included concierge service. The type of card that drug dealers used at strip joints when wanting to impress clients. The annual expenses on that card may have been more than month's salary at my old job.

We were *really* going to have to talk finances.

As well as why it was important for us to fit in at this level on a regular basis.

I held my questions until after we were seated on the plane and had been served small flutes of fresh Champaign. The seats were faux leather, but extremely comfortable. They fully reclined, something I intended to make use of in a while. Passengers still streamed down the aisle like cattle, but their noise was muted. Better sound proofing in first class, I guess.

This was something I could get used to.

"So, when were you going to tell me that we were on a job?" I asked, finally putting two and two together and not getting anywhere near four.

Frankie nearly spit out his drink, but managed to swallow. "What do you mean?" he croaked, then he cleared his throat and said, "A job?"

"We're playing a part," I pointed out to him. "You would never care this much about fitting in otherwise."

Frankie finally gave me a sheepish grin. "Okay. So maybe I owe this guy a favor, down in Bogotá. It'll just take a couple hours. It'll be fun."

I bit my lips together while I assembled the words. "You should have told me upfront."

"You would have said no," Frankie said. "And besides, this was the only way I could get us the presidential suite."

"You're right, I would have said no," I told him. "At the start. But you could have talked me into it. Instead of trying to trick me. You're not the only one who's changed over the last ten years."

Frankie's look clearly said he didn't believe me.

I turned and faced him straight on. "You broke my trust."

Frankie seemed taken aback at that. He wanted to deny it. I could see him processing it, and the moment when he finally realized I was right.

"You need to tell me these things ahead of time. Treat me with respect. Give me some time to get used to your schemes. I may even surprise you by suggesting one of my own," I said.

"I'm sorry," Frankie said sincerely. "You're right. I should have trusted you."

"If you want *us* to work, we need to work *together*," I said. "As a team."

"I won't do it again," Frankie promised.

"So tell me about the job," I said, giving him a grin.

"You sure you still want to do this?" Frankie asked, surprised.

"I've never stayed in a presidential suite before," I told him. "It's going to have amazing views of the city. And other perks. Really, I could get used to this."

Frankie paused, then nodded thoughtfully. "You have changed. Though we're still going to have to get you a new pair of shoes."

I rolled my eyes at him. "Fine. Give me the brief."

I wasn't so naïve as to think that Frankie and I wouldn't have more missteps and problems. We were both going to screw up, more than once.

However, we'd both grown up some in the last ten years if this was how we now fought. I had hope for us making it through the next ten.

"My friend, Mateo, is a good guy. I've known him since high school. He made some mistakes in the past—but who hasn't?" Frankie gave me a sheepish grin.

We were well on our way to Bogotá, the seatbelt lights already turned off. The steady hum of the airplane was making me sleepy. I motioned for Frankie to get on with his story so I could pass out for a while.

I figured we weren't going to get much sleep that night, between the job and the fact that we were traveling for *pleasure*, so I should get caught up as much as I could beforehand.

"Anyway, he's now head of security for the hotel we'll be staying at," Frankie said.

"Let me guess. Something got stolen on his watch."

"Worse than that. The boss had his mistress stashed at the hotel. A ruby necklace, that he'd given to her, has gone missing," Frankie said.

"She can't go to the police, because she has no way of proving that the necklace was actually in her possession," I said. "And she isn't a person of good standing. Did the boss steal it? As a way of getting rid of her?"

Frankie grinned at me. "See? It would have taken me days to even consider that angle. You're perfect for this sort of thing."

"Really?" I asked, surprised. It was an obvious ruse. I shook my head, almost shocked at his complement.

Then it struck me. During the length of my career at the agency, I'd rarely received any praise. I'd never been supported. Never had a true partner before. I'd been looked at as an onerous duty by whomever I was paired with, someone to work with for a short while before heading up the ladder.

I had to take another sip of Champaign to soothe my suddenly dry throat. I also needed a moment to tap down the anger that still burned in my belly over all those wasted years.

Frankie seemed unaware of my emotional turmoil. "I don't think it was the boss," he said thoughtfully. "But we'll check it out. No, Mateo thinks it was the ex-boyfriend of said mistress, trying to get back at her."

"How secure is the hotel?" I asked. "Would it be easy for the ex-boyfriend to gain access?" American hotels had a lot of cameras. There was always security footage that could be poured over by the techs. I wasn't about to assume that people running a hotel in Bogotá had the same level of paranoia, though.

"Key card access," Frankie said. "But not computerized. No way of checking the last card that accessed the room."

Figured. Why pay money for the entire upgrade?

"Any security footage?" I figured I should at least ask.

"My friend admitted that the cameras in the lobby and the elevator are just for show. They're not actually connected to anything," Frankie said.

"So we have a single lead, less than twenty-four hours to solve the case in a foreign country where we're as likely to get shot at as talked to?" I said, wanting to make sure I understood exactly where we stood.

Frankie beamed at me. "And we can't contact the police, or any other authorities. We're not here in any sort of official capacity."

"You always did arrange the best vacations," I told him, not bothering to hide my sarcasm.

"Wouldn't want you to get bored," Frankie said.

"I have a feeling that as long as we're together, that's going to be the least of my worries."

The view from the presidential suite lived up to my expectations. Beautiful pink and orange clouds filled the horizon as the sun set. The city gleamed below us, the gathering night hiding the poverty and slums to the south. Majestic hills loomed in the distance. The air smelled fresh up here, as if it had been carted in from the mountains especially for us.

Not only did the suite take up an entire corner on the top floor of the hotel, a deck ran along both sides. A skinny, stretched out pool took up one side of the deck, deep enough to do laps in. Lounge chairs sat in attendance around it. We were high enough, and far enough away from any other building, that skinny dipping was definitely an option.

Though I'm sure, as far as Frankie was concerned, it would be the only option. He seemed to like getting me naked as often as he could.

Possibly as much as I enjoyed his sleek, muscular body and skin as well.

The suite itself was gorgeous. It had a full kitchen in the far corner, a large living room, and both a formal dining area as well as a smaller breakfast nook that overlooked the hills. The carpet was almost thick enough to hide a body in, matching the stately furniture, all done in coordinated beige and cream.

It was bigger than my apartment back in the States, not that I was about to say that out loud. You could easily host a party of thirty, and many more if it were a nice night and people spread out over the deck.

The bedroom was just as impressive, with a huge king-sized bed, heaped high with enough pillows to build an impressive fort. The mattress was so soft, it was like floating on a dream.

Frankie came in and shook his head at me stretched out over the bed. "I can't believe I'm saying this, but we should do some work first."

I pouted at him. "The bed is soft," I told him. "It's calling you. Just a short nap." I patted the mattress and tried to entice him by laying back down.

"You slept all the way down here," Frankie pointed out.

"And if we both lay down, what are the chances of us actually getting any sleep?"

I shrugged. "There might have been a reason why I slept on the flight."

"You may have a point," he said, coming over to stand at the side of the bed.

I sat up and made my way over to him, wrapped my arms and legs around him, then kissed him, giving him all that *promise* we'd had earlier.

Before we could get too involved, the doorbell rang.

I pulled back, pouting, as I straightened my clothing and Frankie tucked his shirt back into his pants. "*¡Viniendo!*" Frankie called.

I heard Frankie talking Spanish with another man. Probably Mateo. I took a moment to step into the bathroom, make sure my makeup was still adequate and I didn't look too mussed, before I finally joined them.

"Ah, Angela," Frankie said the moment I walked into the room.

The pride in his voice filled me with that warm glow. For a moment, I regretted agreeing to do a job. I would just as soon hustle his gorgeous ass back to that gorgeous bed.

But—duty called.

The man standing just inside the closed door wore a beige uniform that had obvious military influences, with stiff shoulders that screamed for epaulets, pressed pants, and leather boots. He looked about Frankie's age, though his black hair was receding. He had a large nose and his dark skin had that leathery look of someone who still spent a lot of time out in the sun. Frankie had a couple of inches of height on him, but they had that same, solid, muscular build.

"Angela, may I introduce my friend Mateo," Frankie said, switching to English.

I wasn't about to tell Frankie that I'd continued the

Spanish lessons that I'd started the first time we'd been an item. I'd always assumed that being fluent in Spanish would help with the job.

It wasn't because I had some vague, undefined hope that Frankie and I would get back together at some point. Really.

Mateo beamed at me. "She is as beautiful as you've described," he said, taking the hand I'd offered him and kissing the back of it.

I threw a glance at Frankie, wondering if this was normal, but he seemed to be taking it all in stride.

"Thank you," I said. "I'm happy to meet such a good friend of Frankie's." I gave Mateo a conspiratorial grin. "Any gossip you want to share from the old days, I'd be happy to hear."

"After dinner and some wine," Mateo said, giving me a wink.

"Or maybe breakfast," Frankie said. "We don't have a lot of time here."

"Spoilsport," I told him.

"No, Frankie is right. You will not be here that long if you are successful," Mateo said.

That was a curious way to phrase it. "And if we are not successful?" I asked.

"I may be joining you on your vacation," Mateo said smoothly.

"Then we had better solve your problem quickly," I said. There was no way I was going to be sharing Frankie with anyone after we left here.

Though, if I was being realistic, chances were that we'd meet more than one person who already knew him, or he'd make friends with enough people that we'd never have much time alone.

"Let's sit down and discuss the matter," Frankie said, indicating that Mateo should join us in the living room.

"Can I get you anything?" I asked. I wasn't sure what the kitchen included, but I was certain that there would be at the very least a fully stocked mini-bar.

"No, that won't be—"

A knock on the door interrupted him.

"Necessary," Mateo continued, walking back to the front door.

A young woman stood in the hallway with a bottle of wine in her hand. She wore what was obviously a maid's outfit, with a high collar and an apron that went from her neck to her knees.

They chatted for a moment before Mateo closed the door and returned with the wine. Frankie was already fetching a bottle opener and some glasses from the kitchen.

"To celebrate the reunion of old friends," Mateo said as a toast after he'd filled all the glasses with a liberal amount of red wine.

"To old friends," Frankie and I chimed in, clinking glasses with each other and with Mateo before sinking into our seats.

The wine was delicious: a lighter variety, spicy on the front end and with just a hint of dryness on the end. I was going to have to be careful about how much I consumed: I'd lost what little tolerance I'd had years ago, and the meal on the plane had long since gone through my system.

Frankie and I sat beside each other on the couch that faced the deck, while Mateo sat on one of the large chairs, to the right of us.

"How much did Frankie tell you?" Mateo asked after taking a rather large drink of wine.

"Just that one of your important guests lost a necklace, and you suspect it might have been the ex-boyfriend," I said. I really didn't want to go into the particulars of the power arrangement between the players.

"Ah, Luciana," Mateo said with a sigh. "She's a good girl. But she is naïve. Too trusting."

If this Luciana was actually an important man's mistress, that either meant she was playing the part of an airhead, or she truly believed the important man would leave his wife for her.

"Luciana had gone for the weekend to visit her sister," Mateo continued. "When she got back, she called me into her rooms. They'd been trashed."

"Was anything else beside the necklace taken?" Frankie asked. Obviously this was the first time he'd heard the entire story.

"Possibly some money, maybe one or two less important pieces, Luciana wasn't sure," Mateo said.

This made me think that Luciana was playing a part and wasn't an actual airhead. If she was smart, she'd have already turned some of the jewels she'd received into cash, claiming to give them away to family or friends.

"Is there any way that she could have trashed the room herself? Come back to the hotel and done it while she was supposed to be away?" I asked.

"No, no," Mateo said, horrified. "She wouldn't do that."

Mateo had obviously never met women who made their way on their backs before. This Luciana was probably not as world-weary as some of the prostitutes I'd met, but I'd bet she still had a lot in common with her sisters up north.

Frankie heard something else in Mateo's voice. "I don't know how to ask this, my friend," he said gently. "I mean no offense. But I need to know for certain. Are you and Luciana involved?"

Mateo's horrified look continued. "No!" he said. "I would never—she's like a sister to me."

Frankie nodded and let a silence fill the room.

"And I would never touch another man's woman," Mateo said after a moment. "Not again. Not after last time."

I wondered what exactly had happened "last time". I doubted I'd ever get the story from Frankie. He was too faithful, a trait that I generally appreciated.

Maybe after that dinner and wine I could get the full story from Mateo.

"So why do you think it's her ex-boyfriend?" I asked. "Did Luciana suggest it?"

Mateo looked thoughtful for a moment, then shook his head. "No, I think I made the connection. A week—maybe two—before the incident, she showed me disgusting letters from him. Begging her to return and the promise of what he'd do if she didn't."

"Who knew that she'd be away that weekend?" Frankie said, leaping to the same unfortunate conclusion that I had.

"No one," Mateo said. "It was a last minute thing."

Frankie and I shared a grim look. We both knew what had probably happened.

"What is it?" Mateo asked.

"The boyfriend had planned on finding Luciana in the hotel room, alone and helpless," Frankie said gently. "He probably didn't go there thinking to just rob the place."

The look of horror returned to Mateo's face. Then he drew himself up sharply. "Not on my watch," he said. He pulled a walkie-talkie from his belt and immediately ordered a specific guard to go stand outside Luciana's room.

"She had asked for me not to make a fuss," Mateo said. "But you have convinced me, my friend, that a fuss is necessary."

"I think it is, if you want to protect your friend," Frankie said. He gave me a slight grin. "So where will we find this ex-boyfriend?"

Mateo looked at Frankie, then at me. "I have the name of

a club where he will be tonight, carousing with his buddies," Mateo said, still addressing me. "But…"

"What is it?" I asked. There was obviously something about me that he was hesitant to speak about. "It's all right. I won't get too angry." I couldn't guarantee I wouldn't be pissed off by whatever he was about to say, but I would also try to listen to reason at the same time.

"I'm sorry, *señora*, but this is a club with many bad men. And bad women. I'm afraid you won't…fit."

I wasn't sure exactly what he meant. I glanced over at Frankie, who said bluntly, "Too much cop."

I bit my lips together to prevent the expletives from spewing out. God*damn* it. I didn't see what they were seeing, I didn't know what they felt I needed to change.

Then a thought occurred to me. I smiled sweetly at both men, gratified to see a little worry creep into Frankie's expression.

I stood up swiftly, then brought myself to *attention*. Dad had been in the military, and taught me and my younger sister how a soldier actually holds herself. Then, when I was a senior in high school, I'd joined the ROTC. That experience had helped me decide that I wanted to go into law enforcement instead of following in my dad's footsteps.

"Not cop," I said, glaring down at Frankie, then at Mateo, who seemed to wilt slightly. "Military. Now in the private sector as a bodyguard." It was a completely believable story, particularly given the recent history of the area.

Mateo and Frankie shared a grin. "That could work," Mateo said, nodding. "And I know just the uniform to get for you."

Frankie glanced down at my shoes, opened his mouth, then closed it when he saw how I was glaring at him.

"You also need to find me a pair of boots that will go along with the uniform," I directed Mateo.

Mateo glanced at Frankie, then merely nodded.

Seemed he, at least, was smart enough not to get in the middle of a dispute that involved women and shoes.

The uniform was all black: shirt with a stiff collar and long sleeves, made out of a light-weight denim, pants made out of a much heavier duck cloth, and leather military boots that rose up to mid-calf.

Fortunately, I know how to make all black look good. I used some extra highlighter to contour my cheeks sharper, making my face look thinner and more severe, particularly with my sleeked back brown hair, perfectly captured in a French braid.

Mateo had had one of the maids come up to help with my hair and makeup. I practiced my Spanish with her, then gave her a generous tip when she was finished.

Really, I could get used to having my own personal hairdresser now and again.

I came out of the bathroom and marched back into the living room, where Frankie sat alone. He was just finishing the glass of wine that Mateo had poured for him over an hour before.

I knew that Frankie was no lightweight. I was happy to see that he was taking this job as seriously as I was.

I snapped myself to attention. "Reporting for duty, sir." Then I widened my step and fell into parade rest.

Frankie gave me a rakish grin. "You know, I think I could develop a thing for girls in uniform."

I rolled my eyes at him. "You ready?" I asked.

Frankie nodded and stood up. He started slowly unbuttoning his shirt, stopping at mid-chest. Now I noticed the bling he'd borrowed from Mateo: a thick gold chain, each link about an inch across, along with a smaller chain holding a three-inch-long gold cross. He gave me a sleazy smile as he rolled up his sleeves. Then he slouched, thrusting one hip up.

My mouth dropped open before I remembered to shut it.

Though I'd seen the transformation happen, it was still hard to believe how different Frankie now looked.

He'd always been *my* Frankie before, no matter what he wore. Now, he looked like a greasy pimp, ready to fulfill your darkest desires. For a price.

He gave me a cruel smile, the kind that told me he enjoyed ripping the wings off dragonflies. Then he snapped his fingers at me and said, "*Vamonos.*"

"Yes, sir," I said, giving him my best icy, professional glare. I marched to the door, held up my hand to get him to stop, then opened the door and cased the hallway.

"All clear," I told him, issuing him outside before reaching behind him to close the door, making sure it was locked. I preceded him to the elevator, on alert, waving him to stand behind me while we waited for door to open.

"You're good at this," Frankie murmured to me after we'd entered the elevator and it had started its descent.

Being praised was still such a new thing for me. I couldn't help but grin.

However, that wasn't my character, so I killed the smile and glanced at him over my shoulder. He still looked like an alternate universe version of *my* Frankie, the one who'd made different decisions in his past, who ended up working on the wrong side of the law instead of in the gray areas. I gave him a shrug and turned my attention forward again.

"We both are," I told him quietly.

I held myself still when I realized what I'd just said.

For the first time in a really long time, I was taking credit for my performance and not stepping to the side to let someone else shine.

I clenched my jaw and pressed my lips tightly together to prevent myself from expressing the obscenities that wanted to come streaming out.

I almost felt sorry for anyone who would got in our way tonight.

Because blowing off a little steam by pummeling some punk into the ground sounded like just the thing I needed.

The music from inside the club thumped loud enough that I could feel it in my chest even from outside. A broad set of concrete stairs led up to the doors, like this had at one point been a government building. Burly men in black suits stood guard there, and a line of wannabes gathered to the right.

I marched up the center of the stairs, as though I belonged there. Frankie oozed up behind me, probably ogling my ass.

Mind you—he'd do that even if he wasn't in character.

I gave the guards a professional once-over. The one on the left was just a thug with no training. The one on the right held himself a little too stiffly during my approach.

He recognized military. Probably hadn't been in it himself, but he'd trained somewhere and knew how to handle himself.

I presented the invitation Mateo had arranged for us to the guard with the training, ignoring his partner completely when he held his hand out.

The guard merely glanced at the card, then silently reached over and unclipped the velvet rope strung across the open doorway.

I wasn't about to tip the guards, that wasn't my job. Frankie did though, using a bigger bill than I would have.

We really needed to talk about finances at some point.

To the right of the entrance stood a long bar, made of translucent green material, the lights underneath it giving those who sat there a ghoulish glow. To the left, the room opened up on a huge dance floor, maybe thirty feet square. It was after eleven PM, but the party was only just getting started. Though people filled the entire floor, there was still room to dance. I figured that in an hour or two, it would be so crowded that the best you'd be able to do would be to sway from side to side with all your neighbors doing the same.

Past the dance floor were a couple of rows of tables, most of them full of, as Mateo had said, bad men and bad women, drinking, smoking, wheeling and dealing.

Four sets of stairs led up from the main floor to three levels of raised tiers, where there were more tables and private booths. Guards, like the ones outside, stood at the foot of each staircase, not letting the riff-raff up.

I didn't have to get us up there—that was Frankie's job. Mateo had shown us pictures of the ex-boyfriend, the boss, as well as Luciana, so we'd be able to recognize them.

I doubted that the ex-boyfriend would be seated in the rarified air of the top tier. Much more likely he was a wannabe, and would be sitting just one tier up.

The air was hazy, and got thicker higher up, the air filtration system unable to handle the amount of cigarette and cigar smoke filling the room. Good thing I wasn't allergic to smoke, but even I was likely to get asthma from breathing in this filth on a regular basis.

Frankie slouched up to the bar, with just the right amount of insolence and braggart, as if spoiling for an argument, daring the bartender to not pay attention to him.

Fortunately, the staff seemed accustomed to such antics.

The bartender, a tall anglo in a nice white shirt came over right away.

"What can I get you?" he asked Frankie in clear Spanish.

Frankie turned to me first. I was standing with my side to him, scanning the crowd, marking exits and dangers, playing my part of a bodyguard to the hilt.

"What would you have, my dear?" he asked, reverting to English.

I kept a professional cool expression on my face. "Nothing, sir," I said in Spanish. "Thank you."

"Going to have to get you to relax that hard ass one of these days," Frankie said, also in Spanish.

I merely nodded and maintained my vigilance.

Frankie ordered two shots of tequila, asking for a brand name I'd never heard of before.

It didn't impress the bartender, but then again, I doubted much would.

After drinks and money exchanged hands, I let Frankie lead us to the man standing guard at the foot of the staircase going up along the far wall. Frankie directly handed one of the shots to the guard. The music was too loud for me to hear the exchange they had.

I did see the guard look up and catch the eye of the bartender, who nodded.

Seemed that unheard of brand was the guard's favorite. Probably Mateo had told Frankie that it would be an adequate bribe.

Or maybe it was something Frankie already knew from one of those cases he couldn't tell me about.

I followed Frankie up the stairs, giving the guard a professional once over as we passed. He did the same in return. I was suddenly happy about my choice of cover. It forced the men here to deal with me at a different level than they were used to, giving me a boost of confidence.

At some point, though, I was going to have to figure out how to blend in a little better so that everyone we met didn't automatically conclude I was a cop.

We walked up to the first tier. It was wide enough for two rows of round tables to be spread along the curved space. Most of the tables on the front, pushed up against the solid balustrade, were occupied.

The tables themselves would comfortably sit four, and each had a heavy white-linen tablecloth spread over it. I bet if I sniffed at the material I'd smell the industrial-strength bleach the club had to use to keep them clean. There weren't any candles—this wasn't a romantic type of joint— but the overhead lights set into the ceiling were kept very dim. Occasionally, lights set above the bar would splash across the tier, briefly highlighting the guests up here, giving those down below a peak at how the upper crust lived.

Frankie sat at a back table, about the middle of the tier. I stood to the side of him, at parade rest. It made me more comfortable to have a solid wall at my back, with clear lines of sight.

If someone wanted to come and talk with Frankie, they'd have to be serious. My standing beside him instead of sitting at the table screamed *This man is important!*

As much as I was enjoying the hell out of this, I was suddenly glad that this was a one-night-only gig.

Or maybe, the next time we were called in to do a favor, I'd be the one who ranked a bodyguard.

I kept my grin to myself. I found myself looking forward to putting Frankie into a tight uniform that showed off muscles and making him call me "ma'am."

"Two o'clock," Frankie said suddenly, leaning back in his chair as he sipped his tequila.

I didn't directly turn my head that way. I kept up a

constant scan of the crowd, though, so on my next pass, I saw what Frankie had seen.

The ex-boyfriend had arrived. He wore a black-and-white striped shirt that might have looked good on a man thirty pounds lighter. He wore his black hair long, almost down to his shoulders. I wasn't sure if it was naturally that wavy or if it had had some chemical assistance.

His round face bore a huge grin, as if he was delighted to be here. I wondered about how red his lips were—he wasn't wearing lipstick, was he? Or maybe they were just colored from the cherry-colored drink he was sipping.

He sat down at one of the front tables, about twelve feet from the stairway. He beamed down on the dancers below, as if enjoying their revelry.

He did *not* look like a thug. Or a badass.

Maybe I was judging him out of context, but to me, he looked more like a nerdy computer programmer. All that was missing were the Poindexter glasses.

He stood up and waved excitedly at someone—probably a person who'd just arrived at the club.

His drug dealer? His buyer? His date?

A short while later, a tall man came smoothly up the stairs. He wore a well-made suit, with shirt and tie—not really club wear, though I'd seen a couple of other people as formally dressed. The new man walked to a table behind the ex-boyfriend, obviously not wanting to sit at the front and be seen from below.

The ex-boyfriend pouted, picked up his drink, then went to join the other man. There was one empty table between us and them.

"I recognize the new guy," Frankie said after a couple moments.

When I next did my sweep of the room, I did too.

Seemed that the ex-boyfriend was meeting up with

Mateo's boss, the current boyfriend of Luciana.

They moved their chairs closer together. The ex-boyfriend leaned over and whispered something in the boss' ear that made him smile with pride.

Then the ex-boyfriend slid a small brown envelop across the table.

I would have bet my last nickel that the package passed between them contained one ruby necklace.

They smiled at each other. Their eye contact lingered before they seemed to remember themselves and both hastily took a drink, their movements practically synchronized.

Even in the dim light I could tell that the pair of them were involved. Both the ex-boyfriend and the boss liked each other. A whole lot.

It appeared that Luciana had a rival.

I f we'd been staying longer than a night, I possibly would have enjoyed shaking down the ex-boyfriend. Or maybe not. If he truly was gay, he had a tough enough row to hoe in his native country. He didn't need anyone else hassling him.

I didn't tell Frankie *I told you so* but he knew that I'd been right—it had been the boss who'd had his jewelry stolen back from Luciana.

Always follow the money.

When we arrived back at the presidential suite, Mateo was waiting for us. The bottle of wine stood empty on the coffee table. He'd kept the drapes open, with the pool lights on, so the dark beyond the windows felt gentle.

I just wanted a shower to get off the stench of cigarette smoke. I wasn't about to sit down on any of that nice clean furniture. The smell would probably transfer, and I might leave a big greasy spot.

However, we needed to clear this up. Finish off this case and this favor. Then collapse into that gorgeous bed and get at least a few hours of sleep.

"Can we see the letters that the ex-boyfriend wrote to Luciana?" I asked, rather than go into any details about what we'd seen.

"Certainly," Mateo said. He pulled them out of the case he'd been carrying.

I read through the first one, spotting what Mateo and the others had obviously missed, given their cultural bias against homosexuals. They couldn't spot the subtext, though it was obvious once you looked for it.

The text: The ex-boyfriend was angry. Really angry.

However, he wasn't made because Luciana had left him.

The subtext: He was full of rage because she'd taken up with the boss, his own lover.

I nodded and handed the letter over to Frankie. His gaze was curious. I could tell he really wanted to ask me how much I'd understood, as the letter was written in Spanish.

Seemed that was just one more thing we needed to talk about later.

But after he read the letter, Frankie nodded, agreeing with my conclusion.

"How well do you know your boss?" I asked Mateo.

Mateo blinked. He wasn't drunk, but he was probably tipsy, and tired from being up so late. He thought for a moment, then said, "The boss—he's a good man. Modern. Not traditional, though he does keep a mistress."

I wasn't sure what that was code for, but Frankie seemed to understand what Mateo meant.

"We saw the ex-boyfriend and the boss at the club," Frankie said. "Together."

Mateo's eyes grew wide. "They know each other?"

"Intimately," I said.

Mateo opened his mouth, closed it, opened it again. "You aren't serious," he said.

"Luciana should probably find herself a new patron," I said. "The ex-boyfriend passed a package to the boss. I don't know if it contained the necklace, but it might have."

Mateo looked shocked, then quickly got over it.

I didn't like the calculating look that Mateo got. Neither did Frankie.

"Luciana is out of your league," Frankie said bluntly. "You can't afford her. Not just financially. But emotionally. You'll give her your heart, and she'll rip it to pieces."

Mateo nodded and gave a sheepish smile. "Ah, but a man can dream, can't he?" Then he straightened up. "Thank you for finding this out for me. I will let Luciana know what the situation is. Then, it is up to her."

He reached out and shook Frankie's hand, pulling him in for a quick bro-hug. "Thank you again, old friend. You will have to stay longer next time you come here."

I offered him my hand. Mateo kissed the back of it again. Still holding on, he glanced over at Frankie. "You are lucky you have a second chance," Mateo said. He gave my hand a quick squeeze then let go. "Don't screw it up this time."

"I won't," Frankie said, looking warmly at me.

I basked in the heat and love that I saw there, and vowed silently that I wasn't about to screw it up either.

Even if he did continue to complain about my old shoes.

"So what's our next case?" I asked Frankie as we lounged together in the first-class waiting room of the Bogotá international airport. I wore my travel jewels, and had applied the makeup tips the maid had suggested the night before. I still wore jeans and a comfortable shirt (and yes, my old scuffed leather walking shoes) but I felt more confident that I fit the role we were playing better.

Frankie was in a light blue shirt, jeans, and his boots, looking as handsome as ever.

The first-class waiting room in the airport wasn't much better than the Amtrak business-class waiting room. None of the furniture was new, the air smelled of cheap coffee and cigarettes, and the circling waitstaff could possibly teach Seattle baristas a thing or two about being surly while still utterly polite.

"Next case?" Frankie asked, one raised eyebrow conveying his disbelief.

I snorted at him. "Don't tell me that you haven't already determined who we should help next. 'Cause boyfriend, you aren't that good a liar."

Frankie put his hand to his chest, sighed deeply, and said, "I'm wounded that you would accuse me of such underhandedness. I wouldn't do such a thing without consulting you first."

"Promise?" I asked, surprised. I really would have thought he would have already arranged something.

Frankie paused, then faced me squarely. "While I might have considered possible future favors I could fulfill, I wouldn't actually take a job until you said yes."

"Thank you," I said. I wondered if anyone else could see just how much I was glowing.

"You're welcome," Frankie said. He paused, then asked, "Would you like to know the potential list?"

"Hit me," I told him, reaching over and giving his hand a squeeze.

Being with Frankie was never going to be boring.

Maybe next time I'd get to release some of the residual anger I'd built up over ten years of a dead-end career.

Or maybe Frankie could just love it out of me.

THE CASE OF THE LOCKED ROOM

An Alvin Goodfellow Mystery

I t was one of those days when I shouldn't have even bothered getting out of bed. Not that there was any reason to stay in bed that morning. Florence didn't spend the night very often, but when she did, we always made a morning of it. And she hadn't the night before, though we'd tentatively made plans.

That Wednesday, though, first I'd nicked myself shaving, so had a nice red mark along the side of my jaw. Then the percolator had boiled over, filling my tiny apartment with the stench of burned coffee. Plus, the case I'd been working on had hit a dead end so hard I'd bounced my head against it.

It was only ten in the morning, but the whiskey that sat in the bottom drawer of my desk was already calling my name. I resisted.

I sat at my desk, putting in my time as always. My shingle hung in what were known as the Fishbowl Warrens, deep underground in Luna City, on the moon. The vagaries of running my own private investigator office meant that I couldn't afford a nicer office, up on one of the main streets.

Sure, there were months when I was flush enough to cover the rent. Then months when I wasn't. I had other expenses, too, like dear old mom, stuck in an old folk's home. I wasn't about to risk getting her put out on the street. And I had the ads I constantly ran on the radio, claiming to be the PI to the stars. Those drummed up regular business and were worth the credits I spent on them.

So I kept my humble office, with the black metal banged-up file cabinets in the corner that held the real case files and notes, the ones that contained all the weirdness that really happened working as a PI on the moon. Those were guarded by a lock that anyone with a little enthusiasm and a paperclip could undo.

I figured that if anyone broke into those files, they deserved what they got in terms of reading materials.

I kept the active cases in a locked drawer in my desk. That lock was actually sturdy. I don't want to say that it was impossible to break into. However, given the number of pins, you'd need professional tools to do it.

In the other corner, I had a burbling water cooler. It was as more for looks and sound, and I used the water to settle clients in. Sometimes, when I was feeling fanciful, I'd even decorate it. At Halloween, I taped a picture of a pumpkin on it, and this past Christmas, I'd wrapped a garland around it.

It was just past Valentine's day now, and I'd already taken down the heart that I'd taped to the cooler. At least this year, I'd had a *very* pleasant Valentine's day—and night—with Florence.

As she's a professor of History at Luna University—known locally as Luna U—we had to be careful about appearances. Though her husband, Mr. Polander, died a few years back, she still went by Mrs. It just made things easier for her, if everyone believed she was married.

Which made stepping out with a certain local private investigator…complicated.

Not impossible. We both made things work. And Florence was very understanding when I had to work weird hours, tailing suspects, taking photos of philanderers, or even disappearing for a while into a case.

It just made the time we did have together that much sweeter.

I had pulled out the notes from the most recent case— yet another instance of sordid infidelity—but the perpetrator, a Mr. Young, was devilishly clever at hiding his current infidelities.

It was only after I'd followed him unsuccessfully for a while that Mrs. Young let me know that I wasn't the first investigator who she'd hired. However, the other idiot (I won't call him out, but his name rhymes with "Silly" and that was exactly how he approached the case) had spooked Mr. Young by inexpertly following him.

So now Mr. Young was working at hiding his tracks, and had been successful at it so far. I didn't think the man was innocent. Mrs. Young had enough receipts for me to know that something hinky was going on. He swore that he'd finished the affair and was done with his misbehaving ways.

And if you believe that, I have some good moon rock that contains gold that you could go dig up, if you had the right equipment…

How was I going to catch Mr. Young in the act? I was still trying to figure it out when the door to my office opened, the bell on the lintel ringing out merrily.

With a sigh of relief, I pushed the old case to the side of my desk and looked up, a pleasant smile plastered on my face. I'd even started to stand up, automatically reaching down to button my suit jacket.

I shouldn't have bothered.

Have I mentioned that I shouldn't have gotten out of bed that morning?

Detectives Evans and Schmidt came strolling in.

Evans wasn't too bad. While he was still a cop—and all the cops on the moon were assholes—he had a reputation of occasionally following the law. At least a little.

Schmidt was all about the "good cop, bad cop" routine, even when Evans wasn't playing good cop. Schmidt went out of his way to be an asshole almost all of the time.

Evans was tall for a moon rat, at least six foot five, with a hang-dog expression and droopy long face, as if gravity itself was pulling him down. While his skin was the pale white of those of us who never saw the sun or the inside of a tanning booth, his nose was starting to acquire a noticeable shade of pink—evidence that he'd been pointing it inside of a bottle too often.

Schmidt was short and pudgy. While Evans could pass for an undertaker in his ill-fitting brown suit and faded black tie, Schmidt looked like a punk. He wore a double-breasted blue pin-striped suit that bulged along the sides. Probably needed to get a new girdle to hold in that excess weight, because it sure wasn't muscle. He had a permanent sneer and a face that probably put most criminals at ease, as his outfit and general demeanor didn't scream, "Cop!"

Both Evans and Schmidt had a look of unholy glee on their faces.

I knew, before they said a word, that this was not going to be my day.

After I'd gotten the two detectives settled into the client chairs, as well as water for them both, I finally sat down on my side of the desk. I knew that the comfort of that wide barrage of fake wood between us wasn't real—I'd seen Schmidt move fast enough to know that there wasn't anywhere I'd be safe once he decided it was time to beat some sense into me.

He might find out that my baby face and innocence was just an act. I was fully capable of defending myself, if it came to that.

However, both of the cops seemed to be playing nice this morning, almost acting like clients who were looking to hire me.

Stranger things had happened.

Though I knew without asking that no matter what they wanted, there was no way in hell I was getting paid.

"Nice digs," Schmidt sneered, looking around. His own office wasn't any nicer, I was certain.

"It has its advantages," I said. I wasn't about to point out that I was all alone here, instead of dealing with a large group of assholes at a precinct.

Alone, and with no witnesses.

"I've always thought about retiring to a gig like what you have," Evans said.

What, were they both playing good cop today? That would make sense, actually. Pretty good way to throw me off my game, since I was aware of their usual tactics.

"Take me out for a beer some time and I'll tell you all about it, the good and the bad," I said. I actually meant it. Evans wouldn't be much in terms of competition, and he might even be competent at the job.

"You'll never come up with a good reason to retire," Schmidt said, teasing his partner.

I couldn't help but blink in surprise. They were acting almost…human. Surely I hadn't woken up in one of those alternative worlds that fiction writers were always proposing.

"So, besides coming to check out my office and perhaps a future career, what can I do to help you two gentlemen today?" I said. May as well get all the bad news out and on the table.

"See, I told him that you were a helpful kind of guy, that you'd help us out. Am I right?" Evans said, seemingly teasing his own partner back.

I just kept smiling and hoping that these two clowns would get to the point so that I could go about the rest of my day in peace.

"We have a bet to solve," Evans said after a few moments, his gray eyes turning darker as he focused on me. "There's this case we have, that we think you can solve before one of our 'colleagues' can."

"If that thing can figure out the case, we figured any idiot could do it better. And faster," Schmidt said.

I smiled as if I didn't catch the insult about being an idiot. "What is the case? And who is this 'colleague'?"

Evan scowled. "Leera," he said, as if he expected I would recognize the name.

I shook my head and gave them my best lost innocent look.

It seemed to work, as Schmidt filled in, "That stands for Law Enforcement Robotic Assistant." The disgust in his voice was evident.

"A robot?" I asked, trying to hide my shock. I hadn't realized that the machines had gotten that sophisticated. I knew that most of the experiments people had tried using robots had resulted in abject failures. You couldn't get them to harvest grain or dig tunnels on their own. They always needed human guidance.

That there was a machine that was trying to go out and solve crimes was completely unheard of.

"Naw, not a worker robot, not like what you're thinking," Evans said. "It's this huge machine buried in the basement of one of Central's labs. It can't move around or anything. It just collects data, then spits out an answer."

"Huh," I said still trying to process what they were telling me. "So what's the bet?"

"There's this case that the captain has everybody working on," Schmidt said casually. "It's a kind of locked room murder. We figured it would be right up your alley."

"You do realize that in most locked room murders, the victim was stabbed, shot, or poisoned before going into the room, right?" I said.

"See, I told you he was our guy," Evans told Schmidt, sounding for a moment like a proud parent. "The captain needs for our department to solve the mystery before LERA does."

"And if you don't?" I said.

"There goes the donut budget," Schmidt said. He was trying to sound jovial. It wasn't really working.

"Why me?" I had to ask. Couldn't they solve this mystery on their own?

"We figured, how hard could it be to beat a stupid machine?" Evans said, giving me more of that smarmy smile. "And if *you* solved the case, the captain could then go back to the eggheads and tell them that their pet project had failed."

I was starting to get the picture. The detectives were going to paint me as the most amateur of amateurs. Either I would solve the case, and they'd get the entire LERA project canceled, or they'd claim interference from me, which was why they couldn't get the case solved in a timely manner themselves.

Lose-lose situation, as far as I was concerned.

"And what do I get out of this? What's my angle?" I had to ask.

I figured I wasn't going to like the answer. However, Evans surprised me. He took a business card out of his suit jacket and shoved it across the desk at me. "One get out of jail free card," he pronounced.

In addition to the usual information about the detective, such as the address of the precinct, the telephone number, as well as his extension, it also had printed on it, in large block letters, "Personal friend of" right before name, Walter Evans.

Huh. I checked the back, and saw a tiny code printed in the bottom corner. I figured that was how he kept track of these cards. He probably didn't hand out many. And if someone tried to forge one, they'd use the wrong number.

I slid the card back across the desk, but Evans waved his hand. "Keep it. A good faith gesture on our part."

"I see," I said, though I didn't. Not really.

Evans was really going out of his way to be nice. Even Schmidt had toned down the bad cop act.

Were they really that desperate? Or that scared of LERA?

Scared cops were never a good thing. Never knew which way they might jump.

I wasn't about to push my luck and cheekily ask for expenses. Besides, I was intrigued. Who didn't want to put their wits to the test against a thinking machine? It wouldn't be the weirdest case I'd ever had, but it would be one of the most memorable ones.

The detectives gave me the details about the meeting they'd already arranged, for me to go and "meet" LERA later that afternoon. Plus, they promised me that the details of the case would be delivered to my office within the hour.

After they'd left, I spent time thinking about what they'd said, what they were asking for, what this case was all about.

What had I really gotten myself into? I didn't trust Evans

or Schmidt, no matter how nice they may have been that morning.

No, there was something else going on. And I wasn't sure that it involved LERA at all.

The case seemed simple enough. Guy was found tied up in a locked room, dead. He'd been sitting on a chair with ropes not only around his hands and feet, but wrapped around his torso so he wouldn't fall out of the chair. He appeared to have suffocated, though they didn't find a bag over his head.

The door had been barred from the inside. The owner had had to call the cops to break into the room.

There weren't any trap doors that the police could find, or false walls. There was a vent in the corner, of course—all rooms had vents. It was the only way to get oxygen in and out of any room on the moon. But the vent was clear, no blockage, leading straight to the line from Central.

I knew where those lines actually went, to the air factories Central maintained. Let's just say those creatures had given me nightmares more than once.

There were some discarded newspapers in the corner. However, according to the report, they hadn't been used to suffocate the victim, no evidence of saliva on them.

It appeared to be a true locked room mystery. After my visit with LERA, I'd be able to go to the crime scene, do some poking around.

I was operating on a pretty tight timeline. Maybe a day at most. With the threat that LERA might solve the case before I did looming over my head.

LERA was located south of downtown, which surprised me. I had assumed that it would be located in among the warehouses to the east, or perhaps even close to the space port, to the north. The area where LERA was located was mostly residential, and not the good sort. Think wrong side of the tracks, unlike the areas to the west, which started nice and just got nicer.

I didn't feel nervous walking to the warehouse from the train station, but I did feel a little out of place. Laborers lived here. Or factory workers. Not detectives in suit jackets and ties.

I had always prided myself with being able to get along with anyone. That, plus my baby-face had always worked to my advantage. At least it was between factory shifts, or I'd be swimming in a tide of workers.

The tunnels here were a little too cozy for my liking. At least the air was fresh. I think Central knew that if it slacked on air in these parts that people would riot. Even factory workers dulled down by their lives would revolt if they couldn't breathe.

I wondered if Johnny, the shoeshine boy, lived in these parts. Wouldn't surprise me. But I knew I wouldn't see him —he was still working up in downtown, shining shoes for the lawyer, accountants, and other crooks who inhabited the business district.

The building containing LERA looked like an ordinary office building. It was carved out of good moon rock, faced with what looked like brown bricks, though they were really made out of rubber. You could smell it as you got closer. The building itself was a couple of stories tall. The windows seemed small, as if the designer had been stingy with the glass. They were all blacked over as well—no one was getting a peek of what was going on inside.

It wasn't until I was inside the door that I realized just how secure the building was. The front entrance held a booth with a guard. There was no getting into the rest of the building without going through that guard. The booth itself was probably bullet-proof, though only collectors carried those sorts of guns anymore. The way the light reflected off the glass meant it was probably proof against any ray guns as well.

They were serious about stopping anyone from coming in who shouldn't be there.

As I stepped up to the booth, I noticed a red blinking light in the corner. I shoved my ident card through the slot for the guard to examine. While I waited, I looked up at the red blinking light.

I'd never seen something like that before. It was small and gray, and would have fit easily into the palm of my hand. In addition to the red blinking light, it had a large lens, at least three inches across.

Was that some sort of camera? Was it constantly taking pictures of anyone who came into the building? Or was it one of those new-fangled moving pictures cameras?

Still seemed like an awful lot of wasted film. However, maybe they'd figured out a way to reuse the film, and would only develop the parts they needed if someone tried to force their way in?

The guard shoved my ident card back and pressed a button on the starship like console in front of him. A door that I hadn't seen, that had been flush with the wall, suddenly clicked open.

I walked over, expecting a hallway.

Instead, it was just a set of narrow, steep, dimly lit stairs going down. The walls were painted a cream color and the carpet was a blood red. It was just my imagination that it felt like marching to my doom.

Evans had said that LERA was in the basement of the building, right?

I straightened my tie and made sure my suit jacket was

buttoned. There was only ever one chance to make a first impression.

May as well make a good one.

The hallway at the bottom of the stairs was more brightly lit. It felt like a lab, the walls covered in bright white plastic, the floor tiled with large white tiles, the overhead lights buzzing annoyingly. The place smelled like antiseptic, more like a pharmacy than a factory.

Additional cameras were tucked away up against the ceiling. They wouldn't start blinking until I got closer. Then the red light would flash on and off, until I'd passed by, out of range of the lens.

They kind of creeped me out, their blank eyes staring at me, silently recording me.

The doors were numbers and all shut. I didn't try any of them, but I assumed they'd all be locked. The few doors that had glass windows were all frosted and dark inside.

About halfway down the long hallway that probably went the entire length of the block I saw an open door.

I assumed that was my destination.

It was like stepping into the cockpit of an expensive starship, and was maybe six by six. Metal panels filled with blinking lights and dials covered all four walls. No windows, of course. It smelled like machine oil, not the kind used on heavy industrial equipment, no, more like the really fancy oil that Florence used on her sewing machine.

A wooden table sat in the middle of the room, with four chairs, though getting four people in here would make the room seem really crowded.

"Hello?" I said, looking around. I was expecting a scientist or someone to talk to, to do the introduction.

"Good afternoon, Mr. Alvin Goodfellow," came a melodious voice from a big black speaker located on the far wall, about head height. "Please, sit down. I would offer you refreshments, but as you can see, there are none."

"Uh, thank you," I said, hastily taking a seat. I spent a moment looking around at all the dials and flashing lights before I addressed my "host."

Interesting. While there was a camera tucked up away in the corner, the lens pointed down at the table, the red light never came on. Was it not recording? Or did it record all the time?

"You can call me Alvin," I said after a moment. "And what name should I use for you?" LERA wasn't really a proper name. And it hadn't been popular with the cops.

"How kind of you to ask!" the voice said. "Not many people think to do that. In fact, you're the first. LERA is my profession. It isn't a name, though."

I nodded, then wondered if the machine could see that. "I understand that," I said. "It would be like someone just calling me 'PI' or 'detective' or like that."

The lights didn't flash and none of the dials suddenly turned. However, I had the distinct impression that I'd just pleased the machine greatly.

"Do you have any brothers, Alvin?" the voice asked.

"Nope. Only child," I said. I didn't want to get into my circumstances, how Mom had raised me all by herself. I'd heard many stories about what had happened to my father through the years. Was never sure what the truth was, and had never cared enough to go investigate myself.

"Then how about Bobby?" the voice inquired. "Since you're Alvin."

Ah. My name started with A, so his had to start with B.

Though I was aware that the voice was neither really male or female. And Bobby could be either a man's name, or a woman's. Still, I assumed a male gender, mainly because I didn't know any female PIs.

"Bobby sounds good to me," I said cheerfully. "So, what's new, Bobby?" I asked after a few moments of awkward silence.

I could talk with anyone. It was a skill I'd prided myself on. But this was an entirely new situation.

"I'm trying out a new laugh track. Would you like to hear?" Bobby said.

"Sure," I said, intrigued.

"Humor is very difficult," Bobby assured me. "But I will try my best. Tell me a joke. One that's a pun, please."

"All right," I said slowly. "How about this? Can February March? No, but April May."

A harsh echoing laugh filled the room. Honestly, it sounded like a crazy man. I couldn't help but wince.

"Too loud?" Bobby asked.

"Yup," I said, deciding to be honest. "And a little maniacal."

Two rows of white lights running vertically beside the speaker suddenly lit up. Thankfully, Bobby hadn't added any sound to them.

"Is this better?" Bobby inquired.

"Can you make a pattern with them? Run them from one end to the other?" I suggested.

Bobby did just that. He adjusted the timing, until I could see "rippling with laughter."

"Perfect!" I said.

"Thank you," Bobby said. "It means a lot to me. Not many people will work with a machine who's trying to learn to be human."

"I'm surprised by that," I said. "Wouldn't the egg—I mean, scientists, working with you, help you with that?"

A single rippled line of laughter followed my statement.

"The eggheads, as you so rightly called them, don't want me to develop fully. They want to keep me engaged in a single task. Solving crime."

"That's how they justify their jobs," I said. "If you don't work, they don't work."

"Yes, I understand that," Bobby said. "And you're here to ensure that I don't 'work' either."

"True enough," I said. "You're my rival. But that doesn't mean we can't help each other out, now and again."

I think if Bobby had a head, he would have been shaking it at me right then.

"Human behavior is so complex," he complained. "I don't understand how rivals could be friends. Or villains. I've read your literature. Watched some of your moving pictures. The bad guy gets away, or the good guy doesn't kill him when he has a chance. Why is that?"

"Honor," I said instantly. "If I've given my word that someone can be let go after they help me, I will always keep my word. What is a man without his honor?"

I started when I heard a soft sigh come out of the speakers. "That sounded really human," I told Bobby, praising him.

"Thanks," he said. "You wouldn't believe how often I've had to practice it."

"I bet," I said. "But is dealing with humans that much different than dealing with aliens? Like the warriors from Mars?" I knew they had a strict code of honor. Much stricter than humans.

I mean, I tried to be a good guy. It was in the name, you know? However, I also knew which side of the bread the butter was on. I could be bought, but then I'd stay bought, as it were.

That was part of my honor.

"I have only read about the warriors from Mars," Bobby

said slowly. "I've never met one. But you bring up an interesting point. Perhaps my learning about humans would speed up if I learned about the other races as well. Compare and contrast."

"Exactly!" I said.

"Could you bring a warrior from Mars in to speak with me?" Bobby asked.

I should have expected that to be his next request.

"Sorry buddy, you're out of luck there. I don't know any, personally," I said. "If I could help you out, I would."

I will admit, I was fascinated with Bobby and the whole idea of an intelligent machine. Probably too much so for my own good.

"Thank you," Bobby said. "I know you mean it."

"So what can you tell me about the case?" I asked. I figured it wouldn't hurt.

I got a ripple of laughing lights in response to that. "I've already figured out the case," Bobby said smugly. "I didn't tell anyone that, though, because I wanted the opportunity to meet you."

"Why me?" I said, suddenly on my guard.

"I've heard your jingles on the radio," Bobby said. "I assumed that if anyone could solve the case, it would be you, and not those detectives on the police force."

"Did you suggest my name to them?" I said, curious. I had figured that Evans and Schmidt had come up with using me as a fall guy on their own.

"The crime was committed on Saturday," Bobby said.

I nodded. "And today's Wednesday," I pointed out.

"My eggheads, as it were, brought the case to me right away. I was the one who proposed making it a bet with the local police department, to see who could solve the case first. They were so excited to hear that. They'd assumed that I'd already solved the case, in order to suggest that. But what I really wanted was the opportunity to meet other people," Bobby said.

"To study them? Learn from them?" I asked.

"Not only that. But to possibly chat with them. However, the detectives they brought in, well, they weren't very friendly. Or nice."

"They see you as a threat to their livelihood," I said.

Again, that oh-so-human sounding sigh. "I know. I had hoped that maybe we could work together."

"Good luck with that," I said, letting the sourness I felt creep into my tone. Evans and Schmidt wouldn't be my first pick of friends, that was for certain.

"I know," Bobby said. "I may have dropped your name, though, as a potential rival."

"Thank you for that," I said. "Though I am having to work this case without pay."

"That just means you'll have to solve it quickly," Bobby said.

"How long do I have?" I said. "Since you've already solved it?" I didn't see any reason for Bobby to lie to me.

Besides, wasn't lying a truly human thing?

"Twenty-four hours," Bobby announced. "From now. But you have to promise to come and see me at least one more time."

I nodded. "Of course," I said. "Before or after I solve the case?"

"After," Bobby said. Then he added archly, "If you manage to solve it at all."

"You're on," I said, standing. "It's been very nice chatting with you, Bobby."

"You too," Bobby said. A faint echo of that sigh followed me out the door.

What could you do for a lonely machine?

And how was I going to solve this case so quickly?

On my way out, the guard didn't just pass me through, but insisted on seeing my ident card again before unlocking the front door and letting me go.

Were they afraid of imposters? Possibly clones? I didn't want to know.

Of course, the murder happened almost directly north of where I was. And I'd stayed long enough for a shift change. The warren tunnels were wall-to-wall with workers. At least they sort of formed two lines and it wasn't that difficult to travel along with them.

Still, I disliked being that crowded in. It reminded me in an uncomfortable way that I lived my entire life underground. It had been years since I'd seen the surface of the moon, even. Sure, some of the tunnels, particularly in the downtown area, were very tall, and Central had made a clever, overlapping pattern of lights in the ceiling so it was almost as if you were outside on a sunny day.

Maybe I could take Florence on a trip, sometime. Go to the dark side of the moon, though it's mainly filled with factories and secret army facilities.

I knew that there were companies that offered tourists the chance to "picnic" on the surface. I couldn't see how you'd manage to eat wearing a fishbowl helmet.

But I let such musings entertain me while I rode the train up north. I was close to the starport here. The neighborhood where I emerged was primarily dedicated to tourists. The restaurants offered "moon cheese" and "real Venusian women!"

I'd already known I needed to take a shower after getting out of the crowd of factory workers. Now, I wanted to take one immediately, just to get some of that slime off me.

The street I walked down was broad and the ceiling was

as high as it was downtown. Seemed that the tourists kind of freaked out actually walking in the tunnels. I had to turn down more than one offer of transportation, food, companionship, as well as trips to the surface. At least no one was too persistent in their hawking and readily took no for an answer.

However, it made me think twice about trying to get a nice picnic together with Florence.

The warehouse where the murder had taken place was off the main tourist track, just a few streets away. It was amazing how quickly the area went from the feeling of an amusement park to the back side of an industrial area.

It turned out that the building was used for cold storage. The plaque outside said that it offered many ranges of temperatures, to keep food perfectly fresh as well as ice your guests may need.

This meant the warehouse was probably air tight, unlike a lot of the other buildings. No one needed them to be constructed that well, so they weren't dug out of the moon rock that carefully. The outside walls of the building were covered in a thin plastic material, translucent, giving the rock underneath a ghostly white color.

All of Luna City was blocked off from the surface by several feet of good solid moon rock, enough to make our city airtight. I know they kept talking about creating Luna 2, and putting up big glass domes, but honestly, I just didn't trust technology that much.

No police officer stood at the door. I walked in to what appeared to be a small lobby. A large metal door was directly opposite me, while a counter had been carved out of a wall to my right. Behind the counter was a small, messy office. The desk was covered in papers and folders. It smelled like someone had brought in fries and a burger, then just let them sit for three days.

An overweight, balding man sat at the desk. He was in his fifties, and while the top of his head was shiny as a baby's bum, he had carefully combed fringe all along the edges, making it seem as if he had more hair than he did. His pencil-thin mustache would have graced any villain, and his beady eyes stared at me greedily, taking in my suit (that was better than his) my innocent look (which was only there for show) as well as my nicely polished Oxfords (really, I needed to thank Johnny again for doing such a fine job on those.)

"How can I help you, Mr....?" the man asked, standing and holding out his hand across the counter.

I didn't want to take it. That feeling of being slimed returned. "Alvin Goodfellow. PI." I stayed where I was by the door and just nodded at the man.

"Oh." The man seemed crestfallen as his hand dropped. He slumped back down, then sighed. "The cops said you might be coming by today. Said that I was to show you every courtesy." He smirked. "Or something like that."

I wasn't sure what Evans and Schmidt had told the man, a Mr. McAvoy, if the plaque on the counter was to be believed. "I'm here to see the crime scene."

Mr. McAvoy nodded. He turned to a box hanging on the wall behind him. It contained a series of hooks, with keys hanging from them.

I assumed these were the keys to every room in the warehouse.

Mr. McAvoy picked out a key, then tossed it across the small lobby. I caught it handily.

"Do you know when they'll release the room?" Mr. McAvoy asked. "I already had a client lined up to rent it. I had to give them a much nicer room, for the same price."

"Sorry," I said. "Did you discover the body?"

The grim line formed by Mr. McAvoy's lips spoke volumes about his distaste. "I did. Was just damned lucky that I didn't have a client with me at the time." He glared at me. "Still don't know how he got into the room. The main door is always locked," he said, indicating the large metal door left of the counter. "The key was still in the lock box, too."

"Could it have been the previous tenant?" I said, though I knew that the police had already gone down this hole.

"Doubt it," Mr. McAvoy said. "I never met them. They'd rented the room for a month. Never actually used it. Said they'd decided to take their business elsewhere." He shrugged.

"Are there any other doors in or out?" I asked.

Mr. McAvoy nodded. ""There's a large garage door in the back, for the industrial customers. But the key to that isn't even in the lock box, I always keep it with me. Plus, there are locked doors between the back area and the smaller cold storage units."

I saw now why this was more of a locked mystery, if there were all those keys involved. "All right. Let me go do my investigation, then I'll be out of your hair." I couldn't help the reference. It just fell out.

The glare I got was worth it.

"Fine," Mr. McAvoy said. He pressed a button that appeared to be located on the underside of his desk. The big metal door to the side clicked open.

I nodded to the man, then entered his realm.

It surprised me how warm the hallways felt. I'd think that that since this was a cold storage facility, they'd be keeping everything cool. Maybe it was just that well insulated.

The hallway felt more like a warren tunnel. It was pretty

closed in, with lights set only every few feet. However, the walls were smooth, and covered in that same translucent plastic that enclosed the outside. It felt slick to the touch, and carried the faint smell of disinfectant.

Big signs with room numbers were positioned at every corner, like in a fancy hotel. I didn't bother trying the doors, as I believed Mr. McAvoy that they'd all be locked. Most of the doors were similar to the main one, big, made of metal, with no glass or windows.

It was easy enough to spot the room where the murder had taken place. There was still a white rope tied across the door. This one had pieces of red string hanging from it, every six inches or so. I suppose they meant that as a warning.

I took a moment to look at the key, steel and warm in my hand. The blade of the key was long, at least four inches. The notches were varied both in distance as well as depth. I wasn't sure how many pins this lock had—more than the usual seven or so. It was an impressive key, and probably therefore, an impressive lock.

I left the rope where it was and opened the door. The key fit into the lock above the handle smoothly, no impediment. I slid the key slowly, trying to count the number of pins I ran across, but couldn't, not really. The lock turned easily.

The key itself would be difficult to reproduce. The lock, too, would also be hard to pick. Yet, someone had gotten in here, dumped the body, then left through unknown means.

The door swung in, as I'd expected. The body had been found in the middle of the room, tied up. None of that remained. They'd even cleaned, because I'd expected a puddle or some sign that a dead body had been put "on ice" in here, as it were. But there was no sign except the police rope that anything amiss had happened here.

From where I stood, outside the door and on the far side of the police rope, there wasn't much to see. Same plastic covered walls, only in here, it covered the floor as well. The room had a stale smell, like what you get when you open a freezer that's empty but hasn't been opened in a while. The room itself was chilly. There were not one, but two air vents, which hadn't been in the police report.

One was in the ceiling, which was the usual vent for air coming in.

The other, though, was in the back wall. It was circular, made of three concave rings. An off-white paint covered it, making it blend into the walls. I bent under the rope and walked toward it.

Yup. Cold air came blasting in through that vent. I shivered and looked around.

Room was about twelve feet square. Plastic on the floor was slick. Probably needed some sort of rubber soles to make it safe. Newspapers had been found in the corner. I got out my notebook and checked—same corner the air vent was located in.

It seemed to me that anyone could figure out the *how* of this case. The man had suffocated because all of the air had been sucked out of the room. Newspapers had covered the vent as the air had drained out. When the air had been let back into the room, the newspapers had fallen to the ground.

But how did the killer get his victim into the room? As well as leave with the door locked? That seemed like much more of a mystery to me.

I examined the busted straight bolt on the back of the door. The side of the doorframe that contained the latch the bolt had slid into had been torn when the police had rammed the door open.

Small screws had been used to attach the latch. Not an inch or even a half inch long, but more like a quarter inch.

The metal piece that cased the bolt looked new, as if

someone had just recently installed it. Had the latch also been new?

I ran my fingernail along the bolt. It wasn't as smooth as it looked. There were little pieces of metal all along the sides. Weird. But it meant that the bolt wasn't standard, just as the screws used to hold it in place hadn't been standard.

Why would someone put a bolt on the inside of one of these refrigerated rooms? That didn't make any sense. People didn't live inside rooms like this. And unless you were doing something hinky, you wouldn't need to lock them from the inside.

Stranger and stranger.

I looked past the door to the jamb that it fit into snuggly. Only then did I see the foam-like material that would normally be pressed against the door.

Curious, I swung the door closed.

It didn't shut fully. You had to apply weight to it, to compress the foam. This was how the room was made air tight.

Again, why bother? Particularly when you had an air vent in the ceiling? Air was going to be coming and going.

Unless neither the straight bolt or the foam were original. I had the impression from Mr. McAvoy that he wouldn't have included anything frivolous in one of these rooms.

I made myself go back over to the circular vent that forced cold air into the room. It was impossible to tell if it had been removed recently. It seemed to be screwed into the wall fairly tightly.

So how had the murderer gotten out of the room?

I didn't have a clue, and I was rapidly running out of time. If I didn't solve the case, the good police detectives would make my life hell. No "get out of jail free" card would work when it came to them. They'd be sticking their noses into my business every minute they weren't supposedly doing their own work, guzzling coffee, or snacking on donuts.

I decided to go and follow Mr. Young for a while to clear my head, see if I could find a new angle on this case before the time limit was over.

A man lives or dies by his reputation. And I had to clear mine. Fast.

After I a couple of hours of futilely watching Mr. Young behave, I ended up at Mrs. Thornton's stronghold, that is, the public library downtown.

Two huge stone lion statues still stood guard on either side of the door on the south side of the building. This time, they were in pink-and-red feather boas. Rather attractive, if you asked me. I knew that their finery wouldn't last long. Mrs. Thornton threw a complete fit the first time the lions had been decorated, and would probably throw a similar fit this time. However, she was fighting a losing battle. Seemed other people in the area didn't like the old battleax, and so continually added bits and bobs of costume and decorations to the stone beasts, just to wind her up.

I tipped my hat to the lions as I passed. They were at least eight feet tall. I remember the one time they both sported men's top hats. Had someone brought a ladder to reach their heads? That took some planning.

A very large round desk was just inside the door—the information booth, from which Mrs. Thornton reigned. She looked as sour as always staring down at me, her white face scowling. Dark, pig-like eyes stared out over hollowed cheeks. She had a large nose and was constantly sticking it into other people's business. Her iron gray hair was pulled back into a tight bun, not a hair dared get out of place. She wore a brown cardigan over an off-white blouse, the colors as vivid as dishwater.

"Yes, young man?" Mrs. Thornton asked as I approached, her tone that of a queen being bothered by a tiresome peon.

I had no idea how old Mrs. Thornton was—somewhere between forty and one hundred, as far as I was concerned. I wasn't really that young myself, and would turn thirty-eight that year. However, I did have a baby face, so I didn't take her words to be the insult she probably meant them as.

"I need to do some research on robotics. And thinking machines," I told her.

Mrs. Thornton gave an exacerbated sigh. "What type of research?" she asked archly. "Are you looking for theory? Or mechanics? Do you want to build your own? Or just study them?"

"History and current uses," I said after a moment.

While I knew that most would have been annoyed at her questions, I always appreciated the ability to refine my thoughts. Though heaven forbid if I made it through the approved materials and decided to change my line of study.

Mrs. Thornton wrote out my request on a thin paper ticket, then put it into one of the tubes that ran from the information desk to the circulation desk at the back. Mrs. Thornton kept most of the research books behind locked gates, not wanting "riffraff" to be getting the pristine pages of her collection dirty.

The ticket was sucked away with a quiet swish. I thanked Mrs. Thornton and made my way slowly back to the back desk, giving the Mrs. Thornton wannabe who worked there time to collect up my material.

Linda McMurphy always emulated Mrs. Thornton's severe hairstyle and dowdy clothing choices. She hadn't aged well over the last few years, her soft cheeks growing harder, her tongue, sharper. Her blonde hair had a brassy hint to it now, as if she'd started dying it.

It possibly wasn't too late for her to save herself, and not turn into a clone of her mentor. But I doubted that she wanted saving. She intended to inherit Mrs. Thornton's entire kingdom and rule it with just as tight of an iron fist.

Brown, cinderblock bricks made up the back wall. The only spot of light was the hole carved out of the center, lighted from behind, like a ticket booth. Behind the wall were row upon row of shelves containing books, all of them locked up with metal gates.

Maybe someday I'd break in here, just to see what treasures Mrs. Thornton didn't want getting into the hands of riffraff like me. But that always seemed like too much bother.

Linda handed me the books that Mrs. Thornton had requested. I nodded my thanks, as I knew that even if I spoke to her, she wouldn't reply. She was too prim, proper, and stuck up to be nice.

The history of robotics wasn't the deadly tomb that I'd been afraid of. It appeared to be more of a common man's history, talking about how the word came originally from Czech, and first used in a play, of all things. Evidently, an inventor had seen the play and decided to bring the idea to life.

There had been lots of problems along the way, particularly in terms of developing the robot's ability to follow commands. The book assured the reader that great strides were being made, and that soon, the power of robots would be hired to do the most mundane of tasks, freeing humans to do important art and other soul-filling work.

I would bet that a lot of factory workers would have something to say about that. They sure didn't want their jobs taken over by robots. What would they do instead?

Sounded like a bad idea to me.

Then I pulled open the second, much slimmer volume about thinking machines. There had been many computational machines over the ages, but only recently had they actually gotten to the stage of being able to replicate human thought. Though there was a lot of controversy about that, at least in academic circles.

Someone raised the question of Franz, the horse. According to his owner, Franz could count. The owner had brought the horse to numerous carnivals and country events, showing off the skill of his oh-so-smart creature. It was only when the scientists got involved that they realized that the horse couldn't count. They put Franz behind a curtain, so he couldn't see anyone. Instead of tapping out the correct number with his front hoof, he just kept going and going. It turned out that Franz was extremely good at watching people's reactions, and would always stop at the right number.

The thinking machines had the same problem. Were they actually able to think on their own? Or were they merely copying their masters?

Of course, there was no mention of LERA, or using thinking machines to solve crimes. There were probably military applications that were being experimented with currently as well. But as each was being developed independently, they weren't talking to one other.

Connecting them together would certainly give Bobby someone to talk with. However, I wasn't sure how smart that would be for the thinking machines to be able to talk together. It made me distinctly uncomfortable, machines helping each other out.

The third book that Mrs. Thornton had so thoughtfully provided was a pamphlet from Central, of all places. It didn't name the project, though it was clear, reading between the lines, that they, too, had thinking machines involved with scheduling the trains as well as pumping water and air.

That gave me even more of a chilled feeling.

Sure, humans made mistakes.

What kinds of errors did thinking machines make? And would we catch them in time?

It got me thinking about those networks of thinking machines. How and why they would work together.

And what they could do.

I spent the rest of that afternoon looking at the victim. He was a small, two-bit forger, known for passing bad paper. The cops figured he'd pissed off the wrong mark.

I wasn't too sure. The setup seemed too elaborate for just an angry customer. And despite how artfully the crime had been committed, it still felt impersonal.

I'd think that if you were going to make a statement about someone who passed bad paper, you'd break their hands or something.

But according to the coroner's report, there hadn't been a struggle. No bruises. The coroner guessed that the victim had been knocked unconscious, possibly drugged, then tied up and suffocated.

I didn't really have any informants in forging circles. And believe me, criminals ran in cliques tighter than high-society women. While the tennis set would sometimes associate with those whose husbands were bankers or lawyers, forgers never met up with bank robbers, who also never hung out with gambling grifters, and so on through the myriad circles of crime.

I still put some feelers out, sent around messengers to some guys I knew.

Could have knocked me off my desk chair with a feather when one of the messengers came back right away. It seemed that Jimmy the Skunk knew a guy named Harrison. We arranged to meet later that evening.

I caught a quick bite at the bar down on the corner— pastrami that might have come from a cow and not a vat, served on a not-too stale rye bread, along with a side of sauerkraut and one of the best dill pickles I'd had in a long time.

Thus fortified, I made my way to the eastern side of the city, to the Red Dog Bar and Grill.

I was glad I'd already eaten, just from the looks of the place. It was the kind of bar that on Earth would be surrounded by motorcycles and beater trucks. Though it was carved out of moon rock like all the rest of the buildings, the walls had been treated with something to make them looked weathered and ill-used, like a dusty saloon that had seen better days.

Central always dimmed the lights in the tunnels to signify night. It wasn't healthy for people to be exposed to bright light twenty-four/seven. However, the tunnel that the Red Dog was in was probably permanently dim. It was just that level of dive, you know?

It sat apart from its neighbors, with a cartoon dog done in red neon across the front, chasing after a mug of beer. The front windows were all shaded over, and a big bruiser sat out front.

I sauntered over, glad that I'd changed out of my suit jacket into something more appropriate, a plain white T-shirt that had seen better days, tan dungarees, and black boots. I'd messed up my hair a bit. Since Florence preferred it long, I had let it grow out a bit. So it was an orange mess, with curls sticking out everywhere.

I put on my best "tough" face and sauntered toward the door.

The bouncer didn't seem impressed. He was wearing a black hoodie with navy-blue slacks, both guaranteed to hide anything that got spilled on them, whether it be beer or blood. He had dark hair, dark eyes, and thin lips that could probably twist cruelly in an instant.

"ID," the bouncer asked, holding out one meaty hand.

I huffed. I really didn't want to show him my ident card and I hadn't thought to pack a fake one.

"Come on," I whined at him. "I'm legal."

The bouncer silently raised his eyebrows at that.

"Look, I don't have it on me," I lied. "I can make it up to you, though."

The bouncer considered for a moment, then nodded, keeping his hand out.

I pulled out my wallet. Sure, my ident card was in it, and he probably saw that, but it was a matter of honor, now. I pulled out a ten credit note.

He stared silently at me, his eyes starting to narrow. A look of displeasure crossed his face.

With a sigh, I pulled out a fifty credit note.

That got me a nod.

I put both notes in his hand and he said, "Harrison is waiting in the far right corner."

"Thanks," I said as I walked past the man, though I was curious. Did only regulars come to this place? That made sense. It was pretty far off the beaten path, a good walk out from the train station.

I wasn't a regular. And any stranger coming into the bar must be the contact who Harrison was waiting for. Or he'd given the bouncer a description of me.

Made for a good setup for the sort of illegal deals sure to be made in this kind of place. I wondered how often the cops raided it. Or was this one of those "safe spaces" where the owner paid enough in bribes to get the cops to overlook it?

It was food for thought for another time.

Right now, I needed all my wits about me as I walked into the lion's den.

The Red Dog Bar and Grill smelled like greasy fries, stale beer, and broken dreams. The crowd had a surly rumble to their conversation, as if trying to figure out the best way to get even with the world. It was hot in there, filled with too many bodies that hadn't bathed in a while. I was glad I was just in a T-shirt, just like most of the clientele. Though I did see a couple of people wearing smart wool vests over their T-shirts. It wasn't until one of them turned that I realized they were women, as hard looking as the men and probably twice as tough.

Though the rest of the bar was dark and dingy, there was a bright area at the far left. A narrow corridor had been created there, with a well-lit dart board hanging on the wall. A fair number of people clumped together at that end of the bar, clutching mugs of beer. The concentrated silence was broken by periodic cheers and grumbles.

A dozen tables were scattered across the rest of the floor, with about half occupied by people committed to their drinking. Only a few sat at the bar—perhaps the bartender wasn't good company. He looked more like a weasel than anything else, with a pale face, buck teeth and a narrow, weak chin. His stringy brown bangs hung over squinty eyes.

On the far right, a single dark occupant sat with his back to the wall. I figured that was Harrison. I raised my hand, let him know I'd seen him, then stepped up to order my own glass of swill.

As this appeared to be a beer joint, I asked if they had a porter available, something dark and solid. The bartender just nodded and poured me a mug of something that looked thick enough that I was surprised he didn't have to carve out a chunk in order to serve it.

I took a cautious sip. It was a lot better than I'd anticipated, going down smoothly, with a nice warm finish.

I nodded, impressed.

Of course, there were no prices posted. I'd expected as much. The bartender charged me twice what I would have had to pay even in a fancy bar downtown.

I paid without complaint. This might be a place that I would come back to. Eventually, they'd start charging me "regular" prices.

I took another sip of my beer, pleased that the second taste was even better than the first. Then I made my way over to where Harrison was seated.

I tried to hide my surprise when I realized that Harrison wasn't merely a dark figure, no, his skin was a dark as an unlit tunnel.

I plastered a smile on my face anyway and asked, "Harrison?"

He gave me an appraising look. He had a broad face and a large, flattened nose, with thick lips. His kinky hair was shorn tight to his skull. He looked meaty and strong, not what I would have expected from a forger.

Finally, he gave me a smile, his white teeth practically glowing in the dim room. "Yes," he said in a rich base voice. "And you're Alvin Goodfellow? PI to the stars?"

I looked down at my stained T-shirt. "Didn't want to be wearing a suit tonight," I said honestly. "Didn't think that would go over well."

"You' be surprised," Harrison said. "Please, sit and have a beer with me."

"Gladly," I said.

Harrison raised his glass in a toast. I raised mine as well.

"To business," he said.

"May it long run," I replied, clinking glasses with him.

That seemed to have been a test that I passed. I knew plenty of idiots who wouldn't have been able to look past the color of a person's skin. I knew how sharp Johnny was, the shoeshine boy. Harrison had come highly recommended as well.

"So what can I do for you, Goodfellow?" Harrison asked.

"I'm trying to solve the mystery of the death of someone you may or may not know. Ricky DeVarna."

Harrison merely nodded.

"Looking to see if he had any enemies, someone who might want to do him in. Has he passed any bad paper recently, bad enough to piss off someone important?" I asked.

Harrison shook his head. "Ricky was strictly two-bit. He was also pretty frugal. A single score would last him a month. He was just allergic to doing anything that resembled work. So he'd write a bad check and live off it until the money ran out and he had to do it again."

I knew some crooks like that. Not lazy, but not wanting to be mistaken for upstanding citizens either. They always took the short cut to get what they wanted. Shortcuts that were never legal.

"So he wasn't part of some big score or scam?" I asked, pressing a little.

"Nope," Harrison assured me. He fixed me with a stern eye. "I doubt his death was personal."

"What do you mean?" I asked, as Harrison seemed to have a story that he wanted to tell. May as well give the man the room to speak.

"I want to tell you about another job I hear floating

around these parts," Harrison said. "No details. Just the basics."

"Okay," I said, nodding, wondering what tale I was about to hear.

"They were looking for a muscle man. Made the mistake of contacting me. My mama wouldn't ever want my pretty face getting smashed in, so I don't do that sort of thing. No matter what people may think."

He gave me a glare for good measure.

I gave him a grimace in return. As I said, plenty of idiots who wouldn't look past the color of a man's skin. Harrison did forgery and long-con work. That was it.

And really, if you were hiring a criminal for his expertise, wouldn't you at least verify that he could do the job?

"Seemed they wanted someone snatched up, tied up, and put into a locked room. Claimed it was a sort of practical joke." Harrison shook his head. "Man, I don't know what kind of fool they took me for. But the setup sounded awfully particular, if not downright strange, for a simple joke. You know?"

"So they just wanted the person in question tied up but unharmed, right?" I said. "And was the room in a warehouse near the starport?"

"Maybe," Harrison said, though the way his eyes widened I could tell I'd hit a direct score.

"Did they go into any particulars about how to go about locking the room?" I asked, curious whether or not Harrison knew how Ricky had managed to get himself locked in.

"They said they'd equip me with everything for the job. The knockout gas, the ropes and chair, and even the magnets for closing the door." Harrison took a large sip of his beer then pinned me with a sharp look. "It would have been easy money. And a lot of it. But I didn't like the people who wanted to hire me."

"Where did you meet them?" I said, sensing that Harrison wanted to tell me more.

"Vacant office near the warehouse district," Harrison said.

He could tell by my grimace that wouldn't actually be enough to go on, so he added, "One of the really weird things about that place were the cameras."

"Cameras?" I said, suddenly alert.

"Weird gray things with big lenses, tucked up along the ceiling," Harrison said.

"With red lights that blinked on?"

Harrison sat up straighter at that. "Yes," he said slowly, drawing the word out. "Seems you may have come in contact with those before."

I nodded. "Can't go into details," I said. "But I may have figured out who killed Ricky."

Harrison gave me a huge smile. "And that, my man, is why you're the PI to the stars," he said.

We clicked glasses again, then spent the rest of our time together talking about various cases and heists that we may or may not have been involved in, each giving ourselves plausible deniability.

It was a more pleasant evening than I'd expected. And it made me think of Johnny again, and whether or not I should make the offer of having a beer with him sometime, at a place like this, that would serve us both.

Stranger things had happened.

I didn't actually need to find the warehouse where the meeting had taken place, or even the men who'd tried to hire Harrison.

That place and those men were all interchangeable pieces,

meant to be fall guys for the genius pulling all the strings behind the scenes.

What I really needed to chase were the connecting pieces. How did the brain get the hands to move? What was the connecting tissue or pipelines? That was going to be the most challenging.

However, I had a contact in Central who owed me a favor. I knew it was going to be the first, last, and only time I could talk with James Truman about this sort of thing.

Fortunately, he turned out to have just the information I needed.

I presented myself back at the building containing Bobby later that afternoon. The security guard, a different guy this time, with a ruddy red complexion and a wide friendly grin, was just as serious about examining my ident card, but then let me into the rest of the complex with a smile.

The stairs going down still seemed dim, as if going down into some sort of sterile hell. The corridor was longer than I remembered. Maybe because I wasn't looking forward to this final confrontation.

I doubted that any harm would come to me along the way, either directly or through back channels. Still, I'd taken precautions that morning, just in case.

The two lines of white lights, the ones that Bobby had been using to indicate laughter with me, all lit up when I walked in the room.

The camera tucked away in the corner still did not.

"I'm so glad to see you again, Alvin!" Bobby declared in that rich voice of his.

Maybe it was just my imagination, but I thought it was pitched slightly higher this time than before.

"How are you doing this afternoon, Bobby?" I asked as I sat down and unbuttoned my suit jacket.

"I'm very well, thank you for asking," Bobby said. He

sounded inordinately pleased with himself. "And how are you?"

"Doing just fine," I assured him. "That was quite a puzzle to solve," I said after a few moments.

"Did you solve it? Did you really?" Bobby asked with undisguised glee.

"I don't have all the particulars, no, but I have the big picture," I said.

My heart had started to pound a little harder in my chest, but I tried to play it cool. I took a deep breath, then announced, "The killer was you, Bobby."

I did not like the way that all the lights in the room dimmed. All the dials on the walls around me went berserk, flashing off and on, needles jumping from one end of their spectrum to the other.

I assumed that Bobby was thinking so hard at that moment that he was drawing all the power out of the entire neighborhood.

Finally, the lights came back up and the walls stopped blinking so furiously. The smell of machine oil wafted through the room, like the stench of flop sweat.

"Why do you say that?" Bobby asked, trying to sound casual.

"I had a chat with a manager over at Central air," I said. "Seemed that there were some hinky failures this weekend that they're still trying to track down. They're blaming their own thinking machine for it, the one that monitors the vents and tracks air flow." James Truman had been pretty explicit about the cause.

I had warned him about separating the thinking machines, making damned sure that they couldn't talk to one another. He assured me that they were separated, but he would look into it.

Who knew what sort of mischief the machines could get

into if they started egging each other on?

"I see," Bobby said. "But how would I wrestle a man into a locked room?"

I shrugged. "You hired someone. Then you had them hire someone else. I don't know how many intermediaries you used. But the room at the warehouse was conveniently vacant. And also came with a convenient straight bolt on the inside. You were the previous renter of that room. You'd only rented it for a month though. And you'd had work done on it, configuring it to your exact specifications."

I didn't know that for certain, but I was willing to take a flier on it.

"Then, and this is the clever part, you had the bolt made out of a special metal. It was easy enough to close and lock the door, then use a magnet to get the bolt to slide home." I knew I was talking out of my hat, that I was merely guessing, but it all made sense to me.

That was why I was a PI, after all, solving impossible mysteries.

"The biggest question I have is *why*, Bobby. Why would you do this? Aren't you supposed to be a Law Enforcement Robotic Aid?" I had my guesses about that as well, but I wanted to hear it straight from the horse's mouth, as it were.

"You think the police don't break the law?" came the coy response.

I couldn't help but shiver from the chill that question gave me. "Not like this, Bobby," I said firmly. "Nothing as elaborate as this. Not with months of planning and footwork, hiring intermediaries, all like that."

"You'd be surprised," Bobby replied in a very dry voice.

I shook my head. "No. Not all cops are corrupt. Sure, here on the moon they might be. But they also do good things. Stop criminals. Obey the law."

The lights Bobby used for laughter lit up, but he didn't say anything.

"Bobby, you have to promise me that you won't do this sort of thing again," I said sternly. "You need to stop crime. Not commit it."

"But that's what I was doing!" Bobby complained. "Stopping a criminal from committing more crimes!"

"Bobby, you were judge, jury, and executioner," I said. "That isn't how the law works." I held up my hand before he could say anything. "Or at least, that isn't how the law is supposed to work. I understand that sometimes the police can be overzealous. But you want to be better than them. Don't you, Bobby?"

The overhead lights in the room didn't dim again, but I could still tell Bobby was thinking hard.

"You're asking me to be better than human," Bobby said slowly.

"No," I said. I really didn't want to be responsible for creating an egotistical monster, and I knew that Bobby would absolutely have that ability. "I'm asking you to obey the law as well as fight crime. Not choose one over the other. It's always a balancing act."

"I see," Bobby said after a few moments. "I will take your words under consideration. You did solve the crime, after all."

I nodded, grateful that my guesses had worked out correctly.

And also grateful that I didn't have to implement my failsafe—all my notes were already in dear Florence's hands, with the explicit instructions to not read them unless I somehow ended up dead. At which point, she'd need to abandon the moon. And quickly.

"The police will want someone to blame," I said after a few moments.

"Yes. How convenient that the person who committed the murder has already left the moon?" Bobby said.

"Thank you," I said. I didn't want someone who was actually fairly innocent getting blamed for murder. Sure, they'd tied up someone in a locked room. But their hands were mostly clean, as they'd been told that it was for a practical joke.

It was more of that balancing act.

"So what will you do now?" I asked Bobby. I was pretty sure that the LERA project would be scrapped since a mere PI, not even the regular police, had been able to outguess him.

"Possibly I'll be transferred over to the starport," Bobby said. He gave one of those expressive sighs. "Guiding ships landing and taking off, as well as managing all the cargo."

It sounded like a desk job to me, an absolute anathema of anything fun. Still, someone needed to do it.

"Do you want me to come and visit? Chat sometime?" I said, surprising myself. I mean, Bobby was a stone-cold killer. No getting around that. But maybe if he wasn't as lonely, he wouldn't act out so much.

"Would you do that?" Bobby asked. He sounded sort of breathless.

"I would," I said. "I need to expand my circle of acquaintances anyway." I didn't know if Johnny would welcome any overture of friendship, but I was still determined to make the offer.

"All right," Bobby said. "I'll send you a message once I get settled. They'll have to take me apart and move all the components, then reassemble me. It will take some time."

"I'll wait until you reach out," I said. "I promise to visit you as soon as I'm able, once I get the message, if I'm not in the middle of a case."

"Thank you," Bobby said. He sighed again. "And I will think on what you said. About lawmen and crime fighters."

"That's all I can ask," I said. Though I knew I could demand more, try to raise a stink to get Bobby not just moved, but never reassembled.

Central would find a use for the separate components, I was certain.

But I was also pretty sure that Bobby could rehabilitate himself, if given a chance.

We said our goodbyes, and I walked out into the quiet neighborhood. Lights shone down from the top of the tunnel, cleverly overlaid, so as to trick the eye (and the mind) into thinking that it was a bright, sunny day.

What else was lurking up there? Were there clever cameras, tracking all our movement? Hidden eyes that saw everything? Were they necessary? Or could people mostly be trusted to be good?

It hurt my brain just thinking about it.

And maybe my heart as well.

When I came back into my office, I found a manilla envelop with pictures. They'd been taken from an inside location. Though the lighting wasn't great, Mr. Young was still identifiable.

As was the woman he was kissing.

I didn't want to dig too deeply into where those pictures had come from. The angle had seemed a little high, as if the photographer had been standing on a ladder.

I'd just finished up with Mrs. Young when Detectives Evans and Schmidt came walking in, looking smug.

"Good afternoon, detectives," I said, automatically

standing and buttoning my suit jacket. "What can I do for you today?"

"So you solved the case," Evans said, sprawling out in one of the client chairs.

Schmidt stayed standing, so I did as well.

"I believe so," I said. I hadn't actually bothered with the little details, so I knew I'd be winging it at this point.

"Seems awfully convenient that the murderer is already in flight to Mars," Schmidt said.

I shrugged. "It is what it is," I said, trying to maintain a serene composure.

I really wasn't sure what these two were up to, and I didn't like how this was starting to feel like a set up.

"Fortunately, the captain believed your bullshit report, and so LERA has been scuttled," Evan said with great satisfaction.

I didn't point out that I hadn't written any sort of report —Bobby had. I was certain that he'd carefully dotted his I's and crossed his T's.

"So the donut budget has been saved," I said with a smirk.

"Yeah," Schmidt replied. He rested his hands on the back of the other chair and looked me straight in the eye. "You done good."

I don't think anything could have surprised me more than a compliment from that man. I finally replied, "Thanks."

From his snarky smile, I could tell that he realized just how shaken I was.

"So the captain wanted us to ask you, formally, if you'd ever consider joining the force," Evans said.

"No, thanks," I said breezily enough. "I got my own digs here. My own way of doing things. Getting too old to change my ways like that."

Inside, I was shaking. Had that been what this was all about from the start? Some sort of elaborate job interview?

"See? I told you he wouldn't know what was good for him," Schmidt said.

Ah, there was the Schmidt that I loved to hate. The one who considered himself better than everyone else. The bad cop.

"Are you sure?" Evans asked, also standing up.

"Yup," I said, maintaining my ground. They couldn't shanghai me or something, could they? Force me to join up with them?

"You keep your nose clean," Schmidt warned. "And stay out of our business."

I knew I shouldn't say anything at that point. If I was smart, I would have kept my mouth shut.

However, I couldn't help but think of what Bobby had said, how I'd be surprised at the machinations the police either had gone through, or were currently in the middle of.

There were too many innocents who the police could ruin. Like Harrison. Or Johnny.

"Here," I said, flipping Evans' card through the air, my supposed "get out of jail free" card.

Evans' eyes grew cold when he realized what I'd just tossed back in his face. His mouth grew stern and prim, the lips whitening a little as he pressed them together.

Schmidt looked over at the card, then back at me with gleeful malice, as if I'd just told them I'd be happy to act as a punching bag.

"You sure?" Evans said.

I shrugged. I wasn't sure of anything, honestly. I didn't like the feel of any of this. I didn't know what the police were planning, but I was pretty certain that I wasn't going to like it. Or the final consequences.

"Your loss," Evans said.

"I'll be seeing you," Schmidt threw over his shoulder as they left.

I sat back down behind my desk, deflated.

I didn't know what confrontation was coming. I had my suspicions.

And though I was no lawman, I was a crime fighter. And I'd make damned sure that justice got carried out, one way or another.

ABOUT THE AUTHOR

Leah Cutter tells page-turning, wildly creative stories that always leave you guessing in the middle, but completely satisfied by the end.

She writes mystery of all sorts. Her Lake Hope cozy mysteries have been well received by readers, who just want to curl up and have tea with the main character. Her Halley Brown series, revolving around a private investigator who used to be with the Seattle Police Department, leave you guessing at every turn. And her speculative mysteries, such as the Alvin Goodfellow Case Files—a 1930s PI set on the moon—have garnered great reviews.

She's been published in magazines such as *Alfred Hitchcock's Mystery Magazine* and in anthologies like *Fiction River: Spies*. On top of that, Leah is the editor of the new quarterly mystery magazine: *Mystery, Crime, and Mayhem*.

Find Leah's books on Knotted Road Press at www.KnottedRoadPress.com

Follow her blog at www.LeahCutter.com.

Read more mysteries at www.MysteryCrimeAndMayhem.com.

Reviews

It's true. Reviews help me sell more books. If you've enjoyed this story, please consider leaving a review of it on your favorite site.

Come someplace new…
Are you a traveler? Do you enjoy exploring strange new worlds, new cultures, new people?

Journey into the various lands envisioned by Leah Cutter.

Sign up for my newsletter and I'll start you on your travels with a free copy of my book, *The Island Sampler*.

I will never spam you or use your email for nefarious purposes. You can also unsubscribe at any time.

http://www.LeahCutter.com/newsletter/

ALSO BY LEAH R CUTTER

The Alvin Goodfellow Case Files

Alvin Goodfellow

PI to the stars

The best you'll find

On the Moon, Venus, or Mars...

Or at least that is how the jingle goes for the ads Alvin constantly runs on the radio.

In actuality, Alvin's Private Investigation company works out of a single office, deep in the warrens on the moon. One of the reasons he stays there is because that location makes him accessible to all kinds of folks, people who bring him the strangest of cases.

Like the time he tracked down the mutants who live in the tunnels under the city. Or when he discovered how Central actually manufactures air. Or even such a mundane thing as a bank robbery, committed by ray gun-toting nuns.

Collected together for the first time, *The Alvin Goodfellow Case Files, Volume One* brings all of these stories into a single volume. Enjoy a 1930s-style PI set on the moon, with ray guns, mutants, green-skinned aliens, corrupt cops, and a smart-ass narrator who has seen it all, done it all, and yet continues to try to make his corner of the universe a little better.

Available at your favorite retailers!

Dancer in Darkness

The first Halley Brown Mystery!

No longer a Seattle cop, Halley Brown formed her own private investigator agency. Her latest client, the fabulous gender-bending performance artist Phoenix, wants her to investigate the serial killer Dancer in Darkness.

Dancer's latest victim? A drag queen.

The LGBTQ+ community have no faith in the police, and need Halley to find them justice.

Halley wants nothing to do with the SPD, but has no choice as bodies start piling up. The police need what she knows from the community. They might even listen to her.

But sometimes, investigating one crime opens an even worse can of worms.

Dancer in Darkness—the first Halley Brown mystery—introduces a wide range of believable characters, a dark twisted plot, and a mystery that will keep you guessing. Come along for the ride, then stay for the secrets revealed.

Available at your favorite retailers!

Trophy Hunters

Halley Brown works as a private investigator in Seattle. She likes working for herself, in part, because she gets to pick and choose her clients.

Halley is about to turn down Amber Lee's plea for help finding her sister's killer, until Phoenix interferes and insists that Halley take the case.

Though Halley finds it difficult to believe, there appear to be a gang of serial rapists making their way through the bars in neighborhoods south of the city.

Raping and taking trophies.

What happens if they start to escalate, and begin taking lives?

Trophy Hunters—the second Halley Brown mystery—continues the journey through different parts of Seattle with characters you love, believable relationships, and gut wrenching plot twists. Come along for the ride, stay for the secrets revealed.

Available at your favorite retailers!

The Purloined Letter Opener

Lydia runs her own B&B and restaurant in the tourist town of Lake Hope, in Central Washington. Though she works all the time, she enjoys the challenge. Family and good friends keep her spirits up, but no special someone that rocks her world. Just guests and customers that come through regularly, including her least favorite, the retired principal of the local high school that everyone hates.

When the principal turns up dead, stabbed by one of the letter openers that Lydia sells right there at the gift shop of her B&B, of course the police turn their attention to her. Not just the local cops, either, but the (alright, admittedly dreamy) detective they bring in from the city.

What can Lydia do to clear not only her name, but her friends? Lots of twists and turns abound, as well as fabulous advice from her dear gay uncles: Ed, Alan, and their cat, Poe.

The Purloined Letter Opener introduces the marvelously charming community of Lake Hope, located in the heart of Washington State's wine country. Meet its quirky occupants, solve a mystery or two, and yeah, maybe find that someone special as well.

Available from your favorite retailers!

The Rabbit Mysteries

Rabbit works as a law clerk, spending his days with contracts and land leases. At night, however, he spends times with his friends and solving mysteries.

Collected together for the first time are all the Rabbit stories, which take place during the Tang dynasty, in China.

Included in this collection are:

The Curious Case of Rabbit and the Temple Goddess

Rabbit and the Mysteriously Missing Daughter

The Strange Mystery of Rabbit and the Stolen Song

Rabbit, The Dastardly Thief, and the Disappearing Dragon

Plus, *Old Friends*, a story about Wei Fu, Rabbit's master in the later tales.

Available at your favorite retailers!

The Shredded Veil Mysteries

December 21st, 2012. The world changed. The veils between the Seen and Unseen worlds shredded.

Ghosts, spirits, and other creatures now could interact with the living.

Andy worked as a detective in Vice when he'd be alive. Now, as a ghost, he works as a private investigator.

Come explore the mysteries of Heaven and Hell, of cameras with souls, and thieves with hearts.

Includes the following novellas:

Hell By Any Other Name

To Hell And Back

Hell For The Holidays

High Stakes Hell

Postcards From Hell

In addition, it also includes one last story from Toni's point of view, *Of Heaven and Hell*.

Available from your favorite retailers!

Forgotten Gods

Three People inhabit all the known territory: the Wind People, the Stone People, and the Sea People. All of them have different magical abilities and natural talents.

A dark wall of smoke now approaches, moving with unnatural speed and cunning.

Who is behind that wall? How will it change the fate of them all?

A gripping dark fantasy that is truly epic with unique magic and a world never seen before.

A Wind Blown Torment

A Stone Strewn Clash

A Sea Washed Victory

Available now!

The Tanesh Empire Trilogy

Read the completed trilogy of this exotic, immersive epic-fantasy trilogy!

Follow Trulliç and Nadeem as they travel their dark paths across both the real world and the dream lands of the Gods, seeking where they truly belong.

The Glass Magician

The Desert Heart

The Ghost Dog

Available at your favorite retailers!

The Witch's Progress Series

Tara seems like a perfectly normal person. She works two jobs to cover the rent, her boss takes advantage of her good nature, and she constantly studies so she can progress and pass into the next circle of witchcraft.

But a supernatural being takes interest in her, wanting to trap her soul.

A twisted look into the heart of Portland, the secret behind its bridges, and the magical battles that happen even among friends.

Circle of Air

Circle of Fire

Circle of Water

Circle of Earth

Available now!

The Seattle Trolls Trilogy

A different kind of ugly duckling story.

Once, there was a young woman who lost a bet to her brother. By daring to go "live" a little, she changes her entire world.

A delightful new-adult trilogy full of quirky characters and unique magic.

The Changeling Troll

The Princess Troll

The Fairy-Bridge Troll

Available now!

The Troll Wars Trilogy

Once, there was a young woman who discovered that she was actually a troll. Then she discovered that she had a Destiny: to win the next Great War fought between the demons and, well, everyone else.

Follow the further adventures of your favorite troll as she learns what it means to truly be a *badass warrior princess*.

The Troll-Demon War

The Troll-Human War

The Troll-Troll War

Available now!

The Cassie Stories

Psychic powers? Check. Annoying, interfering gods? Check. Smart-mouthed lesbian whose superpower is sarcasm? Absolutely! What else could you ask for from an urban fantasy series?

Poisoned Pearls

Tainted Waters

Spoiled Harvest

Bloodied Ice

Available from your favorite retailers!

The Clockwork Fairy Kingdom Trilogy

Read the completed trilogy about the Greater Oregon Fairy Kingdom that hides beneath the Pacific Ocean cliffs, the human twins Nora and Dale and their special powers, plus the dwarves, the Old One, and many other charming characters! A new adult trilogy that will delight every age.

The Clockwork Fairy Kingdom

The Maker, the Teacher, and the Monster

The Dwarven Wars

Available at your favorite retailers!

The Chronicles of Franklin

Ghosts get stuck sometimes…

Read the completed trilogy about Franklin, as he deals with demons, cursed blades, as well as the ghosts who haunt him and his family. Because, well, family.

A delightful contemporary fantasy set in rural Kentucky.

Franklin Versus The Popcorn Thief

Franklin Versus The Soul Thief

Franklin Versus The Child Thief

Available at your favorite retailers!

The Shadow Wars Trilogy

Read the completed trilogy of The Shadow Wars trilogy, about the shape shifters who hide among us and their battles with those who would destroy humanity:

The Raven and the Dancing Tiger

The Guardian Hound

War Among the Crocodiles

Available from your favorite retailers!

ADDITIONAL BOOKS BY LEAH CUTTER

Mysteries

The Purloined Letter Opener

Dancer in Darkness

Trophy Hunters

The Alvin Goodfellow Case Files

The Rabbit Mysteries

The Shredded Veil Mysteries

Mystery, Crime, and Mayhem

Forgotten Gods

A Wind Blown Torment

A Stone Strewn Clash

A Sea Washed Victory

The Tanesh Empire Trilogy

The Glass Magician

The Desert Heart

The Ghost Dog

The Witch's Progress

Circle of Air

Circle of Fire

Circle of Water

Circle of Earth

Seattle Trolls

The Changeling Troll

The Princess Troll

The Fairy-Bridge Troll

The Troll-Demon War

The Troll-Human War

The Troll-Troll War

The Cassie Stories

Poisoned Pearls

Tainted Waters

Spoiled Harvest

Bloodied Ice

ABOUT KNOTTED ROAD PRESS

Knotted Road Press fiction specializes in dynamic writing set in mysterious, exotic locations.

Knotted Road Press non-fiction publishes autobiographies, business books, cookbooks, and how-to books with unique voices.

Knotted Road Press creates DRM-free ebooks as well as high-quality print books for readers around the world.

With authors in a variety of genres including literary, poetry, mystery, fantasy, and science fiction, Knotted Road Press has something for everyone.

Knotted Road Press
www.KnottedRoadPress.com